Books by Solara

EL*AN*RA:
The Healing of Orion

The Star-Borne:
A Remembrance for the Awakened Ones

The Legend of Altazar:
A Fragment of the True History of Planet Earth

Invoking Your Celestial Guardians

Inside the Doorway

Solara

Star-Borne Unlimited

Star-Borne Unlimited
2005 Commonwealth Dr.
Charlottesville, VA 22901 U.S.A.

First Edition published June 1992

ISBN # 1-878246-05-4

Cover Design by:
Solara & AArela

Cover Photograph by:
AYA

Illustrations by:
AArela Antara

Book Design by:
Solara & Garjon

Typesetting by:
Garjon

Printed in the United States of America

This book is gratefully dedicated

to all our Starry Family worldwide

who opened the Doorway of the 11:11.

TABLE OF CONTENTS

THE ACTIVATION OF THE 11:11

THE DOORWAY OF THE 11:11

THE OPENING OF THE DOORWAY

THE JOURNEY THROUGH

11:11 is a pre-encoded trigger

placed within our cellular memory banks

prior to our descent into matter,

which, when activated, signifies

that our time of completion is near.

The 11:11 is hereby being activated. . .

The Activation
of the 11:11

The Door Before

The Doorway of the 11:11 is not the first portal of ascension to open on this planet. A long, long time ago we experienced the opening of another doorway. Here is a fragment of my memories of the Door Before. Perhaps, it shall spark your own remembrance...

To remember this previous portal of ascension, we must go back to a far, distant age. It was so long ago that the memories have only recently resurfaced, triggered by our efforts to activate the 11:11. It was the time when the great civilizations anchored at Shamballa in the Gobi Desert and AN located near Lake Titicaca disappeared from the physical plane. Many great beings made their departure from the cycle of incarnation and stepped off the Wheel of Birth and Death. These Great Ones are those whom we now refer to as *Ascended Masters*. Up until the moment when they passed through the portal of ascension, they walked openly upon this planet amongst us, just like we are doing now.

When this doorway opened, many of us were given the choice of whether to ascend or stay. Since I had already made my vow to serve as a Bodhisattva *(one who chooses to stay and serve as long as there is a need)*, my decision was clear. I would remain in service upon this planet until the next doorway opened – sometime far into the undefinable future. *(Being an ancient First Waver now, it's interesting to remember when we were fresh and full of enthusiasm for the times to come.)*

All of the Bodhisattvas who were to remain on Earth were carefully taught and prepared by the departing ones. Sceptres of responsibility would be passed and we had to be ready to wield them by ourselves. It was our turn to serve as the Pillars of Light upon the planet. We were to become the next wave of Great Ones. We were greatly aided by those of the Devic Kingdom – fairies, elves, gnomes and nature devas, all of whom had also chosen to stay. At that time, they were openly visible to everyone.

We were shown that the next cycle upon the planet would be a challenging one, for much would be forgotten. Many of our touchstones with the Greater Reality would seem to disappear. We would have to discover them within ourselves. It would often appear as if we were totally alone and unsupported from On High. Our very links to who we truly would seem to fade away. No memories would remain of the star lineages of EL AN RA except the presence of Orion itself. The Family of AN would forget that AN had ever existed, yet spend lifetimes searching for those elusive *others.*

We were told that we could remain on Earth for one more turn of the spiral which represented the completion of a major cycle. And that *we* would be responsible for opening the next portal of ascension. It was strongly emphasized that when the new doorway opened, it was essential we move through it, for our time in duality would be complete. *(Bodhisattvic Vows are in effect for one complete cycle of evolution. Thus, when I was given the opportunity to renew them in this lifetime, I declined.)*

14

It was also made clear that if we somehow missed the next opportunity to ascend, we would no longer be able to serve in duality. Instead, if we stayed past our allotted time span, we might enter a cycle of degeneration, traveling on a reverse spiral into the worlds of anti-matter. Although it wasn't explained in great depth how this would manifest, we were deeply impressed with the importance of departing through the next doorway of ascension.

Each of us who was on Earth at the time of the Door Before carries the memory of that momentous event. And we are the ones who surely must understand the significance of the 11:11. We hold the responsibility not only for our own sucessful passage through the door, but for giving our Starry Family the opportunity to ascend with us.

Once again sceptres are being passed. Now it is our sacred duty to prepare the ones who choose to remain in duality for that time in their far, distant future when yet another doorway will open. They need to realize that by the end of 2011, many of us who have long served as Pillars upon this planet will be gone. Then it will be up to their efforts. So even if you choose to remain in duality, it is time for you to rise into full empowerment.

The beloved Family of AN is being Called homewards. The Devic Kingdom shall be departing as well. Some of them will return to their starry homes in the Great Magellanic Cloud, while others will continue on to Octave Seven with the reborn Earth to help recreate nature in alignment with the new Starry Grid. They all will depart from duality. Even those who ascended through the previous door will be joining with us. The same is true of the ancient dragons, unicorns, whales and winged lions. If you are one who knows any hidden pockets where they still live on the planet, please call to them that the time is at hand.

Preparing for the shift through the Doorway of the 11:11 is a huge responsibility. The help and participation of everyone is needed. Some of us *must* go through this door; it is not a matter of choice, but of timing. Each of us who is an awakened one already has our ticket Home. By flying together as One in the formation of our Birdstar, we can clear the channel so that many may ascend. No matter where you choose to anchor your being, there is work to be done. This is the largest doorway we have ever faced since we first descended into matter.

The Door Before was a portal of ascension, *but it was not a shift in templates.* The Doorway of the 11:11 is our first opportunity to change spirals of evolution and move into a Greater Central Sun System! Let us join together as One that this great task may be brought to completion!

The Doorway of the 11:11

This book is about a journey – the most important and exciting journey we shall ever take. It is our journey Home.

The activation of the 11:11 is not a random event that took place on January 11, 1992. It is the beginning of our life's work. It is the fulfillment of our Divine Missions upon the Earth. It heralds the completion of duality and the anchoring of the Template of Oneness.

The 11:11 is not another stargate; it is our bridge to ascension. It is our doorway Home. We have waited aeons for this moment to arrive. We have struggled and toiled, yearned and prayed for this to happen. And together as One, we have called it forth to be!

If you are one who participated in the Wheels within Wheels on January 11th, you have already experienced the power of the vast love which was anchored into the planet on that blessed day.

If you chose to be part of the Master Cylinders in Egypt and New Zealand, you were indelibly transformed. You are now ready to enter the First Gate of the New Octave.

If all this is new to you, there is still time to make your commitment and join with all your Starry Family in conscious Oneness that together we may manifest our Unified Presence!

What is the 11:11 about? It is about completion, graduation, mastery, empowerment, embodying our Highest Truth, freedom, sacred union, True Love, One Heart, Oneness.

This is the Time of Completion. We are being called Home. The Golden, Solar Angels of the Great Central Sun, the great star lineages of EL, AN, RA, the Legions of Archangel Mikael, the Order of Melchizedek, the Annuttara; all of us, the vast collective Family of AN, are being called Home.

11:11 is our wake-up call. It is our map for the next twenty years. Now is the time!

*Here we stand, poised on the brink
of a great adventure, that we, ourselves,
have called forth to be!*

The Call to Activation

Here we stand in the midst of great changes. The survival of planet Earth and all of its inhabitants is now on the line. We are constantly being pulled back and forth between an ingoing and an outgoing tide. This is causing turmoil, confusion and fear. The outgoing tide is composed of the third and fourth dimensional energies rooted within the Template of Duality. Hence duality's final battle for supremacy and control is now taking place.

The ingoing tide represents the awareness of our inherent Oneness. It resonates with our new Divine Dispensation and is our Call to Completion and Freedom. It is our graduation from illusion and the next step on our journey homeward. We must now fully anchor our beings on the Template of Oneness to maintain our balance within this transitional zone between two very different energy patternings.

Ahead of us lies a tremendous task – to pass through the Doorway of the 11:11, thus moving onto a New Octave of awareness. In order to achieve this, to survive these tumultuous times, we must align ourselves irrevocably with our Higher Purpose. No matter what is happening on the outer levels, we must keep a positive outlook! Remain centered and remember at all times what is truly real. Do not allow yourself to feed duality by giving it any more of your energy. Do not propagate doom and gloom. Remember that all of the dire future prophecies are based on third dimensional patternings. They do not emanate from the Greater Reality.

Whenever you begin to get drawn into the illusion of duality, simply pause and realign your being while quietly stating that you do not accept this reality. Remain focused on the Great Awakening that is presently in effect on Earth; remember who you really are and visualize the open Doorway of the 11:11. This newly activated Arc of Light serves as our bridge to New Octaves of harmony, peace and Oneness.

This anchoring of your being into the template of Oneness is crucial to the fulfillment of the Divine Plan on Earth. Your total commitment is needed now!

Here we stand, poised on the brink of a great adventure, that we, ourselves, have called forth to be!

The time has finally arrived which we have long awaited. Truly, do we stand poised on the brink of a great adventure! This great adventure is the fulfillment of our Divine Missions on Planet Earth. It is our graduation from the Template of Duality enabling us to rise up into true Mastery and Freedom. We are now entering upon the time of completion. This is the beginning of the next phase of our journey Homeward.

We have long carried within us, *pre-encoded into our cellular memory banks,* the memories, knowledge and sealed orders which shall serve us in these times of completion. These were placed within us long ago, prior to our initial descent into matter.

The fulfillment of our Divine Missions is the reason we chose to come to Earth in the first place!

Throughout our cycle of embodiments upon Earth we have laboriously prepared to be ready to serve in our fullest capacity when the preordained time arrived. And the time is now. The Call to Awaken has already resounded across the Celestial Vastness calling us to remember and ultimately, *to embody*, that which we truly are in our full magnificence and empowerment.

Now we are issuing the Call to Activation. This activation entails that each of us faces a decision of tremendous importance and lasting consequence. Our choice is whether or not we will answer and serve this Call with the fullness of our beings and with unshakeable commitment to serving our Higher Purpose. We must now decide where we choose to anchor our beings. Shall it be on the Template of Duality or on the Template of Oneness? These choices must be made now. Please, choose wisely with your full consciousness, for the results of these choices shall be with you for a very long time and will affect all levels of your life.

Great times require both greatness of spirit and greatness of action.

Together we have much to accomplish. What we are being called to achieve is of a scope far greater than anything we can presently imagine. The Earth herself, is nearing her time of graduation from the patterning of duality and she who has succored our needs for so long, now needs our help to birth her into a New Octave of Oneness. And by serving as Earth's midwives, we, *the awakened humanity of Earth*, also birth ourselves onto a new spiral of evolution.

Our first task is to transform ourselves into fully awakened multi-dimensional beings, thus fully merging the fourth and fifth dimensional frequencies into the third. It is the inner union between Earth ascending and Heaven descending. This sacred merger has already been achieved by many of us and numerous others are awakening daily as the Call steadily intensifies. We are reclaiming our Divine Birthright and Heritage, remembering that we are Angels incarnate, vast starry beings of Light who are no longer limited to and bound by the illusions of time, space and matter.

Now we are ready to join together as emanations of the One. Indeed, this is of primary importance, for the great work in front of us requires that we unite as a collective whole. The new doorways cannot be opened or passed through by any of us still operating as individual units of consciousness. They are brought into manifestation through our Unified Presence, through our focused intent, through our total commitment to serving our Higher Purpose as One.

The Activation of the 11:11

We hereby announce the next major planetary activation on January 11, 1992.
This is the Opening of the Doorway of the 11:11.

This is the most important evolutionary step we have ever taken on planet Earth! It heralds the completion of the spiral of evolution which we have traveled upon since Earth's inception. The activation of the 11:11 signifies a time when the planet and all of humanity shall be given the opportunity to move onto a new spiral of consciousness.

The 11:11 is the bridge to an entirely different spiral of energy patterning.

It is the step *beyond* this known dimensional universe into a new patterning of Octaves. It is a journey into the Unknown which shall lead us ever closer Home. The Opening of the 11:11 is a major planetary activation on a scale never before experienced.

The Call is hereby issued to you from On High.

The symbol of 11:11 was pre-encoded into our cellular memory banks long ago, before our initial descent into matter. It was placed into us, *seared into the very fibers and DNA of our beings,* as part of our preparations prior to beginning our cycle of incarnations upon the Earth. The 11:11 has rested dormantly within us since that faraway time, positioned under a time-release mechanization, complete with sealed orders which would only open when the 11:11 was fully activated. It has been gently sleeping, awaiting its moment of triggering. And now the 11:11 is finally being activated...

11:11 is the pre-encoded trigger that our time of completion is near.

Many of you have recognized this symbol as something of great significance, yet have been unaware of its true meaning. With the advent of digital clocks many years ago, the presence of 11:11 began to make itself felt, often appearing on the clock at times of accelerated awareness. For those of you who have known that 11:11 was something special, we ask you to come forth into positions of leadership for you hold important parts of the key. Let your sealed orders be now opened!

Sealed Orders

Many of us have long felt that we carried sealed orders embedded within our beings. These sealed orders were encoded within our cellular memory banks back in the Starry Councils before we ever descended into matter. For many, they have been a source of major frustration, for sealed orders simply will not open before their time of readiness. Over the years I have encountered many who have tried in vain to decipher their sealed orders. They have attempted various methods to force them open, blasting them with their wills, visiting various psychics and channels, but always the orders have remained locked.

The reason for this is quite simple. These sealed orders contain the blueprint for fulfilling your Divine Mission and are not to be opened until you have fully awakened and merged with your vaster, Starry Selves. The Divine Missions are not to be achieved solely by your third dimensional fragment. They require a whole, complete being who is anchored firmly into the Template of Oneness.

If you are one who carries sealed orders and desperately wants them to open so you may proceed with fulfilling your Divine Mission, there is only one thing to do. Simply forget about those secretive sealed orders for the time being and

26

focus totally on reuniting with your Higher Self, with your Angelic Presence, with your Starry Overself. Only when you truly embody your Full Presence here on Earth, *in the physical body,* will your sealed orders be revealed.

It must also be stated that often the very nature of our chosen Divine Missions is so awesomely vast that if they were revealed to us before the appropriate moment, we would be simply overwhelmed with shock. I'm afraid that many of us would react with panic: "Oh, I couldn't possibly do anything that grand, that important," and we would probably *literally* go hide ourselves in the back of the nearest closet!

The way it happens is that after we have merged with our Greater Self and we are quietly going about our lives, doing the best we can in any given situation, then suddenly, without any warning at all, something shifts and opens up. And we discover that our sealed orders *have* opened and we *are* fulfilling our Divine Mission!

The important thing is to relax and stop thinking about sealed orders. Simply acknowledge that they are there, sleeping dormantly within you, ever awaiting their moment of activation. As long as you are giving your fullest commitment to embodying your Truth and serving the One, you are doing your utmost to fulfill your Divine Mission.

The Star-Borne

**We all come from the stars;
we all originate from the One.**

The Star-Borne are all of us presently incarnate who know that we originate from somewhere beyond this planet. We remember that we chose to undergo incarnation on Earth in order to serve in the transmutation of matter. And that once this was achieved we would be able to move both the planet and the portions of humanity who will choose themselves onto an entirely new evolutionary template.

Right now at this very moment, a mass awakening of the Star-Borne is taking place on Earth. This awakening is of utmost importance. It is the time that we have long awaited – yearning for in the depths of our hearts while calling out to our starry brethren at night.

In truth, all of us here are Star-Borne. However for greater clarity, I delineate the Star-Borne into three main groupings. The first group contains those who remember who they are; we shall call them the Awakened Ones. The second group are those in the process of remembering. And the third group are those who choose *not* to remember.

The Awakened Ones are those who remember. Each one of them is a blessing to all. Encountering one another throughout the planet and working together is one of our greatest joys. Whenever we meet, there is always deep recognition and respect, followed by loving support and trust on all levels. Since we have transcended our egos, there is no processing, strain, or adjustment necessary. We simply join together in Oneness to complete whatever task needs doing. Knowing that there are others, fully awakened and giving of their total Selves in loving service to humanity makes our load lighter. Each of us is like an activated Pillar of Light upon the Earth. We are the real vortexes!

The main focus of our work at this time is twofold. We will continue to anchor our beings in Oneness and proceed on our journey through the Doorway of the 11:11. This we must do regardless of whether it is a small group of us or all of humanity. It is our prime task which needs to be achieved no matter what else happens.

Secondly, we have the responsibility of awakening and activating Starry Family in the second group – the ones in the process of awakening. Remember: We are in the time of the Great Awakening. It takes very little to awaken those who are ready and there are millions upon millions of us who are currently poised on the brink of remembrance. This is why I have felt a tremendous sense of urgency and traveled extensively for the past several years trying to reach as many as I can.

The third group of Star-Borne are those who choose not to awaken right now. It is important to remember that they are fine just as they are. Our job is not to force anyone into awakening before they are ready. We certainly have enough to do without arguing and struggling! All of us know many people in this category; we often live and work with them. We must honor each person's right to make their own choices and if some choose duality, we must lovingly accept their choice. It is not our function to push people through the Door. Our challenge is to continue to stand firmly in our own Beam and not get polarized back into duality.

Activations
Leading to the 11:11

We have been experiencing a series of major planetary activations to prepare us to open the Doorway of the 11:11. These activations began on December 31, 1986 with the World Peace Meditation brought forth by John Randolph Price. On this day, millions of people came together worldwide to consciously meditate for world peace! This was the first time that humanity joined together on such a large scale. The World Peace Meditations have continued each year on December 31st.

Next was the Harmonic Convergence on August 16 & 17, 1987, activated by José Arguelles which anchored the fourth dimension. Once again millions of people participated at sacred sites throughout the planet. Although the Harmonic Convergence was mocked by some of the media, many people experienced lasting breakthroughs in consciousness from our unified focus.

Then came Earth Link in February 1988, centered over Uluru *(Ayers Rock)*, in central Australia. Here a shaft of electric blue Light was brought down and anchored into the crystal beds under the Earth. This further activated our cellular memory banks and brought forth new levels of remembrance.

The last big activation was Earth Day, celebrated on April 20, 1990. Millions celebrated their loving concern for this planet through festivals, concerts, and various ecological events.

Concurrently, we have had a series of smaller planetary events, such as Star Link in June 1988 – activating the Angelic Vortex in Los Angeles, California, Crystal Light Link – activating the crystal grids in April 1989 and Time Warp in November 1989. Each of these important activations has served to bring us into a new global awareness leading to a heightened sense of Oneness – healing, transforming and ushering new levels of consciousness into the planetary Logos.

In 1991 the activations greatly increased in intensity. On July 11th was a powerful solar eclipse which cleared the channels for opening the Doorway of the 11:11. For those receptive to the energies streaming onto the planet on that day, full access was given to journey all the way to Beyond the Beyond. It was quite a taste of the powerful times to come. This eclipse penetrated deeper into the Earth than any we have experienced in several hundred years. It represented the Father penetrating into the Mother and helped us to further unify our polarities, thus preparing the way for the Template of True Love to be anchored in 1992. Then on November 11, 1991 came the Activation of the Order of Melchizedek, which flung open the doors to the ancient wisdom and secret Halls of Records that had long been hidden.

All of these quantum leaps have brought us to the place of readiness where we stand right now. We are in the midst of the most important activation ever experienced on Earth. This is the Opening of the Doorway of the 11:11.

Preparations

In order to move through the Doorway of the 11:11, there are some important preparations to be made. These will enable you to complete your cycle of service upon the Template of Duality and step forward into the New Octave which awaits. . .

Letting Go

You can begin by cleaning out your lives, lovingly discarding any outmoded habits and thought forms rooted in the illusion of separation & denial. Go through your closets, both literally and figuratively, shedding anything that no longer resonates with the highest Truth of your Being. Simplify everything so it vibrates in accord with you, leaving space for the introduction of the New. Free yourself of any unnecessary activities. Consciously complete any unfinished business, any unresolved relationships, anything which keeps you smaller than you really are.

Clear up any fears you may have around the issue of power. We have all misused power at one time or another. It was simply part of the third dimensional experience. Set aside your guilt and forgive yourself for any previous transgressions. As you remember who you are and begin to anchor your Higher Self into your physical body, your ego will become smaller and smaller. Your vast, Starry Overself containing unlimited amounts of love and wisdom will begin to see through your eyes, think through your mind, etc. – thus transforming everything! Then please, bring forth the courage to openly be your empowered magnificent Selves!

Many of us are experiencing this completion of the old as a massive death process. This is not only appropriate; it is quite accurate. *The old, outmoded parts of ourselves are dying.* This is necessary to make way for the New.

Whenever you find yourself in the midst of a death process, it is important to stay with it. Fully acknowledge the energies and emotions you are experiencing, feel them coursing throughout your being. Remember: We are also letting go of denial. But at the same time, it is important to remain aware of the Master Plan. Retain at all times a greater perspective. From the vantage point of your Starry Self, look down compassionately upon the small fragment of your old self who is dying. Now send yourself waves of love, encouragement, strength and understanding.

In the midst of grieving for what is dying away from you and your life, focus on the fact that you are simply clearing space for that which is in more perfect alignment with the Highest Truth of your being. My mantra for this process is: *"Completing the old frees me for the New!"* As you set your course for the New, learn to focus on that which endures.

Death processes are never fun or easy, however with greater understanding, we can pass through them quickly. One thing which I do whenever I find portions of myself dying is to take advantage of these energies and work with them. I put as much as I can into the open grave of my dying. This transformation is known as the great Pluto

Initiation wherein our old selves die that they may give birth to the Phoenix. Times of dying can be utilized positively if you surrender freely, with total abandon.

Remember: Anything which resonates with your Highest Truth will remain!

We truly have nothing to fear. The greater the death, the greater will be the rebirth which follows. And that rebirth is inevitable, for each completion is *always* followed by a new beginning. Learn to die freely, letting go of any resistance so you may move through quickly into the new beginning.

Laying the New Foundation

After each period of dying you can begin laying the foundations of the New by organizing your life into greater efficiency to support your Higher Self. Be sure you take the time to nourish yourself in whatever ways are needed. Incorporate into your daily schedule some things that give your pleasure. This can be as simple as a long bubble bath, time spent working in the garden, reading a magazine, buying yourself fresh flowers, whatever. Something that gives you joy and makes you feel cared for.

No matter how busy your life is or how many people you share it with, it is essential to spend some time each day by yourself in silence. This time can be utilized in meditation, but it doesn't have to be. Sometimes just sitting silently and staring blankly at the walls can be most beneficial. This is your time to integrate all that you have taken in. It is when you can open to inspiration and guidance, when you can reanchor your being on the Template of Oneness.

And of course, give yourself time for relaxation and play. It is a great way to facilitate your assimilation and integration of the incoming accelerated frequencies. Romp with your dog and children, do something extremely silly, watch a funny video, go dancing, let go of all your lofty intellectual and spiritual concepts for a minute and have a good time being playful. *(This is one of the things I like about the work I do. At Reunions and Workshops, our staff gets together in the evenings or at staff meetings and we get really silly. You should see us practicing Barat-Natyam, a classical dance of India, riding camels in Egypt or trying out new ways of wearing our halos. We have fun together!)* Remember, Angels take things lightly. We have to, since our work is basically so serious.

Don't forget to develop your self esteem, for we must love and honor ourselves before we are ready to receive love. And we must learn to give *and receive* love before we can become embodiments of love.

Whenever you feel the human emotions of anger, sadness, impatience, disappointment, etc. course through you, do not try to suppress them. Allow them to express themselves freely. At the same time, from the vantage point of your True Self, see them for what they are and for what they are not. Observe these emotions calmly. "Oh look, now I'm feeling angry." While you are feeling your emotions, you don't need to totally identify with them. Allow them to pass through you quickly, all the while remembering who you really are and that these emotions belong only to your third dimensional fragment.

Join with others who support your continuing growth. This is most important. If you are willing to let go of those people who keep you within narrowly defined roles, those who tend to mock your higher aspirations, you will find yourself making room for new friends who vibrate at the same level of Oneness as you. Our Starry Family is the best support system we could possibly ask for. We are scattered all over the planet. Seek us out, for we strengthen each other tremendously. Even when you are alone and feel overwhelmed, remember to call upon our Unified Presence. You will feel us with you, showering you with love, healing, courage and support.

Focus on the whole instead of the fragments of the whole.

See all of humanity as one vast starry being, held together by love. Feel the interconnectedness between us all. *There is nothing separate from the One.* This is one of the new foundation stones of the Greater Reality. Once you have accepted this great Truth in the depths of your heart, put it into practice. Try going out in the world and observe all the people whom you encounter. Remember: They are all parts of the One, of our Unified Presence. Each person is doing the best that they can at the present moment. Of course, we often see lots of room for improvement in behavior, but that is no excuse for becoming judgmental. Instead, try developing your sense of compassion. Love them for both what they are and for what they are not. Love them simply because they are part of the whole. Love them as you would love your elbow, your toe, the hair on your head. We are all of the One. See how freeing this is?

Contact your Golden, Solar Angel. Bring it in and embody it in your everyday life. Knowing that you are an Angel consciously serving on Earth definitely lightens your burdens and clears your way. It is the path homeward through the heart, for it is impossible to know that you are an Angel and to keep your heart closed. Remember that you are no longer alone; there are millions of us here.

Ask for your Angelic or Starry name, and once you receive it, begin to use it. These names are profound triggers which aid in our transformational process. They dissolve the rigidity of old third dimensional patternings and align us to the New. They are one of the most powerful tools presently available. Your Angelic, Starry name is *your* name, your personal resonance, the unique vibration of your ray of the Star of One. Emanating from the other side of the Doorway of the 11:11, your name opens up and strengthens your pathway Homeward.

Head & Heart Alignment

Here is a simple practice given to me in meditation many years ago. It came at a time when I was having great difficulty aligning my head with my heart. I was receiving quite a lot of amazing experiences and revelations through my meditations with various personal, inner teachers. However, I was still working through my doubts and fears. "Maybe I am making this all up?" "Perhaps I'm losing my mind?" I'm sure many of you have known this scenario. Logic and intuition were waging a huge battle inside of me. While I thrilled to the experiences I was having, I was afraid to believe that they were real.

Finally it all became too confusing. So I asked to be given a practice that would align my being into Oneness. I only used this exercise for a few days; then knew that the task was complete. My doubts and fears had transformed into a new, heightened knowingness and confidence in my own inner voice which has never left me. So I pass this on to you, to use as needed.

Stand with your arms outstretched. Now envision a rainbow which begins at the palm of your left hand, goes through your left arm into your chest, through your heart to your right arm, all the way into the palm of your right hand. From here the rainbow arcs up into your head, passing right through your brain and arcing back into the palm of your left hand.

Make the sound of EEEE. As you make this sound, envision the EEEE sound making the rainbow circuit within you. Repeat this for a few minutes whenever needed.

Focused Intent

We all contain in varying degrees the gap between what we truly are and what we embody in form.

Our challenge is to align our beings into conscious Oneness, so we can embody our vast storehouses of Love, Wisdom and Power. The gap is within all of us, but as we continually raise our bottom lines, the gap narrows. Our focus is shifting from reaching up to the stars to raising the level of our foundation, *or bottom line,* so we can be totally anchored on the Template of Oneness.

It is of utmost importance that you merge with the full magnificence of your Starry Selves. What is needed here is your 100% commitment to embodying the Truth of your Being. A 99% commitment will not do, for whatever you hold back will become magnified until you deal with it. It will keep you from moving through the Door into the New Octave. This is like the old story of the monkey who had his hand in a jar. He wanted desperately to get his hand out, but was not willing to let go of the nut he was holding. We must let go of everything and give our full commitment before we are free to pass through into the new spiral.

Another area which we must deal with has to do with compromises. We have become so accustomed to making compromises in our everyday lives that often we don't even notice when we are making them. We have assumed that they were a natural part of life. But they are not; compromises are an illusion created in duality for the purpose of keeping us smaller. Compromises are simply not an acceptable reality for any of us anymore. Now that the 11:11 is open, compromises will serve to hold us back. We simply cannot make ourselves smaller for anyone or anything. And although some of you might feel that your entire life would fall apart if you let go of your compromises, you might be quite surprised to discover that the opposite is true. Your life will develop much more smoothly when you uproot all vestiges of compromise from your being.

Restructurization

Our process of restructuring has been continuing unabated. There is no part of our beings which is not being affected. We are changing from carbon based bodies into silicon bodies of Light. The scope of this transformation is enormous! Hence we are continuing to experience many strange physical and psychic symptoms. Some of us are developing irregular rhythms in our hearts. This happens to me whenever I experience a quantum shift in energies. It often takes a few months for my heart to calm down.

Another interesting thing concerns our vision. Many of us are discovering that we can't see as well as before. This is because we are moving out of the third dimensional reality. Actually our True Sight is becoming much keener, enabling us to see into the Invisible. These symptoms are nothing to fear; they are simply indications of the vast changes we are undergoing in order to move onto a new spiral.

Even our wings are transforming. When we initially begin to perceive them, they are often white in color. As we become increasingly empowered, our wings turn golden-white and then golden. The next step is crystalline wings. From there they develop glints of iridescence. Eventually, our wings disappear, leaving only some iridescent sparkles. Each of these shifts in coloring perfectly mirrors our progression through the various stages of anchoring our full Presence.

Often when we are undergoing a period of intense restructurization, we will find that we develop colds or the flu. This serves to lessen our physical activities and keep us quiet so we can better assimilate the incoming changes.

It is helpful to constantly remind ourselves of the vastness of what we are experiencing. *We are shifting Great Central Sun Systems after all.* That is an unspeakably huge change, so it is no wonder that it strongly affects our physical bodies. This is another reason why it is good to join together with other members of our Starry Family. Sharing our symptoms of restructurization, we are able to discover that many of us are experiencing the same things. And we can refocus on our Purpose and continue on the Homeward Journey.

Archangel Mikael

The activation of the Legions of Mikael or Michael began in February 1988. Since then many have risen into empowerment. Archangel Mikael has long served as the Overseer of our awakening. He has been watching over our evolutionary progress since we first came to Earth.

Already, the commanders of his Legions presently incarnate upon Earth are being drawn together in order to prepare for this vast quantum leap for humanity. The Call resounds across both Heaven & Earth in order to awaken, activate and empower all who serve in this vast Legion of Light. Indeed, the time is at hand which we have long awaited. Each of you is needed in your full Presence, for we must join together as One in order to fulfill our Divine Missions and complete our Earthly span of service.

A mass activation is now in effect.
You have hereby been placed on full alert!

Mikael's focus is that of empowerment. Power has long been the most misunderstood and the most feared energy on Earth. Many have taken on a tremendous amount of guilt over our misuse of power in previous lifetimes. We have judged ourselves as too unworthy and impure to reclaim our Divine Birthright and Heritage. We felt that

41

we deserved to experience punishment and suffering, hence we kept ourselves small by continually feeding our pain. It is now time to let all of that go. Let's cast aside all illusion and see ourselves in the Light of the Greater Reality. First we shall return to the Starry Council. That's where we gathered together to prepare for our initial descent into matter. Maybe you remember now, that exquisitely beautiful, circular, starry temple where we sat in rows upon rows, rising upwards like an amphitheater...

In the center of the floor is an opening through which we could see into myriad dimensional universes. There we were in our vast, starry bodies of Light, bristling with excitement at our impending adventure into the world of form. We gazed with wonder down upon the tiny planet Earth which appeared as a small blue and white orb. This was when we were given the opportunity to choose our entire cycle of Earthly embodiments. We were like actors in a repertory company choosing our next season of plays. And we chose carefully, picking numerous, widely diverse lifetimes in which we would experience the full spectrum of human life, because we didn't want to miss anything!

At that time we weren't afraid to pick incarnations where we abused power or were victims of abusers of power. Sitting in the Starry Councils in our full Presence, we realized that all our experiences upon the Earth would be mere child's play in the illusory drama of duality. Yet, we also knew well that we would be fulfilling a Higher Purpose by descending into density and transmuting matter.

Now when you take part in a play and the performance is over, what happens? We remove our costumes and makeup and return to our everyday reality. We don't carry guilt with us because we happened to play the part of a villain. So why have we allowed ourselves to do that here on Earth? Why have we judged ourselves to be *bad* and unworthy because of the various roles we have chosen to play?

It is important to remember that only a small fragment of our true Self incarnates at all. It is now the time to remove our old costumes and disguises and remember who we truly are and who we always have been. And above all else, to step forth openly as that which we truly are!

It's interesting how the cycle of misusing power manifests itself on Earth. This cycle is actually quite short in duration, although its memories tend to stay with us for a long time. It begins gradually until we finally work ourselves into a really heavy lifetime. First we start by being petty and mean, maybe as a shopkeeper or landlord who is selfish and cheats on his customers. After we have gotten a taste of distorted power, we are on our way.

The cycle continues with ever greater abuses of power until we come to our really big one. This is the incarnation where we are the mean ruler who causes great suffering to his people, or the evil witch who uses her magic to manipulate and control. Or maybe we played it out with more dramatic scenarios, by annihilating entire civilizations or blowing up planets.

The good news is that after our most massive abuse of power, we usually see the error of our ways and sincerely vow never to misuse power again. We do our utmost to avoid positions of power and authority, attempting to hide any strengths or capabilities we may have accumulated. For above all else, we don't want any attention drawn to us. We want to stay small so we can become harmless! This is when we usually take the Sword of Empowerment handed to us by Archangel Mikael back in the Starry Councils and place it somewhere inside our body, so the constant pain of it will remind us of the dangers of power.

Then comes the twist of fate; this is the lifetime which actually damages us the most. A possible scenario runs like this: You are born into a ruling family, but feel safe because you are the youngest. However, everyone older than you gets incapacitated, so guess who is thrust into the position of power? Or perhaps you are a lowly officer in the heat of battle, grateful for the anonymity of your humble position. Those in authority above you get killed and suddenly you are in charge. You get the picture...

Now here's the ironic part. This time when you are placed unwillingly into a position of authority, you do your utmost to serve wisely, to be a good ruler, to help your people. But in spite of all your sincere efforts, you are severely ostracized and often killed. You tried to use power wisely and it still didn't work! This is when you vow never to have anything to do with power or authority again.

Now it's time to move into the next phase called the Cycle of Atonement. Here you willingly choose to be a victim, so you will never again be tempted with power. The Cycle of Atonement is of extremely long duration for masses of victims are needed as fodder for the abusers of power. Many of us are just now emerging from this cycle.

Remember: Power is simply an energy.

There is an endless supply of power available to us from the One. True power is nothing to be feared, nor can it be owned, hoarded or manipulated. It simply is... I have to sigh sometimes when I hear of all the classes teaching people how to reclaim *their* personal power, how to manipulate it to serve their own needs, and sometimes even how to steal it from others. Sooner or later, they will learn that the most powerful thing is No-Power. A total absence of power which is achieved by letting go of all the personal power which you worked so hard to acquire.

Standing openly with No-Power is where you find absolute protection, total purity, and an unlimited supply of clean power. To stand directly in the beam of our Star with our hearts wide open is true empowerment! This gives us direct access to an unlimited supply of Love, Wisdom and Power which must be wedded together within us in perfect balance. None of the elements of this sacred trinity can be held onto or possessed by anyone. For as soon as we try, they begin to distort, suffocate and disappear. And why should we want to, as there is a limitless supply of Love, Wisdom and Power for everyone.

What is desperately needed upon the Earth today are ones who can serve as clean instruments of power, beings who have activated and united within themselves the sacred triangle of Love, Wisdom & Power. Only after this is achieved, will we be able to fulfill our Divine Missions and complete our journey through the Doorway of the 11:11.

And here's another amusing thought... After all the work we have done in fully activating the Legions of Mikael so that we can ride forth as one unified, Legion of Light here on Earth, this facet of our destiny is nearing its chosen end. On December 31, 2011 when the Doorway of the 11:11 finally closes, the Legions of Mikael shall be disbanded. For our work here will be complete.

The first level of Mikael's work is healing our issues of power and helping us rise into full empowerment. However, each of us, Mikael included, holds a new sceptre of responsibility within the Template of Oneness. In the context of the 11:11, Archangel Mikael's Divine Mission could be described as:

He aids in the transition from the old patterning of duality into the new patterning of Oneness. Mikael is the primary Overseer of our transformation from 3D human selves into starry beings. By bringing the small white birds, *(us as awakened Star-Borne)* into the patterning of the Birdstar, Archangel Mikael activates the many, bringing them into the potential of the One.

45

The Order of Melchizedek

On November 11, 1991 there was the long awaited activation of the Order of Melchizedek. Melchizedek serves as the Overseer of the Lords of Wisdom, those Holders of secret ancient knowledge. All that which has been hidden away in the Halls of Records, buried in sealed up caverns, whispered to only a few initiates, is under the leadership of the Order of Melchizedek. The ancient tribal peoples who have quietly kept alive the Higher Wisdom such as the Australian Aborigines, the Dogon of Mali, the Mayans and the Hopi are aligned with Melchizedek.

With this most important activation of Melchizedek, there will be an increased externalization of that which has long been hidden. Some of the Halls of Records shall be found and opened. The secrets of the Dead Sea Scrolls will finally be revealed. Also there shall be an externalization of the hierarchy. What this means is that many of the hidden masters will now step forth. We are not talking here only of those masters long rumored to be living in secret caves in the Himalayas; although some of them will definitely be making their Presence felt.

But there are hidden masters all over the planet who will now be coming forth with their great reservoirs of Love,

Wisdom & Power. And guess who these hidden masters are? That's right, it is us, the awakened Star-Borne! We are the hidden masters, we've been here all along, and now it is the time for us to reveal ourselves, to walk openly amongst humanity.

The New Sceptres

As we have mentioned before, sceptres are being passed. These are the sceptres of responsibility which we chose to carry back at the beginning. As we complete our long cycle in the patterning of duality, we are now free to hand in our old sceptres and to receive new ones which we shall wield in the Template of Oneness.

Melchizedek, as well, carries a new sceptre. His could be described as a Rod of Power. As the Order of Melchizedek rises into full activation from November 11, 1991 to the end of 1995, his Rod of Power will be sending forth a bolt of lightning like energy which shall be stimulating our internal rod of power. This will serve to anchor the Yods of the New Template into the Earth and to further activate our cellular memory banks. With his Rod of Power, Melchizedek shall be quickening the Birdstar, transforming the many into the fully manifested One.

47

Preparatory Initiations: Part 1

Throughout 1991 I was sent off on a series of journeys to many different parts of the world. Two months of the year were spent in the Southern Hemisphere, first in Australia and New Zealand, later in Brazil. Part of my task was to awaken our Starry Family. And such magnificent ones I met; some of whom have become dear friends. Everywhere I traveled, there was a huge response to the message of Star-Borne and the 11:11.

During my travels, I also found myself involved in a series of activations and initiations. Some were highly personal in nature, while others involved preparing the planet for the opening of the Doorway. The Template of Oneness was anchored in some key planetary vortexes. This work was aided by members of our Starry Family who always came forth to serve when needed. It would not have been achieved without their help and support for which I am deeply grateful. Here are a few stories from my journeys:

Hawaii

In Spring of 1991 I traveled extensively throughout Australia and New Zealand activating the Star-Borne. My journey back to the heart of Lemuria began in Hawaii where I visited volcanos and rain forests on the Island of

Hawaii and gave a talk in Honolulu. At sunset I walked the lava flows as fresh, molten, golden swirled lava streamed into the ocean. I met with my friends Makua and Reta AnRa, sharing remembrances of celestial navigation and finding our starry origins to be similar. Makua told me of the four pillars which mark the boundaries of this dimensional universe. Most of the time they are angled into the center, keeping the door closed. Now they are open for those who are ready to journey further. Standing upright, the four pillars form an 11:11.

From the first morning in Honolulu when I gazed at the distant, lush green mountains to my favorite bird sanctuary on the Big Island where I walked through lava tubes, visited with the little people and remembered timeless initiations long ago, there was a gentle, yet persistent singing which followed me everywhere. Repeating some of the words to Makua, I was told that it was ancient Hawaiian! He said that in order to go home, we must complete our migrations back to the place of the beginning, that was why I was making my pilgrimage to Lemuria. On my last night, after giving a glorious talk in Honolulu, draped in numerous flower leis, feeling somewhat like a Lemurian Princess, I departed for Australia.

Australia

The response in Australia to Star-Borne's message was phenomenal. Although I was not well known upon my arrival, our Starry Family in Australia was *ready* to be activated! And what dear, dedicated family we have in Australia. Thirteen talks and six workshops were given throughout the country, all well attended.

The highlight of the trip was a special gathering at Uluru *(Ayers Rock)* in Central Australia over the Easter holiday. For five days, twenty two of us came together from all over

Australia to anchor the Template of Oneness into this sacred power point. It was an important step in my own cycle of initiations, for this was the place where Altazar, the beloved High King of Lemuria had reached a state of full remembrance. So this was a major completion for me.

Upon my arrival at Uluru, I went immediately to Mutujulu Springs and asked for a sign that this work of anchoring the new template would be achieved, and that I was truly the one to fulfill the prophecy of activating Uluru into the Template of Oneness. If all this was true, I wanted to find a feather as instant confirmation. Stopping on the path, I looked down at my feet. There was no feather in sight. *(Great, I thought with relief, that's one less thing to do!)*

Then I glanced to my right where there was a dry river bed. *(It had not rained at Uluru for thirteen months.)* There in the river bed were hundreds of small white feathers! I heard a voice say, "Are these enough feathers for you or do you need more of a sign?" Feeling very humbled and awestruck, I was told to look under a small arched rock for a feather to take home with me. Sure enough, a beautiful, long white feather awaited.

That night the rains came – filling up all the waterholes. The magnificent red rock of Uluru streamed with myriad waterfalls as it poured for two more days. On the third day our group walked all the way around the perimeters of the Rock, around 7 km., so we got to know this amazingly powerful vortex more intimately. Uluru is considered to be either the heart or the solar plexus of the planet, and both seem to be true since it is a powerfully loving place.

Easter was extremely intense. The energies were so strong that a few members of our group became unbalanced, resulting in a period of chaos. It was an intense challenge for all of us; but many broke through, sealed orders popped open, veils dissolved; we played out our various roles and finally, the Template of Oneness was anchored!

The next morning a few of us drove out to Mutujulu Springs to say our farewells and see if the energies of Uluru had changed. The Rock had never looked so bright and shining; it was streaming with the Light of Remembrance. The energy had magnified and clarified immensely. We could see with our physical eyes the vast extent of the shift which had been accomplished.

New Zealand

Two weeks before I was to arrive in New Zealand, my organizer there suggested that I should cancel my trip. There simply wasn't enough interest to fill a workshop. But I felt a real calling to activate the Star-Borne in New Zealand, so I asked him to proceed with organizing the four talks and workshop, for I knew that the right people would come. *(This is not unusual when I travel, for usually I am sent to those places where I am not well known.)*

Shortly thereafter a miracle occurred. My workshop was scheduled for the Tauhara Centre, a beautiful Light Center on Lake Taupo in the middle of the North Island. *(Lake Taupo is known as the heart center of New Zealand and it definitely is!)* What happened was; one night all the clocks at the Tauhara Centre stopped at 11:11. Then the folks there knew that something special was up and started signing up for the workshop which ended up having 120 people! Several Maoris attended and shared of their legends about the return of the New Star Tribe who come together in Oneness from all over the world.

A few days later, four of us set off for the South Island to locate and activate the new Master Grid Vortex. Our small group of intrepid adventurers discovered that we all needed

51

to be dressed in white, so off we went to purchase identical outfits topped off with white hats from Te Anau. *(Talk about trying to keep a low profile!)* Then came the perplexing job of locating the new Vortex. By night, we studied topographical maps; by day, we drove all over the South Island until we arrived at Milford Sound.

Anchoring the Vortex at Milford Sound

A funny thing – on our way to the Sound we passed almost thirty tour buses going in the opposite direction. When we arrived at Milford's only hotel, *without a reservation,* we discovered that the hotel was virtually deserted for the night. In the early morning we took a boat tour through Milford Sound in misty rain. The boat was practically empty and we were the only ones standing outside on the upper deck. *(Everyone else was inside the lower deck keeping warm and dry.)* As we traveled damply through the Sound getting increasingly wetter, we all knew that although one could not say that this *was* the Vortex, this was where we were to anchor it.

Suddenly the skipper cut the boat's engines and announced that we were in a special place. The four of us went to work on the upper deck, reaching through the Doorway of the 11:11, taking hold of an iridescent thread from the other side and anchoring it here on Earth. The skipper waited patiently until we were done. The passengers remained downstairs. Time stopped as we moved into that eternal, enduring moment of No-Time and with great ease, the job was done! Returning to the hotel, we discovered hoards of people and tour buses swarming everywhere! Somehow, all the tourists had been kept away for one night so we could do our task undisturbed. Perfect, isn't it!

Solara doing her mudra at Lake Taupo, New Zealand

To complete the trip, I was given the gift of three days of silence in the retreat cabin of the Tauhara Centre. New friends took turns bringing me the most delicious, nutritious meals *(Tauhara is famous for its food)*, then with a quick smile and a flash of their mudra, they were gone. Here I slept deeply, *(I had about four free days in two months of intense traveling)*, drank thirstily of the pristine silence, passed through unspeakably subtle iridescent realms, and finally finished writing my book, *EL*AN*RA.*

First and Second Wave

Prior to our descent into matter when each one of us chose our destiny pattern in the Starry Council, we became aligned with either a First or Second Wave patterning.

The First Wave beings chose to come to Earth in order to irrevocably Anchor the New. They are the ones who have experienced countless embodiments upon this planet, thus have been the holders of ancient wisdom as well as the leaders, prophets and visionaries. First Waves have seen everything and been everything. They are aligned with the number eleven. Because of their long cycle of experience here, most First Wavers are profoundly weary and longing to return Home. It is difficult to get many First Wavers enthusiastic about anything on the Earthplane except for the task of completing their Missions and moving onward.

The Second Wave's Purpose is to Build upon the New once it is firmly anchored. Aligned with the number twenty-two, they have had far less Earthly experience. This does not mean that they are less advanced, rather that they have spent more time off-planet than on. Second Wavers are the future leaders, the artists, the sacred architects; the ones with new forms of healing, music, creating and community. Bristling with energy to manifest, the Second Wavers have also been riddled with impatience to create!

Some of the First Wave have been hiding away for years in quiet and seclusion, feeling that they had no more energy to serve; that they had already given their fullest in times past. Many others are still serving as the Doers, *exhausted for sure*, but still making certain that the New gets anchored.

Since the activation of the 11:11, many of the First Wavers have been stepping forth openly with their fullest commitment to facilitating not only the opening of the Doorway, but helping to prepare our Starry Brethren to make the shift into the New Octave of Oneness. This is the Call to Homecoming that they have awaited, that they, themselves have called forth to be!

And let us say that many of the First Wavers have a deep understanding of the full significance of what this shift in spirals entails. They still hold the remembrance of the last doorway aeons ago when many ascended from this planet. They remember the dedication and enthusiasm they felt to help create the New, much as the Second Wavers feel now.

Many of them are ready to take the leap and move into the New. Of course, it can be a challenge for First Waves to clear out the myriad layers of clutter, disappointment, sadness and fatigue which they have accumulated throughout their cycle of incarnations. They are the ones who are learning just how much illusory debris they have picked up during their Earthly journey. And as I have discovered myself, *we must now be prepared to let go of everything!* This includes our vast earthly histories, storehouses of memories and knowledge, antiquated narrow habits and patterns, even our most holy, sacred altars. We must willingly, lovingly surrender anything inside or outside of ourselves which serves to limit or define our beings within the parameters of duality. And for us First Wavers, this has proven to be an enormous task in itself!

Now for a Second Waver, this is not nearly so difficult, simply because they haven't accumulated as much baggage along the way. Hence you will often find Second Waves somewhat impatient at the snails pace which the First Wave exhibits in releasing old patternings. Through a First Waver's eyes, the pace of letting go is fast, often *brutally* rapid. It often feels as if they are continuously undergoing a prolonged death experience.

Which brings us to another difference in perception between First and Second Waves. The Second Wavers often think of the First Wavers as full of fascinating information and experiences; but frankly, not very much fun. That's because First Wavers really don't want to do anything unless there's an important reason for it. Their idea of an enjoyable way to spend their rare free time is to sit at home staring at the flashes of sunlight delicately dancing upon the walls or out in nature watching the water running over the rocks in a stream. They've already read all the books and listened to all the music, discovering a boring sameness to it all. Perhaps, if there was something which was truly different, which came from a new energy source . . .

First Wavers often feel like tired Grandparents to the Second Wave, watching with bemusement while the Second Wave keep themselves busy with endless activities and chatter. They listen patiently to the creative visions of the Second Wave, encourage them on, yet are deeply grateful that these tasks are to be achieved by others.

The Second Wavers find themselves easily bored with inactivity. They love to go out and explore new things. They like to keep moving, experiencing and learning. They can't understand the concepts of weariness and struggle carried by the First Wave. Life on Earth is a glorious adventure!

However, not all First Wavers crave the silence. Some have become so jaded by their prolonged immersion into the third dimensional world that they require constant, outer stimulation in order to feel alive. You will find large collections of this type living in our biggest, cosmopolitan cities where the constant interplay of noise, activities and confusion helps to cover over their numbness. By over-developing their intellects, they have long forgotten the beauty of being natural and simple. They have lost touch with the purity of their true natures and have assumed a thick veneer of cynicism which barely masks the empty despair of their souls.

Thus, these ones are difficult to activate. Sometimes you can touch them deeply for a time; but they are often unable to sustain this new heightened sense of lightness, innocence and freedom. They are afraid to believe that the time which we have long awaited is truly here. Sadly, we watch them sink back into the morass of their old habits.

Throughout my life, I have seen so many bright beings rise up into remembrance, regain their true magnificence, then slide back into sleep. This had caused me much sadness and challenged me to continuously release all expectations and allow each one to freely make their own choice. At times, it feels like we are living in a war zone. I try to hold fast to the Golden Beam and carry on as best I can in the midst of tremendous carnage, watching many whom I have grown to love disappear back into a state of numbed amnesia. When this happens, there is nothing more which we can do to reawaken them. There are no more words or actions which will trigger remembrance. By forgetting who they are, they have also forgotten who we are. All we can do is to lovingly release them onto their chosen path of destiny and continue on. Everything serves the perfection of the Divine Plan, whether we understand it or not.

Another interesting phenomena is that of the Beginners, those who are newly awakened. A friend of mine calls these ones *the Pop-Ups*, for they are just like mushrooms which suddenly pop-up in a forest right after a rain. They are the ones who are always apologizing for being so new in the spiritual world; the ones who haven't read many of the books or spent years wading through various spiritual paths. I also tell them that they can't fool me, for I know how advanced they really are.

Back in the Starry Councils, before we ever descended into matter, these *Beginners* were wise enough to decide not to reawaken until it was the time of the Great Awakening. Therefore sparing themselves all the layers of illusion from which the rest of us are still trying to extricate ourselves. So if you regard yourself as a *Beginner* to the spiritual path, you can now start to congratulate yourself for a wise choice. I have personally found that Beginners not only are free of most of the old baggage, but once awakened, they are ready to give their fullest commitment to fulfilling their Divine Missions with strength, boundless courage and total dedication.

It could be stated that generally, the Second Wavers are having a much easier time on Earth than First Wavers. Naturally, they are impatient to get on with Building the New and manifesting their creations. But while they are waiting, they are finding this planet a fascinating place to visit.

What the Second Wavers have not understood until recently is that the New cannot be created within the old dimensional patterning. It will manifest on the other side of the Doorway of the 11:11 in Octave Seven which could be called Second Wave Paradise! To try to manifest the New into form within the Template of Duality is like trying to place a round peg into a square hole. However, as more of us consciously anchor our beings into the Template of Oneness, we will serve to bring the other side of the Doorway *here* into the physical and Second Wavers will find increasing ease of manifestation.

Now there may be some of you who are still not sure which Wave you belong to. Possibly you feel like a little bit of both? Then you are probably a First Wave who will choose to remain in Octave Seven and join with the Second Wavers to Build the New. You see, once the First Wave passes through the 11:11, their contracts are complete. They are free. But each of them will be given the choice as to whether they wish to stay in Octave Seven with the Second Wave and Starchildren or to journey onwards to Octave Eleven and beyond.

First and Second Waves bring each other great gifts: experience and wisdom combined with energy and enthusiasm. We all need the qualities which the other Wave brings to our Unified Presence. And it is now of utmost importance that we unite together with focused intent in order to move through the Doorway into the new Divine Dispensation.

Starchildren

Enlightened, pure beings from the stars have been incarnating on this planet in ever increasing numbers. These are the ones we call Starchildren. The earliest forerunners of the Starchildren came in about twenty-five years ago, but their incarnations stepped up considerably around fifteen years ago with ever larger numbers in recent years.

These already awakened ones have come here from the other side of the Doorway of the 11:11. They arrive on Earth with their memories intact, emanating a powerful purity of Essence. Starchildren are like fresh troops upon this planet – bright, clear members of our greater Starry Family come to help lead us through the Doorway. Each Starchild already has their return ticket home.

Starchildren incarnate under an extremely different patterning than the ones of us already here. They have not been through the mill as most of the weary First Wave has, nor are they here predominately to experience as the Second Wave has been doing until recently.

They are on Earth to hold the resonance of the Template of Oneness for all of us until we also resonate in accord with the Greater Reality. Therefore it can be stated that Starchildren have a different vibratory rate than most of us. They are already operating from a new internal grid matrix that the newly awakened Star-Borne are just now moving into. This has a highly calibrated rate of vibration. Starchildren shall be serving us as Celestial Navigators as we move through the 11:11 into the New Octave. *(That's why they are so good at those lightning fast video games. It's all just practice for them to keep their skills honed.)*

Once we arrive at Octave Seven, Starchildren will be moving into positions of leadership, working alongside the Second Wavers. They are the visionaries of the new template, each of them containing within them the hologram of the New Octave.

Naturally, Starchildren need to be treated differently than *normal* children. Some of this has been already mentioned in my book, *The Star-Borne*. They require *and deserve* lots of respect from us. But this doesn't mean they should be placed on little silk pillows and catered to. *Starchildren need boundaries in their lives.* Here I want to stress the difference between boundaries and limitations. In no way can we hamper or limit their spirits, yet it is most important that we give them enlightened parameters. They need to know what is not acceptable behavior. Otherwise we're going to end up with spoiled, self-indulgent children.

It is most helpful if we are clear with them about the differences between life in the 3D and the Greater Reality. Starchildren need to be aware of their responsibilities both in the world of duality and as starry beings. If they can see each reality system clearly, they will be better able to maintain their integrity and balance.

Starchildren also need quiet, although many of them will not willingly seek it. It is beneficial if they can have their own personal space and are given time alone there. This is to replenish their energies from the onslaught of the world of duality. Often they will become engrossed in distractions, from television to myriad activities and forget to take time for themselves. This is where you can help them as an enlightened parent. Set the boundaries so they can get plenty of rest and time to ground their energies.

Starry teenagers, in particular, are having a difficult time. It's not easy to carry the knowledge that they do and deal on a daily basis with the soap opera world of modern high school life. Here they are faced with crowds of less enlightened beings and the social pressures of sex, drugs, alcohol, popularity, as well as academic demands. Many of them are more mature than their peers and teachers, yet they still have the teenage abundance of energy, wild hormones and the need to break free of all constraints.

The need is great to create schools for our Starchildren so they don't have to be barraged with the illusions of duality. They need inspiring places where they can be treated with respect, taught not only basic skills, but the underlying Purpose behind the world of duality. They need the opportunity to create their visions. Hopefully this will come about as our Islands of Light are formed.

The most important thing that we can do for Starchildren is to be our True Selves around them. They do not need to be immersed in any third dimensional patterns of thinking and being! They truly need us to be in our fully empowered, awakened Presence, communicating with them as one starry being to another. We can serve as the other's link between the Higher Realms and the world of matter. And then we can enjoy the delightful blessings which Starchildren bring us – joy, fresh energy and insights from the New Octave!

Pregnancy

Since Starchildren originate from a more finely calibrated resonance than the Earthly frequencies, on occasion this can make pregnancy difficult. The problem occurs as the Starchild's frequencies begin to anchor within its mother. It is like an alignment of two templates. Now if the mother has not fully anchored her Starry Overself and if the baby is arriving with a highly refined Starry Template, *which they increasingly are,* then sometimes there will be the possibility of miscarriage. This situation can be easily averted and transformed. What the mother needs to do is to extend her internal template and grid patterning from that of duality into Oneness.

She can achieve this by anchoring and embodying more of her Higher Self, Angelic Presence and Starry Overself – each of these being various levels of the same Essence. It is also important to activate your Greater Heart so you and your child can align into the One Heart. I have seen dramatic transformations from problematic pregnancies to a pregnancy of total ease. This is because the Template of Oneness cannot anchor itself into the Template of Duality until duality has been transformed into Oneness. Once this is done, the pregnancy will proceed with ease. So being pregnant with a Starchild is an excellent opportunity to transform yourself into more of who you are. Remember: Communicate with your Starbaby, not just as parent to child, but as starry being to starry being. Honor this new member of our Starry Family!

Partnerships

Once the Doorway of the 11:11 is opened, there will be a vast shift in our current mode of partnerships. For those choosing to anchor their beings in the New Octave of the Greater Reality, the old form of third dimensional relationship between two incomplete fragments will die away. Many of us have already found this old way of relating not only unfulfilling, but impossible to attempt. After you have merged with your full Presence, it is pointless to try to relate on an intimate level to one who is still anchored in duality. Thus many of the Star-Borne have spent the past several years without a love relationship in their lives.

This period of solitude has served us greatly. Here we learned what we want and don't want in a relationship. We had the time to discover just what true relating is all about. *(Then of course, when we are in a partnership we put all our great revelations to the test.)* Being alone also gave us the opportunity to put our full attention on the awakening process. We have discovered who we really are, adjusting to our own internal rhythms. Learning to live alone, we have made friends with the silence. If needed we could be up during strange hours of the night – writing, meditating or simply sitting in silence. We have been given the time to allow our own inner process of integration of the higher frequencies to take place unhindered. Loving our shadow selves into Oneness, unifying our polarities, cleansing ourselves of old habits and patternings – the time in solitude has surely been a blessed gift.

Others of us have not been so fortunate. They are the ones who have continued to hide themselves in unfulfilling relationships. You know what kind of partnerships, the ones which have required us to be less than we really are. They are defined by the rules, regulations and morals of accepted third dimensional behavior. Initially many of these relationships were entered into out of innocence, for we knew not who we truly were. But often, we have stayed in limiting relationships out of fear – the fear of truly being ourselves, hiding from our own magnificence.

Much of this has stemmed from our memories of previous misuses of power in times past. We have feared that if we were liberated that perhaps, we might run amok again. So we simply deemed it safer to remain in the confinement of an incomplete union for it represented the safety of the Known. This did serve to give us a false sense of security from which we could build our lives in the third dimensional framework.

The sad thing is that while we allowed ourselves to be subjugated in these outmoded relationships, we developed a deeply ingrained victim attitude, often blaming our partner for our own lack of courage. "Of course, I would like to be doing my utmost to fulfill my Higher Purpose, but I have to think of my marriage." If you find recognition here, maybe this insight will jar you into finally taking full responsibility for your own being. No one keeps you from fulfilling your Divine Mission, but yourself! No one holds you back from embodying your full Presence except yourself! Whether you are willing to accept it or not, it is your own choice that keeps you smaller.

Unfortunately, many great ones have allowed themselves to be limited in this manner. And it has truly not served you. In your years of compromise you have not had the opportunity to clean out the hidden pockets of old patterns and habits. In order to keep justifying the untruth of your everyday reality, it has been necessary to continually strengthen the ego. "This is *my* life; I'm going to do it *my* way!" This illusory sense of assertiveness merely covers up your deep, underlying discontent. It is particularly touching in the case of First Wavers, who just might miss their opportunity to move onwards.

Luckily, the Call of our Unified Presence is getting stronger each day. It is becoming increasingly difficult to deny. Many of the ones who have been shutting their ears for years are *nevertheless*, hearing and responding to this Call. The Great Awakening is getting impossible to ignore. At the same time, the solidity of the third dimensional patterning is fading away. What is left to do other than to follow the inner promptings of our Greater Hearts, choosing love and true, spiritual union over fear?

Sceptres are being passed. The transfer is in position. For everything that dies, something new is reborn. For each letting go and surrender, there is the gift of the New. All of us must periodically tip over the chalice of our beings, emptying it out completely that it may be filled anew. To put it simply: When you are faced with a need to surrender; surrender completely. Let go of absolutely everything. There is nothing that you need fear losing. For what truly belongs to you, whatever resonates with the *Highest Truth* of your being will remain! Why hold on to anything less?

This is especially true in the area of partnerships which are undergoing tremendous, cataclysmic upheaval. Many are finally gathering the courage to step free of outmoded, third dimensional relationships. It is simply a decision to choose the Greater over the lesser. It is part of our process of becoming free of duality. There are practically no partnerships which are untouched by the massive shifts we are currently undergoing. Even *successful* relationships are finding it necessary to move their union onto higher levels of consciousness in order to continue to grow and evolve.

From Soul Mates to Twin Flames

There are vast changes ahead of us in the area of partnerships. For woven into the very fabric of the Greater Reality is the Template of True Love. This heralds the entrance of the new form of partnership which many of us have been anxiously awaiting... The reunion between you and your True Love on the physical plane.

I know there has been a lot of talk about Soul Mates, Twin Flames, inner polarities and now here is the introduction of your True Love. What is the difference between them? Soul Mates are those with whom we share a deep inner affinity. We always knew that we had several Soul Mates scattered about the planet at any given time. What was not realized before, is that we are all Soul Mates to one another. It is the alignment of individual Essences into Oneness, and as we increasingly step into the New Octave, the fact of inherent Oneness becomes evermore obvious.

Twin Flames are our counterparts who live on the other side of the Doorway of the 11:11, either in Octave Seven or Eleven. They rarely step down into matter and when they do, it is unusual to experience an enduring romantic relationship with them. Often the energies are too intense to remain together. Most of the time when Twin Flames come to Earth they serve to trigger us into greater levels of awakening, then mysteriously disappear from our lives. I

myself, have experienced this many years ago. Here is my
story which I have shared with few people:

Δ   Δ   Δ

It was the Summer Solstice in London. The year was 1968,
when London was in the midst of the grand and glorious
hippy days – a magical time laced with lots of illusion that
presented a taste of Oneness of the times to come. There
were several public gatherings and concerts that evening.
All of my friends were going to the Royal Albert Hall, but
for some unknown reason, I knew that I had to go to a
different event. It was very unusual for me to go somewhere alone, but I felt a strong calling.

I had two large faceted amethyst pendants which had
belonged to my grandmother. For some reason I felt it
important to string one of the amethysts upon a necklace
of clear beads and wear it that night. After I arrived at the
concert, I truly didn't know why I had come and was sorry
that I hadn't gone with my friends. I didn't know anyone
there so I spent the next few hours standing by myself
feeling shy and awkward.

It was when I was standing there aimlessly watching the
light show, feeling totally perplexed, that I felt an immensely powerful energy coming at me from behind. This
energy was so strong, it felt as if I was standing in a wind
tunnel; it almost blew me over. Finally I turned around to
see if there was anything behind me. And there he was,
this intense dark haired, handsome man with wild eyes
which stared into the depths of my soul. The energy
became even stronger... Finally, I managed to stammer,
"Who are you?" "I am Tah-na," he replied. His voice was
both strong and reassuring with a mysterious, unrecogniz-
able accent. When I heard its resonance, I felt safe as I had
never felt before. The energy intensified.

"Where do I know you from?" he asked with a deep sense of urgency. "From another time," I responded unhesitatingly, then was surprised at my answer. "Yes, but of course," he said and gathered me into his arms. The energy became impossible to describe... Dissolving together to a degree I never knew possible... After we slowly parted our embrace, we stood making shy conversation. *(I did find out that he came from Turkey where his name means, Man Who Walks in the Dawn.)* Somehow none of the details of our third dimensional lives had any reality; they simply didn't matter. Whatever the connection was between us, it was absolutely timeless. Then a woman approached us whom he introduced as his companion. Numbly, for I was still in a state of profound shock, I managed a bit of polite conversation and excused myself.

An hour later found me sitting in the deepest, darkest corner of the hall in a state of stunned silence. What was that all about? Who was that man? I wondered. Obviously he was the reason why I was called to come here. A voice suddenly interjected into my thoughts. "Ah, I finally found you; I've been looking everywhere." There he was again, standing before me! Tah-na said that he had taken his companion home; he had explained to her that it was important that he talk to me and everything was all right.

My surrender to this man was instant and total. Our connection emanated from a Greater Reality which superseded anything else I had known. I would follow him to the ends of the Earth if necessary. He was the only person I have ever known whom I worshipped. I would have gladly given up my life for his without a moment's hesitation.

We left the hall and walked for hours through the deserted streets of London, vaguely heading back to my flat on the other side of the city. Our strides matched in perfect unison, walking as if one being. Gazing at his strong features and flowing black hair, I noticed how regal he looked, almost like an Emperor. (*Now this is something if you stop and think about it. For how many men do you know other than Sean Connery who even look like kings, much less emperors?*) We didn't talk much; it didn't seem necessary. We just strode along like two people who had finally reunited back together into One. It was quite something.

Arriving at my flat, we spent a few hours sitting on the living room floor with our backs against the wall, silently holding hands. There was no need to talk or kiss or do anything to break the spell of our perfect Oneness and our joy at finding each other. Never before had I felt so full!

Shortly before the dawn we walked down to a small park on the River Thames. As we entered the park, a most amazing thing happened. The doors of remembrance began to open! I saw that we had been together on this planet once before in the times of the Incas. I was a young maiden when first I married him. He was always incredibly wiser than I. While we walked along, it was as if with each step we were becoming progressively older and I evolved more and more into his equal partner and Queen.

Sitting quietly on a park bench, we both were given the realization that we would not be together in this lifetime, that we had much to achieve on our own. He said that there was one way that we could be together forever which was to live our lives with such purity and dedication to our Higher Purpose that we would complete our Missions upon the Earth and never have to return again. Immediately I made my full, unswerving commitment and felt a deep shifting within my being. Then I gave him the amethyst I was wearing and said that I would wear the other one. And now it was time for us to part.

I know that this makes a good ending to my story, but it wasn't destined to complete yet. What happened is that after two joyous weeks, I began to sink into a profound despair. I could not bear to remain on the Earth if I couldn't be with my Great Love. Then a few weeks later at a reception, there he was again. His companion had returned to France and he was going to stay and work in London for the rest of the year. We both still knew that we weren't meant to have a relationship, but that there was something for us to do.

This amazing man was so spiritually advanced; he always seemed to be several steps ahead of me. This served as my method of propulsion to awaken quickly, so that we could stand on an equal footing. I was consumed with a burning desire to learn all I could, as fast as possible. My time was now spent delving into all the spiritual realms I could access. I didn't just go through new doorways; I blasted my way through.

We didn't call each other on the telephone or spend much time together. What would happen is that every few weeks, I would be off on some errand in a random, always different section of London and all of a sudden, there he was, coming towards me with a large smile on his face as if expecting me! He would always take me in his arms and reassure me that everything was all right. And suddenly, it was. Often we would then go have a cup of tea. I would be anxious to show him how much I had progressed, almost to the level where he had been during our last encounter. But each time, he was far ahead of me. He told me many things which I did not understand at the time, but wish I could remember now.

Finally, it was the end of the year. For the first time I was visiting him in the place where he lived. We both knew that it was the last time we would see each other. I cried and cried, knowing the truth of this, but not wanting to let go. With a final embrace I was gone, traveling for over an hour on the Underground to my flat. When I got home, I climbed the stairs to my room and sat on my bed to cry. That was when the amethyst which I always wore around my neck fell out of its setting.

I never saw Tah-na again on the physical, yet his Essence has merged within me. I know that he performed a great service to me, by helping with my awakening. However, our story is not quite complete. Back in 1982 I was sent to Lake Patzcuaro in Mexico to perform a private ceremony for a special alignment of planets. Surprisingly, Tah-na's Presence began to come in strongly. This was unusual for I had not thought of him for several years. Then one night I had a dream ...

In my dream, he was a great spiritual master who was visiting New York City. I spent much of my dream trying to find him, arriving at one location, only to be told he had just departed for the next. Finally we were at the same place, but we were separated by a locked door. He talked to me through the door, asking me to release him from his promise to be with me after this life was complete. This was like knocking the foundation out from under my being. I hadn't realized until this moment just how much strength it had given me. I couldn't agree to this, even though I knew that I should. "Ask me in person," I stubbornly replied.

A few months later, I awoke in the middle of the night, grabbed pen and paper and wrote a poem releasing him from his promise. So now we are totally free and on our own again. And this is how Twin Flames can manifest in our lives.

From Twin Flames to True Love

As you can see from my story, Twin Flames can serve as our cosmic carrots. Whether they appear in person within your life or call to you from the other side of the Door, they serve to raise us to ever higher levels of consciousness. They are our sacred Beloveds, the missing parts of our being who propel us to achieve completion and union.

Another category is our inner polarity. Each of us has a male and female polarity. They represent the two poles of our internal being. On the higher realms our natural state is androgyny which is when our inner polarities have merged into one being. It is an important part of our process of completion that we heal our inner male and female and bring them into total union. My book, *The Star-Borne* deals with this subject more extensively. *(Also I have a tape called, Unifying the Polarities which is a meditation to bring them into balanced Oneness.)*

Now what is a True Love? A True Love is another physical being with whom you can unite in conscious Oneness on all levels. This being is not your Twin Flame, but it is enlivened or quickened by your Twin Flame so they can serve as your True Love. Although you will be in a relationship with only one True Love, until that one firmly anchors in your life, there are many on this planet who have the potential to serve in this capacity. Once a potential being is quickened and activated by your Twin Flame, then they become your True Love. And of course, when this happens, you will also be quickened by their Twin Flame so you may serve as their True Love.

What is absolutely fascinating about this time is that many of our True Loves are going to manifest into our lives in 1992 and 1993. This is another good reason to lovingly let go of those old relationships which are anchored in duality, which don't bring love, expansion and joy to those involved. Remember: By holding onto a partnership which has run its course, you are not just holding yourself back, but you are also keeping your partner from finding their

True Love. In the Template of Oneness, there are no winners and losers; it is simply Win-Win.

As many Star-Borne proceed with total commitment to our awakening process, we are becoming increasingly more whole and complete within ourselves. This is the new bottom line which has to be reached before we are able to unite with our True Love. Compromises are no longer an acceptable part of our everyday reality. We yearn for nothing less than unobstructed, perfect union on all levels of being. And that is what the anchoring of the Template of True Love brings to all of us who have chosen Oneness over duality.

Two complete beings joining together in love, trust, openness and respect. As we unite, we shall discover that we form one unit. Not the old kind of self absorption in the 3D relationship, but a complete unit with focused intent, who live and serve as One. Our Oneness will be so strong and irrevocable that it will allow us to serve humanity with the fullness of our Presence with barely a sideways glance. We become like two horses working as one team, pulling the wagon of the fulfillment of our Divine Mission. That's focused intent. It's easy and effortless. It's fun and nourishing. And the quality of love between you is limitless.

The Earth

Lest you think that we are concerned only with the stars and have forgotten this planet, we shall now turn our attention to the Earth. What happens to her as we prepare to move through the Doorway of the 11:11? Is she going to be abandoned by us? Of course not, for the Earth is as involved in this process as are we. She is undergoing the same transformations that we are, preparing to ascend.

The Earth is a starry being, just like us. She is reclaiming her Divine Birthright and Heritage and donning her form of Light. Earth is transforming into a star! She will be traveling through the 11:11 in the heart of our Birdstar.

You might ask, "But what of the terrible pollution ? How is Earth ever going to be healed?" She is in the midst of her healing process right now. Again we must release our old attachment of focusing merely on the physical. As our physical forms represent but a small fragment of our totality, so the Earth's physical body is but a tiny fragment of her vastness. When you allow yourself to connect with Earth's Starry Overself, you will see that she is even more pristine than when she was newly created. *This exists right now in the Greater Reality!* It is not something that we have to strive for; it already is. We simply have to allow ourselves to see it – to look larger. If we take a glimpse into the Unseen, we will see the Earth's true form.

As our true nature is whole and complete, so it is for the Earth. If you really want to heal the planet, simply enlarge your vision and see that all the pollution and corruption is an illusion. She is already perfect and pristine. Her true nature resides beyond time and space and is eternal. By embodying our Highest Truth, living in a state of No-Time and moving through the 11:11 into the Greater Reality, we serve as the midwives for our planet's rebirth. This is how we become the ultimate environmentalists.

Shedding Her Skin

At some point before the Doorway of the 11:11 closes on December 31, 2011, a mighty separation is going to take place. This is when the Template of Duality and the Template of Oneness move out of positional alignment. The two spirals of evolution are going to separate once again. When this happens, planet Earth will shed her skin. This is much like peeling the skin off an apple in one fluid, spiraling motion. All that is anchored in the Template of Duality will be removed. This includes not only the environmental pollution, but the portions of humanity who choose to remain in duality. All of this is going to take place painlessly, in the flickering of an instant.

The old skin of the Earth is going to reform itself around another planet which has already offered itself in service. Life in duality will continue on as if nothing has happened. For example, say you have chosen to stay in duality and live in New York City. One night while you are sleeping, the planet is going to shed its skin. In the morning, you will wake up and continue life as usual. New York still looks the same. Duality will continue to play itself out at the normal rate of evolution without the heightened energies of the past several years. The only difference is that some of us are missing. This isn't as grim as it may sound, for the very memory of our existence will fade away instantly, so you will have no one to miss.

Actually, the separation between those who choose duality and those who choose Oneness takes place gradually. This process has already begun. The ones who are entering the 11:11 have started their journey into the realms of the Invisible. Although it takes twenty years for the complete passage through the Eleven Gateways inside the Door, we are already moving into the subtle currents of the Unseen.

This means that those anchored on both the templates of duality and Oneness will become increasingly invisible to each other. An example of this would be a husband and wife who live together. One chooses Oneness and the other chooses duality. Gradually, subtly yet steadily, they become invisible to one another. Finally, one morning, the man wakes up in bed alone. At the same instant, the woman wakes up in bed alone. The two templates have effortlessly moved out of positional alignment.

If you are one who chooses to remain in duality, the important thing to remember is that it is all right! You are not doomed or damned. Eventually there will be another opportunity like this one for graduation and ascension. Meanwhile there is always more to learn and experience in the playing fields of duality. There are some highly advanced, bright beings who are going to *consciously* choose to remain in duality in order to serve. This is what we did last time, when the previous door was opened. It's the path of the Bodhisattva – choosing to remain and serve when you have the opportunity to move to a higher level of awareness. Remember: There is no judgement here; it is simply a matter of choice. Service is needed on all levels of evolution.   77

Children

People ask me about their children. Will they get the opportunity to move through the Door? Firstly, all Starchildren already have their tickets home. Since they originate from the other side of the 11:11 and have incarnated here to remind us of our starry origins, they will return to the New Octave effortlessly.

As to other children, you must remember that although they are children in this present incarnation, their souls are timeless and mature. On the soul level they are fully capable of making their own decisions on whether they wish to graduate from duality at this time. Then they will choose a life situation which enables them to achieve their goal. For example, a child whose soul desires Oneness will find itself with parents who are also choosing that path. Remember: There are no innocent victims in this process. Each person on this planet must make their conscious decision on where they want to anchor their being. And please choose wisely, for the results of this decision will be with us for a long time.

Crop Circles

For several years, mysterious flattened circles have been appearing in the fields of England. Although scientists have tried to come up with logical explanations for this phenomena, such as random whirlwinds, the mystery remains unsolved. What is known is that farmers often hear low humming sounds on the nights that they appear.

Another interesting fact is that the molecular structure of the crops within the circle have been deeply altered.

Beginning in May 1990, the patterning of these crop circles has changed dramatically. The designs have become more elaborate. There are often multiple circles with key shaped formations protruding from them. Some of these new crop circles measure over 300 feet across. When one enters into the crop circles, a heightened energy can be experienced.

It is fascinating that several of the new crop circle formations are in the shape of a dumbbell . And on either side of the line connecting the two circles are very large elevens, forming an 11:11. This design brought to the planet from On High shows our two spirals or Great Central Sun Systems connected by the Doorway of the 11:11!

As with many *unexplainable* mysteries, the crop circle phenomena is being subject to a government cover up. Dubious individuals have come forth stating that they created all the crop circles. Although physically impossible due to the quantity of crop circles appearing not only in Britain, but in many other countries, the media has given this supposed hoax full coverage. Hopefully, world governments will realize one day that humanity does not need to be protected from the existence of mysterious phenomena. Many of us are already aware of the myriad manifestations of the Unknown. And in the times to come there will be increasing occurrences of the unexplainable.

My personal feelings on the crop circles is that they, or most of them, are real expressions from On High. Their symbols are powerful triggers to reactivate our cellular memory banks. And even if they were all man-made, then I would have to say that whoever created them was definitely inspired from Higher Planes of consciousness.

Animals

What happens to the animals when we move through the 11:11? Will they come too? Animals are similar to people; they represent a multitude of levels of evolution. We have now sufficiently awakened to set aside the outdated metaphysical concept that all animals are inferior species compared to humans, and that they are anxiously striving to evolve into human beings. Undoubtedly this is true for some individual animal souls, just like some people want to be horses or lions in their next life. However, if you observe animals with a greater degree of awareness, you will see that many of them are highly evolved starry beings who have chosen their present physical species because it is their most appropriate vehicle for learning and serving!

Take ordinary household cats for example... Many of us live with cats in our homes. Now in spite of the fact that they eat mice *(we eat some pretty strange things too)*, you can see that many of these cats are special beings. They are starry beings who have come to Earth to serve with us in the transmutation of matter. In fact, they are probably more highly evolved than many of us. Look how smart they were to incarnate as cats! They don't have to work for a living or wrestle with the material world and they have lots of time to meditate and work on the inner planes. They have trained us to meet their physical needs of food and shelter and enjoy a certain independence which many of us have yet to achieve in our own lives. Love and affection is always there for them when they want it, yet they aren't dependent upon it to define who they are.

Cats are particularly adept in working with us on the subtle realms. I have two special cats who are highly attuned to the work I am doing. Often when I am working with accelerated energies, I will find them positioned by me, triangulating and anchoring the energies. Cats are great healers as well. When we need healing, they know just where to place themselves on us, so that the healing transmutation of energies can occur. I believe that most animals, if not all of them, understand everything we say.

Dogs too can be highly evolved starry beings, although their work with us tends to be more concerned with levels of protection and companionship. They are immensely faithful and loyal guardians. And if you look at your dog more closely, you will see that they have wings too.

Domestic pets work with us on very intimate levels. They serve with us on a basis of equality and it is important that we show them the respect which they deserve. By aligning ourselves more consciously with the service they are doing, we can work together on more powerful levels.

Each species of mammal, bird, reptiles, insects, etc. has highly evolved starry beings serving in positions of leadership. Each species brings a great gift to all of humanity and to the planet herself. *(Look at the efforts of the Spotted Owl to help save our ancient forests.)* However some species are reaching their time of completion on the Earth and it is all right to lovingly release them to move onwards.

An excellent example of this would be the rhinoceros. This extremely ancient beast is about as First Wave as you can get. Just look at its physical body, so ancient and heavy.

Rhinos have completed their Divine Missions upon the planet and it is time for them to move on. This doesn't mean that we should go out and shoot all remaining rhinos, but it brings into question whether we should go to extremes to preserve them in zoos through artificial insemination. Maybe you can look inwards and see the Rhino Home Planet in a distant corner of the galaxy in the Star System of Monoceros. There, in Rhino Paradise, they drop their weary, heavy forms and don their bodies of Light. They are dancing the dance of freedom and completion.

Dolphins and Whales

Dolphins and whales are in a category by themselves. They are great Masters who have been living amongst us since the beginning, overseeing the fulfillment of the Divine Plan. Whales are more aligned with First Wave energy and originate from the Star System of Canopus, stepping down to Earth via Sirius. They are the Record Keepers of this planet, like great floating libraries. What is interesting about the immense knowledge that the whales hold, is that it is embedded deep within their cellular memory banks in a dormant state and awaits activation. Presently, they don't know the extent of what they know. Possibly this is why they have been beaching themselves. Could this be their way of calling our attention?

Whales have an important role to play in our Homeward Journey. It is of utmost importance that their knowledge be activated. We are the instruments for their activation. They will not be able to fulfill their Divine Missions unless they are activated soon. The whales also have an important role to play in the completion of the Isis/Osiris legend which will further activate the Template of True Love.

Dolphins come from Sirius and act like Second Wavers, bringing in the New. Whales and dolphins could also be perceived as two lineages deriving from the same Source, much like AN and ON. While the point of merging of the latter is the energy known as Metatron, whales and dolphins unite in the starry Presence of A-Qua-La A-Wa-La.

Although fewer whales and dolphins are living in the oceans of our planet than in times past, many dolphins are incarnating into human forms in order to aid our ascension process. There have always been a few dolphins experiencing human embodiments during Earth's history, but now increasing numbers of them are coming into human bodies. These dolphin people are unique unto themselves. They have a highly unusual patterning of energy which enables them to serve amongst us as great healers, helping us to align our physical bodies into our starry body. Energetic, playful and highly sensual, they bring a sense of exuberant joyousness to everyone whom they encounter.

If you are attuned to dolphins, you might want to turn inward and visit with the Dolphin King at Sirius. He's a very accessible being and openly shares his insights. You will find him standing upright on the tip of his tail. A broad smile of welcome shines across his face. Hovering above his head is a circlet of tiny, real stars. Although there were very powerful Dolphin Temples on Earth during the time of Atlantis, some of the purity had already been dispersed, so you would do better to go straight to the Starry Dolphin King or A-Qua-La A-Wa-La herself.

And what of the so-called mythical creatures such as the unicorns, dragons, and winged lions? They definitely exist, but on a higher level of reality. As we develop the ability to see into the Unseen, we shall be able to perceive their presence. They have been on the Earth since the beginning of time. Many of us have been working closely with them all along. They are aligned with the First Wave energy patterning and will soon reach their time of completion.

Islands of Light

There are some portions of the planet's surface which will not be peeled off during the final separation between duality and Oneness. These places are called Islands of Light. They are communities of those who have anchored their beings in the Template of Oneness. A few Islands of Light may already exist. Soon we will see many new ones being created and begin to blossom. Here will be established a new form of community living which is anchored in the Greater Reality.

Most of the Islands of Light will be established in remote areas of the planet. Their function is to anchor the Template of Oneness, creating an island of energy which is aligned with No-Time. *These are the key points on the planet for our future endeavors.* Each Island of Light will be self sustaining, yet they shall align with each other, creating a mandala pattern across the planet. This mandala is the blueprint for the new Starry Grid.

As we move through the Doorway of the 11:11, we will feel drawn to join together with others who have woven themselves into the cloth of One. This is because we are moving into the subtle currents of the Invisible. As duality no longer becomes our predominant reality, we shall feel the need to live within a new band of energy – that which emanates from the New Octave. We are already feeling the intensification of this calling.

Many of us still have no idea where our particular Island of Light will be located. They could be anywhere on this planet. Yet I know that the time fast approaches to find them. Again this is not a matter of personal preference. It is merely an harmonic resonance which calls you together. I do know that all over the Earth there are people who have acquired large parcels of land or resorts who are consciously serving as caretakers until the time is at hand for the Islands of Light to be created. Then each one will be led to their proper place.

Meanwhile, there is much to do. This is an excellent time to release anything which no longer sings to your soul, which no longer resonates with the Truth of your being. Do you really need all that old furniture, books, records, high school momentous and accumulated clutter? If not, clear it out, sell it off and make room for the new. Let's get light and clear and ready for our Islands of Light!

Life in our Islands of Light will enable us to totally surrender into the subtle vibrations of the New Octave. Although some of us, especially Second Wavers, will choose to serve as interfaces between the Island of Light and the world of duality, others amongst us will surrender completely into fully embodying the New. We shall make the transition from doing into being.

Since the Islands of Light will be existing on a different band of energy than the rest of the world, we will not be as susceptible to the fluctuations of duality as before. Here we will be able to move through the Eleven Gateways inside the 11:11 with ease, surrounded by members of our Starry Family who are at similar levels of consciousness. It is important that these Islands of Light are created in a state of utmost purity. They are not places of compromise, rather they require the full embodiment of who we are. They will be simple, filled with Light and new! In some ways they resemble colonies of hermits where each one is given their private space yet are indelibly united into a collective whole. Light, white, transparent and starry – and totally anchored in the One Heart!

Preparatory Initiations: Part 2

Hawaii

In August I returned to Hawaii for two weeks, giving talks in Honolulu and Kauai and a workshop in Honolulu. I knew it was most important to visit Haleakala Crater on the island of Maui and had arranged to meet with my dear friends Makua and Reta AnRa. What we hadn't expected was the arrival of a hurricane off the coast of Hawaii!

(However this is not uncommon to my travels. A few years ago I was driving down the center of Florida when a hurricane and a tropical storm were simultaneously approaching both coasts. Two weeks before, a renegade Star Commander had been in Florida telling everyone to evacuate since a major flood was coming. Or there was the time when I was driving through Las Vegas, Nevada when a rocket fuel plant blew up, knocking down twelve buildings, but miraculously with few casualties. Like many Lightworkers around the planet, I am often used to transmute energies so catastrophes can be averted. To be perfectly honest, this is not one of my favorite areas of service.)

Anyway, as we drove up the winding road to Haleakala our small rental car was buffeted by 60 mph gusts of wind. The park rangers advised us to turn back. Makua and I looked at each other and decided to proceed. On the way up I began to receive the vision of the arrival of the First Light at Haleakala, which is mentioned later in this book. The road became overrun by torrents of water, but we finally reached the parking lot at the summit. At least we were alone. *(This is one way to avoid crowds of tourists!)*

Stepping out of the car, we were instantly drenched. The winds were so strong we could barely walk. I felt exhilarated by the powerful prana swirling about me. While the others quickly returned to the car, I was drawn to follow a small path which wound upwards along the edge of the crater. I knew that there was something that I must do here and asked to find the proper place. Walking in bare feet on the lava, I left the path and was led to a small circle in the rocks. Here I did my mudra and other sacred movements. Then I was told to look downwards for a gift. I replied that I didn't need a gift, that being here was enough of a present. Look under the rock at your feet, the inner voice insisted. A small white feather peeked out of the lava at my feet, which I gratefully accepted.

The next day we went to the beautiful Eo Valley, the burial site for many of the Hawaiian Kings and Queens. It was so familiar; I felt that I could stay there forever. Then we drove out to some hidden sea caves. The water was *icy* cold, but as Makua gestured to us to get in, we did. Following him to the back of the cave, he suddenly disappeared from sight! Then we discovered that by swimming under the back wall of the cave we could enter a hidden chamber. Here the water was an indescribable aqua in color. All was embraced in a delicate stillness. Makua showed me a stone seat underwater, advised me that this was the place where you could ask for anything and left me alone. What an exquisite place of initiation.

On Kauai, my daughter Nova and I discovered the place where we had first arrived on the planet. We stood on the edge of a deep chasm, bombarded by an unrelenting wind;

the two of us filled with an indescribable exhilaration. Time stopped and we felt that we had returned to the beginning. We had been drawn here by looking at a map. The place had called to us to come. Something powerful was completed within us that day.

Next we traveled to the Big Island of Hawaii, revisited Pele at Kilauea Crater and my favorite lava tubes. Then it was time for the Hawaiian ceremony of Ho'oku'ikahi or Unification which was a preparation to return to the stars. An historic encounter between two rival Hawaiian Kings was reenacted with amazing costumes. This time it was played out differently, which healed old patterns of duality and brought reunification to all.

Brazil

In September, I journeyed to Brazil, which was yet another step in my series of preparations for the 11:11. I spent most of my time in Saõ Paulo which is the largest city on the planet and defies description. *(Imagine New York City spread out as far as you can see in all directions!)* Immediately I got a pinched nerve in my back which meant that I spent most of my free time lying down in the hotel. This gave me lots of time to contemplate.

What Brazil did for me was to deepen my compassion. I delved into all the questions of what happens to those who remain in duality, did we really need to go through the 11:11? *(we do)* and what gift can we leave behind to clear the path for others? It was a powerful time of healing, revelation and initiation. I was deeply moved by the strong love, dedication and beauty of our Starry Family in Brazil. These were the first talks and workshop which I had given with an interpreter and it flowed effortlessly. Differences in language are no barrier when it comes to speaking the language of the heart!

The Lessons of Orion

The constellation of Orion is of vast importance in our sacred quest for full remembrance since it is the Master Template of Duality for this dimensional universe. Ever since we first descended into matter, we have been subject to the law of duality. Almost all of our experiences on Earth until now have been set within the parameters of the patterning of duality. The exceptions would be the occasions when we stepped into No-Time and the Greater Reality or merged together with our Angelic Presence and Starry Overself.

The map of Orion is also the map of the Antarion Conversion. This map defines not only the boundaries of our experiences within duality, but it also contains the key for completing duality and moving into conscious Oneness within the New Octave of the Greater Reality.

Orion is divided into three zones. The upper zone is ruled by the star Betelgeuse. Located here are the Councils of Light. The lower zone is controlled by the star Rigel and is the home of the Dark Lords. In the central portion of Orion is a Zone of Overlap which contains the belt of EL*AN*RA. This area could be referred to as the Great Light for it represents the sacred, alchemical union of dark and light merged into One. The Zone of Overlap is served by Lord Metatron and the Council of the Elohim.

The need for a true understanding of Orion is so great, that I have devoted an entire book to the subject, *(EL*AN*RA-The Healing of Orion)*. Thus I will not spend much time here in covering the same information. It is important for us to realize that every one of us has experienced numerous embodiments both on this planet and

The Antarion Conversion

EL AN RA

on larger playing fields, such as the area which I term Intergalactic. All of these incarnations were subject to the fluctuations of duality. Many of them were experienced as parallel realities, which means that while one part of yourself was whizzing around in starships, participating in huge intergalactic wars, another fragment of you was simultaneously having a lifetime on Earth! If that boggles your mind, try this one – *none of those embodiments has much significance, because they were all anchored in illusion.* And they all occurred to only a small portion of our True Being.

What you can be certain of is that each of us has spent numerous incarnations as Lords of Light *and* Lords of Dark both here and in the intergalactic realms. We came into form in order to enact the full spectrum of the human experience, remember? This means that each of us has been everything – over and over again. Like a well seasoned repertory theatre, we have played every role. Donning those dark robes, wearing them with our full conviction; then discarding them for robes of light. Going back and forth until it finally fades into a blur and we begin to wake up and see that we were never just light or dark. That

91

in the Highest Truth, we are all of the One, the Greater Light which contains light and dark wedded together in sacred, alchemical union.

The first lesson of Orion: It enabled us to experience all extremes of the Template of Duality.

Unacceptable Reality

The second lesson of Orion can be discerned by studying the map of the Antarion Conversion. In the center is found the diamond shaped Zone of Overlap. Here all polarities have merged into conscious Oneness. This shows us what we must do in order to graduate from duality. We can choose to anchor our beings in the Template of Oneness, thereby loosening the bonds of duality. They begin to fade away as soon as we realize that they are not real, that they have been illusions all along.

We have now entered upon the path of true freedom. Once we refuse to feed the illusion of duality by regarding it as real, its life force begins to dissolve. This is the needed step into mastery which must be completed by each of us before we can begin our journey through the 11:11.

Here is a simple story that I have shared in numerous talks around the planet to illustrate this point:

Δ   Δ   Δ

A few years ago I was readying *The Star-Borne* for publication. I had been sent a friend's beautiful, multi-colored foil business card. This would be perfect for the cover of my book! I checked with several printers in my area, but none of them could do this process. Calling my friend, I asked her where she printed her cards. "Oh," she said, "that was when I lived in Santa Fe. But I can't remember the name of the printer." This wasn't the most encouraging news.

"But isn't there some way I could find them?" I asked, knowing that I would be passing through Santa Fe in a few weeks. "Well, yes," she replied. "You can go to a certain natural foods store, then stand facing the front door. Now raise your right arm to the side. Follow that direction, crossing the road and going behind all the buildings that you can see. There you will find the small printer." Writing down these unusual directions over the phone, I was sure I would find this elusive printer.

When I arrived in Santa Fe, I went straight to the natural foods store. Not wanting to get the directions wrong, as I was only in Santa Fe for a few hours, I now stood in front of the entrance and raised my right arm. Crossing the street I went behind all the buildings that I could see. Miraculously, there in the back was a tiny printer. I was elated. My long search was over! Well, not quite, as it turned out. . .

I now discovered that the front door of the print shop was closed. A sign stated in large, firm, irrevocable letters – "Closed Wednesday". Well, you can probably guess what day of the week it was! Now, what makes this story interesting or even worth retelling, is my reaction to this new development. In times past I would have reacted in one of three ways. Either I would have moved into victim mode. "Oh, poor me, I've come all this way only to experience such a cruel twist of fate. Why is life so mean to me?" You probably have known that one yourself now and then.

My second probable response would have been to get angry. "How dare they close on Wednesday! What kind of business is this?" Possibly punctuated by a few kicks at the door. Familiar, huh? Or the third response, which admittedly takes a little personal power. For this one you stand strongly in front of the door, feet planted solidly on the pavement, sending out willful energy from your solar plexus and third eye. Commanding, "Door open now!"

Anyway, to make a long story slightly shorter, I'll divulge that for once I didn't react in any of the above manners. Without thinking, without any premeditation, I simply stood there quietly reading the sign, well aware that it was a Wednesday. And without any emotion, without giving it any energy at all *(pay attention, for this is the most important part)* I silently observed to myself, **that this was not an acceptable reality.** And as I calmly stood there noting the fact that this was not an acceptable reality, I happened to glance at the window, which was open a crack. Peering into the crack, I saw a ceiling light was on. Putting my mouth to the crack, I called, "Excuse me, if anyone's here. . . I know that it's a Wednesday, but I've come a long way. Could you please let me in?" And they did!

Now none of this would have happened if I had reacted in the old ways of duality. I discovered that I had found a major key in freeing myself from duality. Since then I have used this tool innumerable times as have many others. And you know what? It works! So the very next time that duality tries to pull you in and convince you that it is real, remember to call its bluff by noting that *this is not an acceptable reality* and see what happens. Watch it fade away before your very eyes. . . Try it on all those extremely realistic appearing major obstacles in your life and see them dissolve into nothingness. "This is not an acceptable reality." Of course, your being has to be anchored on the Template of Oneness in order to carry this off.

The second lesson of Orion: Duality is not an acceptable reality.

Realignment of the Stars

The three stars in the belt of Orion, what we call the EL*AN*RA *(Mintaka, Al Nilam, Al Nitak in traditional* *astronomy),* are the main control points or pins which hold our dimensional universe into position. Along with Polaris, the Pole Star which aligns our planet to its rotational axis keeping it pinned on the Golden Beam, these three stars are the key areas to watch during our impending passage through the 11:11.

Interestingly enough, ever since I was a little girl, the first thing I do when I am outside at night is seek out the EL AN RA. Once I have located Orion's belt, I can relax, knowing that my doorway home is still available. During the past few years I have encountered many others who share this experience.

This is directly tied in with the Realignment of the Stars which started becoming apparent in early 1988. Already there are reports of astronomers discovering stars in previously empty sectors of space. The heavens themselves are indeed shifting and realigning as are we.

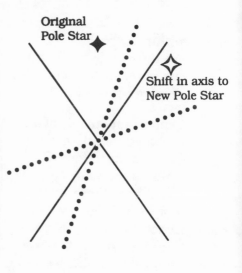

Original Pole Star

Shift in axis to New Pole Star

Sometime before the 11:11 closes on December 31, 2011, the Earth is going to shift off its axis, moving out of its positional alignment with the Pole Star in order to anchor itself onto a new axis within the Greater Central Sun System of the New Octave. Already there is a great loosening of the underpinning of this axis due to the planetary wobble currently in effect.

Probable Realities

In Quantum Physics there is something called Probable Realities which delineate the parameters of what is available for us to experience within our present dimensional patterning. These probable realities are circumscribed within the cones of past and fu-

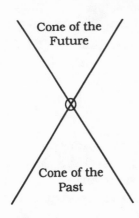

ture. These cones contain all of our potential experiences. In other words, something must be within either the cone of the past or the cone of the future in order for us to have the possibility of experiencing it or *of even being aware of its existence!* It is important to remember here that these cones pertain only to the Template of Duality.

I wondered for years what existed *beyond* the parameters of our probable realities within the realms of the Unknown or the Invisible. These are the new frontiers into which we shall be traveling on our passage through the Doorway of the 11:11.

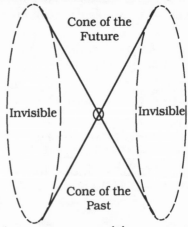

I know that outside of our probable realities there exists a new Pole Star, which is not really new for it is already there, but it *is* new to us. When we experience the shift in positional alignment sometime before 2012, we are going to hook into this new Pole Star which will pin us into our new position.

In order for this to happen, we can also expect a loosening of the three stars of EL AN RA. Already this is beginning to happen. Many have noticed that they are no longer in a direct line; the central star is becoming higher than the rest. Eventually they shall triangulate which will signify the final completion of duality. *(Late at night during our 11:11 Ceremony in Egypt, an Egyptian astrologer whom none had seen before, approached my friend Kumari. He said that he had heard that she too, was an astrologer. This mysterious man told her that the Egyptians had been waiting ages for the three stars in the belt of Orion to form a triangle and that they were very happy that we were doing this ceremony! Then after imparting this information, he disappeared from sight.)*

The third lesson of Orion: Orion is the map of our probable realities within the Template of Duality.

Orion is a large Antarion Conversion. Within its Zone of Overlap, all dualities have merged. Our present challenge is to create that Zone of Overlap within ourselves until we are irrevocably anchored into Oneness. Once we stand within the Zone of Overlap, we are ready to journey through the 11:11, for this is where the Doorway begins.

It is through the central star in Orion's belt, the star of AN or Al Nilam, that we shall travel as we make our homeward journey. This star contains the All-Seeing Eye of AN which is the entry point for the Doorway of the 11:11. J. J. Hurtak's amazing book, *The Keys of Enoch* refers to the alignment of the Eye of Horus with the All-Seeing Eye of God in the apex of the Great Pyramid. *(Key 205)*. This describes the same process. It is the alignment of the All-Seeing Eye of AN with the One Eye. When these eyes overlap, both within us and without us, the Doorway is opened. . . The Great Pyramid has become an Antarion Conversion. . . The Zone of Overlap activates. . . And our vast journey begins. . .

97

Metatron

Metatron is the Overseer of the Zone of Overlap, that place of merged Essence in the center of the Antarion Conversion in the constellation of Orion. This does not mean that Metatron is from Orion, merely that it is the location of the Zone of Overlap. Here Metatron anchors the Template of Oneness within the spiral of duality.

By embodying Oneness, Metatron shows us the way to master duality, for he is the Master of Duality. His true form is as one vast, invincible shaft of Light, emanating from the Star of One. He is an embodiment of the Yod serving as a stabilization pinion of the New.

Metatron could be called the Keeper of the Door. Until the Doorway of the 11:11 opened, he regulated who was allowed to pass through into the new template. Metatron stands in the center of the conversion/inversion zone. He could be perceived as standing in the middle of an X directing the in-going and out-going flows, not only of energy but of beings who pass into and out of this dimensional universe. And as Keeper of the Door, Metatron will be responsible for closing the Doorway of the 11:11 at midnight on December 31, 2011. He will be the last to leave the Template of Duality.

Another of his functions is to stand at the center of the Council of the Elohim. All of us, in the form of our Angelic Presences, sit upon this Council. Metatron helps us to fully anchor our Angelic Presence on Earth. The Council of the Elohim is now preparing to anchor itself for the first time into the Zone of Overlap, signifying the completion of duality. Metatron is also the temporal head of the Family of AN. All polarities are united within him into perfect, pristine Oneness. From him emanate the two twin rays, ON & AN of the Beacon of AN.

The Three M Activation

Within each of us is a sacred triangle which must be activated before we are free to move through the Doorway of the 11:11. The three points of this triangle are Love, Wisdom and Power. Archangel Mikael holds the position of Power = physical; Melchizedek is the holder of Wisdom = mental; and Metatron embodies Love = emotional. Each of these aspects of the sacred triangle are found within us. It is our task to undergo separate initiations with Mikael, Melchizedek and Metatron to fully activate Love, Wisdom and Power within our beings.

Love
Metatron

Wisdom
Melchizedek

Power
Mikael

In the Mikael Initiation: We stand firmly anchored in the Beam, thus achieving true empowerment. This leads us to the Melchizedek Initiation: Being empowered opens the doorway to the hidden wisdom, giving us complete access to the One. Then comes the Initiation of Metatron: By embodying our full Presence we become the One. Once this is achieved, we are ready to experience the Three M Activation.

The 3M Activation can be perceived as three Ms approaching each other and forming a triangulation which unlocks the Zone of Overlap. *(Diagram #1.)*

This creates three passageways for the lineages of EL AN RA to enter for their final completion from the Template of Duality. *(Diagram #2.)*

During this initiatory process the three aspects of Love, Wisdom and Power are indelibly fused into inseparable Oneness. We become powerfully loving and powerfully wise. This is when we don the garment of our Starry Overself. Now we are ready to fulfill our Divine Missions with the vastness of our true Beings. It is time to begin our uncharted voyage into the Greater Reality.

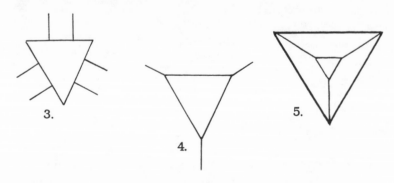

Family of AN

The Family of AN are those of us who are choosing to move into the Template of Oneness. AN *(pronounced On),* can be spelled AN or ON. These different forms of spelling denote the primary method of step-down from the Starry Overself to embodiment as humans on Earth. The AN lineage stepped down through immersion in the Celestial Realms. Here are found the Angels. So if you identify with the spelling of AN, you have spent much time immersing yourself in the Angelic frequencies.

The ON spelling denotes more of an intergalactic connection. Here we find the various levels of Star Commanders and Celestial Navigators as well as those connected to the Intergalactic Confederation. For example, the Trons.

Both lineages of AN and ON emanate from the energy source known as Metatron centered in the Zone of Overlap in the belt of Orion. They all belong to the Council of the Elohim. Although you might feel more of an affinity with one or the other derivations of AN/ON, in truth we have all traveled upon both of these roads. Remember, we have all been everything!

AN represents the union of Sun and Moon. In ancient Egypt, one of the earliest sites of initiation was the Temple of AN located within the settlement of ANU, later called Heliopolis. The Egyptian God AN united the Sun and Moon within one being. This God was instrumental in the founding of Egypt. Within the Earth's history, the AN lineage had a profound influence on the Egyptian, Assyrian, Druid and Inca civilizations. To find the presence of AN in times past, simply look for places where the Sun and Moon were worshipped equally and where brother and sister became husband and wife, ruling as king and queen. *(In my book EL*AN*RA, the marriage of the Star Commander AAla- dar & the Angel Kurala represents the union between ON & AN.)*

There came a time upon the planet when the lineage of AN disappeared from sight. Most of the outer signs of its existence simply faded away. All of its great civilizations had either reached their time of completion or become diluted in Essence. The Beacons of AN were silenced. The memories of AN slept dormantly in the hearts of humanity. It was as if the remembrance of the greatness of AN had been covered by a thick blanket of amnesia. At the height of this state of forgetfulness, the Annuttara slowly began to retrieve their memories.

The high level of initiates called Annuttara within the Starry Brotherhood of the Og-Min, form the Overseers or Elders of the Family of AN. Many of them who are presently incarnate here are devoting their lives to bringing the Family of AN into full remembrance. The Activation of AN has begun. As the Annuttara will be soon departing the Template of Duality, they are attempting to awaken the rest of their family that they too, might have the opportunity of ascending into the New Octave.

In regard to the three stars in the belt of Orion, AN *(emotional, union & Love)* holds the central position in order to merge the opposite energies of the EL *(mental & Wisdom)* and the RA *(physical & Power)* into triangulation. AN is the central portal through which the Doorway of the 11:11 begins its journey into the New Octave. This is made possible through an alignment and overlapping of the All-Seeing Eye of AN with the All-Seeing Eye of God which makes visible the Great Central Pillar, also known as the Tower of Light of AN.

As we plant our beings firmly within the Great Central Pillar of our Star, the Tower of Light of AN activates. This opens the channel through which we shall travel. See it before you, vibrantly shimmering. . . open. . . ready. . . waiting for us to enter.

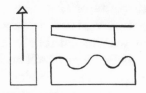

Egyptian hieroglyph for the Tower of Light of AN.

Anaho

This is a fragment of remembrance from the time when the newly created planet was first colonized.

Back before the period known as *the colonization of planet Earth*, several contingents of God-like giant beings descended to the planet at various, widely scattered locations. Their mission was to establish large ceremonial complexes to be used as Beacons of AN and stepping-down stations for the arrival of the star-seeded ones. Such a site is our beloved Anaho. *(Anaho is the ancient name for what is presently called Pyramid Lake, in Nevada.)*

On the island of Anaho was constructed a large step pyramid filled with various chambers. This was later a site of a great mystery school where the star-seeded initiates were schooled in the practical techniques and tools needed for the fulfillment of the Divine Plan for Earth. This pyramidal structure was not constructed by the ordinary means in effect today. It was created by utilizing beams of light combined with highly specialized vibrations of sound.

Before coming to this planet, each star-seeded initiate was immersed in areas of knowledge needed to fulfill their part of the Divine Plan. Pre-encoded patterns were imprinted within their cellular structure to be activated at a much later date. This was done with pulses of Light and sound currents in what we would currently term a holographic patterning. This form of encoding sent frequency pulsations to preset the inner circuitry of each individual into a unique mandallic pattern.

These highly calibrated attunements were placed within a delayed frequency sequence. What this means is that certain vibratory frequencies were programmed to be fully activated for a specific time phase. The holographic patterning then entered into a state of suspension or pause until its time of reactivation at some point in the distant future when the pre-ordained conditions had been met. Among these conditions was a certain level of vibratory acceleration for the planet itself, as well as a heightened degree of consciousness and commitment from the individuals involved.

Let us return to the ceremonial complex at Anaho. Once the God-like beings had completed their preparatory tasks, many of them chose to leave this planet and return to the realms from which they originated. A few remained in position to activate the site and fulfill its Purpose.

The star-seeded ones had volunteered and prepared themselves for their descent to Earth. The roster of participants was exalted indeed. We would do well to remember that Earth was not seeded by the dregs of humanity, but by some of the finest, purest beings from myriad dimensional universes, united together under the banner of loving, dedicated service to the One.

They included Suns of Arcturus, daughters of Andromeda, sisters of the Pleiades, Sanat Kumara and members of his immediate family – the royal Kumaras of Shamballa and

Venus. There were numerous others from distant universes who rarely venture this far. Never before had such a rare assortment of beings gathered together.

These Star-Borne volunteers came together knowing the full value of the Earthly experience. All willingly surrendered their natural forms; be they forms of Light with wings, transparent forms of flowing liquid, star rays, forms resembling mammal, reptile, fish & bird, forms of pure geometry, or forms of sound. All donned a human garment of physical flesh.

You might say that their sacrifice was great indeed and that it was. For although each individual being had chosen to serve in this great adventure of colonizing Earth, they gave up much in order to come. Not only did they surrender their true forms and leave their homelands for an undisclosed period of time, but they gave up their limitlessness, their timeless sense of freedom and Oneness.

As the pre-ordained heavenly alignment approached, the volunteers went through intensive procedures, altering their molecular structures to assume physical forms. Their new human bodies came in two predominant sizes. Some were taller than what is perceived as the norm today, (*around eight to ten feet in height*) and some were much smaller, (*from two inches to two feet*).

The star-seeded ones pulled large helmet-like devices over their heads. These were to aid in the changeover of atmospheric content during the journey. The helmets monitored the air intake, regulated the inflow of certain elements and slowly altered the mixture of elements until it was compatible with that of Earth's atmosphere.

Once the helmets were in position, the volunteers were carefully placed in individual pod-like containers. These pods resembled eggs in shape, large white hollow ovals composed of crystalline matter. Then the star-seeded ones entered into a state of suspended animation. While this state may resemble sleep to the casual observer, it is actually a mode of heightened awareness, of being so perfectly centered in the present that no movement is necessary. Thus they were ready to depart.

When the correct alignment of heavenly patterns presented itself, all was in readiness. The beacons in the pyramidal complexes were activated throughout the planet, transmitting a similar high frequency signal up through the overlay of dimensional universes.

On Earth the main ceremonial pyramid complexes throughout the planet were fully activated at the same moment in which the pods were released from the Heavens far above. The pods spiraled down the starwaves of the Celestial Seas, tumbling freely, over and over. Centrifugal force realigned the inner crystalline structure of the pods creating exquisite mandallic patterns which radiated outwards. These mandalas remain to be seen today inside the discarded fragments of the pods at Anaho.

The transmissions from the pyramid's beacons were stepped up and extended far upwards slowly drawing the pods into the gravitational field of Earth. At various preordained locations, the skies filled with clusters of pods raining downwards. Thus it was at Anaho.

Here as at the other sites *(such as Lake Titicaca and Lake Victoria)*, many of the pods had their impact softened by landing in the waters of the lake. They bobbed and floated in the now steaming waters until they cooled down sufficiently to be plucked out of the waters by the hands of the giants. And sadly enough, some of the pods missed their target and smashed into the ground, creating craters both large and small. Their long journey had been in vain.

The cooled down pods which had been removed from the lake lay scattered about the shore like dozens upon dozens of white eggs until gently warmed by the sun. As they heated enough to crack open, the air was filled with the sounds of rending fissures, until one by one, all of the pods had opened.

Inside reclined the star-seed traveler strapped in his seat with helmet on. A high pitched frequency was emitted from deep within the step pyramid on the island of Anaho. This was somehow projected and magnified within the helmets. Finally hands began slowly to move, fingers stiffly unbuckled safety straps, the headgear were gently taken off. Laboriously crawling out of their pods, the travelers lay weakly in the warmth of the sun. Their hair was damp and clung to their heads as did their loose clothing to their wet bodies. Lying limply in the sun, they soon fell asleep.

When they awoke, much had changed. The giants had been busy stacking the pods into hills, burying the helmets under a pile of rocks, removing all traces that anything unusual had ever taken place. *(However, if you search carefully, the Hill of the Helmets can be found today at Anaho.)*

Next, the new star-seeded arrivals were boarded onto a flat barge and ferried out to the Island of Anaho, welcomed and taken inside the step pyramid. Their Earthly Initiation had begun. . .

In the final parting of the curtains of duality
before the glorious new dawn,
walking my last steps through the corridors
of the Temple of Initiation,

I pause... waiting for a sign,
lest I make a mistake,
lest I step off course,
lest I fail to complete my final testing.

Slowly, but steadily,
I feed the totality of my being
into the sacred fire
waiting for a sign of renewal.

I, who have given my all for aeons,
who has served with total obedience,
must face yet another challenge,
must purify ever more layers of my being
until that most private inner core lies naked...
wide open... unprotected... vulnerable.

Welcoming the final annihilation
that I may be released of all illusion,
that I may rise like the wondrous Phoenix.
Reborn anew... Unfettered... Free...

The Time of Completion

We are in the midst of the Time of Completion. This occurs whenever two templates overlap and create a Zone of Transition. *It signifies the simultaneous beginning and ending of two major cycles of evolution.* The journey through this transitional zone is full of immense challenges.

Passing through this Zone of Transition is like living in two vastly different worlds with two sets of boundaries. You might experience this as trying to cope with two juxtaposed realities, both totally unrelated to the other. For example, some days you may notice that the Template of Duality is having a terrible day while the Template of Oneness is experiencing a day of loving ease. Not only is this confusing, but it is also a tremendous challenge to maintain our balance in the midst of two, separate reality systems. Our weather patterns also reflect this – one minute it will be brilliantly sunny and the next, raining ferociously. Weather is becoming more erratic and unpredictable, serving as an excellent mirror of the shifting energies around us.

Being in transition is causing many people to go a little crazy. Even those of us who are aware of what is happening can find it quite difficult to maintain our equilibrium and focus. We will probably see many people choose to make

110

their transition by dying. Some are doing this because they have completed what they came here to do; while others are choosing to leave their physical bodies rather than to see this process through. During the more intense periods, it's as if we were in the midst of a battle zone.

It's a powerful and challenging time. Times of completion always are. They are similar to the process of labor which we undergo in order to give birth. Our pains are necessary to birth the New. It is not an easy time and it is essential that we maintain our total commitment and focused intent for that is what will see us through.

The Out-going Tide

We all know that duality is dying away and its myriad illusions are being exposed. Every day the news is full of shocking revelations of corruption, deceit, decadence and greed. The misusers of power are being steadily unveiled. Everything which has been built upon a foundation of illusion is crumbling. Our most hallowed institutions, be they government, religion, education, medicine or business are being shaken to their cores. The world economy is extremely fragile, the environment is still being raped and exploited, the rich continue to enslave the poor, diseases run rampant. Violence is endemic not only within the shifting zones of war, but in our major cities. It is brought into our houses daily via television, newspapers and films until we become hopelessly numb to the fact that violence is not an acceptable reality.

These are all merely signs that we are in the Time of Completion. We have been living with this sickness buried deep within for a long time, as has the planet Earth. At least now it is finally rising to the surface like a boil or pimple, that it may be cleansed, purified and healed. This mirrors our own individual purification process as well. When children are abused, this means that parts of hu-

manity are abusing their inner child. And when the equality of either women or men is suppressed, it is a sign that
our polarities are not balanced.

With the dissolution of the Soviet Union we are seeing a
huge increase in nationalistic fervor. However this should
not be construed as a movement away from Oneness. As
the I Ching so aptly states: "We must separate in order to
unite." One must first discover who they are and stand in
their own beam of empowerment before they are ready to
join with others in Oneness. It will eventually come. . .

It is most helpful during these trying times to maintain
your sense of overview. An easy way to do this is to rise into
your Starry Overself and look down upon the planet.
Watch history play itself out in the Template of Duality
just like a film. *(And don't forget your popcorn!)* Calmly
observe all the cacophony, the strivings, the hot blooded
drama of it all. Watch while empires rise and fall, great
dynasties are born and die away, see us repeatedly fall in
and out of love – each time thinking "This is finally it!", as
we slip into and out of countless embodiments as easily and
mindlessly as changing clothes.

After you have seen enough to get the picture, *the big
picture that is*, don't be in such a hurry to make yourself
smaller again and jump back down to disappear into the
little picture of duality. Maybe you have seen enough to
realize that you don't want to return to the little picture.
But you don't need to go running and screaming from the
theatre either. Possibly you might be ready to try something different? Like maybe experiencing something enduring and real that is based on Oneness?

At this point you can choose to live in the big picture, rather
than the little one. This is *anchoring your being in Oneness*. It is possible to live our lives on Earth in this manner.

Actually, it's not only possible, it is highly recommended. After all, everything will make a lot more sense! More than that, it's an issue of survival and mastery. This is graduation and what we are choosing to graduate from is all the chaos, craziness, instability and illusion of duality.

Once you have anchored your being in Oneness, it's going to become easier, although the challenges are going to continue until we live in our Islands of Light where we can exist in our own band of energy. We are still going to undergo the continual process of letting go and surrendering all of our residue of duality. This will constantly be brought up to the surface of our beings so we can deal with it. It's not one of the most pleasant aspects of our journey, but it is most necessary in order to continue on.

We are also faced with the continuing challenge of integration of the New, grounding it into our physical reality. Everything must be worked through the body into full assimilation. The higher frequencies of our Light Body must align themselves perfectly with our physical body until there is no more separation. We must learn when to pause and give ourselves time to integrate what we have experienced. And then with that old 100% commitment, we must continue on, focusing on that which endures.

The Final Days

We are entering the final days of the Time of Completion. This period extends from the beginning of 1992 to the end of 2011. What we will experience during this time is a massive completion, almost impossible to imagine. Just think about it for a moment. By the year 2012, this is what will be achieved:

We are leaving our Great Central Sun System, departing the Template of Duality. We will master the map of the

Antarion Conversion and turn Orion inside out. The three great star lineages of EL, AN, RA will finish their cycle of service upon Earth. The Legions of Archangel Mikael will disband. The Order of Melchizedek, having revealed its secret mysteries, will return to the cave heavens of the Og-Min. The Annuttara will no longer incarnate into physical bodies. We will be reunited with our True Loves. Fairies, gnomes, elves will be returning to their homes in the mists of the Magellanic Cloud. First Wavers will have completed their contracts and be free to journey to Octave Eleven. Second Wavers will build on the New in Octave Seven. The Earth shall be pristinely pure again. The Ascended Masters will be freed of duty within the world of form. We will become the next Ascended Masters.

The Completion of Myths

Another fascinating thing which is happening during this time period is the Completion of Myths. Some of the hidden parts of our worldly mythology which have not yet been completed, will now play themselves out. For example, there are elements of the Isis/Osiris legend which will find completion in 1992. *(I will write about this in my next book, but don't want to say more until it has been achieved.)* Many of the ancient peoples of this Earth have legends and prophecies concerning our impending return to the stars. The signs are already manifesting, signifying that the time is at hand. The great mysteries of Atlantis and Lemuria will finally be revealed in their entirety.

Completing these myths during these final days brings the circle back to the place of the beginning. Our initiatory cycle on Earth draws to a close. As the Ouroboros takes the last bite of his tail, it irrevocably links together the cycle of Earthly Initiations with the cycle of Starry Initiations. As this happens, we will see that the Purpose behind all the Earthly Initiations was our return to the stars, to full remembrance, to the One!

Preparatory Initiations: Part 3

In October 1991 I embarked on yet another journey which was to clear the path for the opening of the 11:11. What I had not anticipated was the depth of transformation that I myself, was going to undergo. Its stunning totality came to me as a complete surprise. I can truly say that I returned home as a very different being than when I had left only three weeks before.

Our first stop was London. Four talks and one workshop were scheduled in Britain. London felt wonderful – both comfortable and exhilarating – quite like being home again, for I had spent five years living in London twenty years ago. Successful talks were given in Edinburgh, London and Portsmouth. We encountered lots of bright, starry beings in service to the One.

Stonehenge

Then came the drive to Glastonbury. . . Passing by Stonehenge, we decided we might as well stop by for a few minutes and have a cup of tea at the little refreshment stand. I was not too interested in Stonehenge for I had visited it many times before and was certain that its energies were now going to be rather lifeless and old. Was I ever wrong in this assessment!

115

Walking innocently up to the rope encircling the huge standing stones, I gazed at them in wonder. They were already anchored in the Template of Oneness! I could feel it strongly. Stonehenge was ready to move through the Door! There wasn't the slightest hint of old, musty energy. It was streaming with iridescent Light.

What was totally unexpected by me was my strong reaction to these dear, ancient rocks. I recognized them as part of my Family of AN. It was amazing; each stone was like a beloved family member. I knew their names and personalities with great familiarity. Overwhelmed with love and tenderness, simultaneously crying and laughing, I began to speak to them. They welcomed me so sweetly, happy to see me again, wanting to hear of my experiences out in the world. It was like a family reunion. Even the Queen, a tall, thin, delicately flat monolith, allowed me to see her beautifully subtle face as she conveyed her love to me.

I had the sudden realization that once, long ago, I had been one of them. Maybe I was one of the missing stones. I communicated to them about the 11:11 and helped them further prepare for our homecoming.

Glastonbury

Arriving later that afternoon in Glastonbury, we headed straight for the Tor. Because Glastonbury has been one of the most powerful vortexes on the planet, it has also served as a major battleground for duality. Climbing the spiral path up the hill to the summit, I carefully sensed the energies which felt as if they still needed some cleaning up. Once we reached the top, I sat down, checking to see if the mound still felt hollow, which it did. I could feel it breathing underneath me.

Glastonbury Tor always gives me the impression of hollowness, as if it is composed of a piece of stretched canvas with dirt and grass placed on top of it to look natural. But it's not a real hill. It is hollow inside and alive. As I had on my last visit over twenty years ago, I traveled down into the tiled chambers deep inside. There were fountains of the purest spring water surrounded by luminous, blue tile.

A feeling of weary sadness rolled through my being like a wave of ancient mist. Poor, old First Wave Glastonbury – so tired and still serving, still enduring the misuse of its energies, being bombarded with duality. I promised to aid it in whatever ways I could.

That weekend we held a dynamic workshop in Glastonbury. Participants came from all over Britain, including a sizeable contingent from Scotland. There were even two visiting Australians who had attended my workshop in Melbourne earlier in the year and friends from America. It was an extremely advanced group of beings united together in focused intent. So great was our Oneness that we kept moving into the level of consciousness known as the Council of One.

Together we called down the Template of Oneness and anchored it deep into the Tor. Now this doesn't mean that Glastonbury Tor is totally pristine; that will take a while yet, for so many people go there with such varied energy levels. But I do know that a hard knot of dark magic was dissolved forevermore and although outer forms may continue on, the root is gone, so the outer expressions will become increasingly transparent until they fade away into perfect Oneness.

A curious thing happened while we were having dinner after the workshop. Two of us were in an Italian restaurant when a waiter who was working in another section came up to us and began speaking to me in Spanish! I don't know how he knew that I spoke some Spanish and my companion did not. He explained to me about a special rock which he

117

had carried with him for the past thirty five years. He said that it was the most precious thing which he possessed.

His rock had told him that he was to show it to me. A large, smooth stone was then placed in my hand and my fingers wrapped around it. The waiter ran off. Without looking at it, I closed my eyes. Yes, I could sense that this was a most special object. Waves of energy were coursing through my body. The rock was soft and smooth and emanated what I can best describe as empowered love. Finally opening my eyes, I saw that the rock was pale orange, yellow and white, possibly alabaster or some other soft stone, of an unusual, conical shape and quite unlike anything I had ever seen.

When the waiter returned I asked him in Spanish where he had found this beautiful stone? In Egypt, he replied, in a pile of rubble near the Great Pyramids when he was fifteen. Hours later I could still feel the changes in my body caused by holding his rock and knew that somehow this was preparation for my impending trip to Egypt.

Sweden & Norway

Arriving in Stockholm for two nights to give a talk, we were told that we would no longer be staying in a hotel. Instead we had received an invitation to stay at a most unique house, a Center of Light, about an hours drive north of Stockholm on the Archipelago. At first, I wasn't too enthusiastic, for I have stayed in a lot of strange places on my travels and now prefer the quiet anonymity of modern hotels. But I decided to check it out.

The outside of the house was simple and plain, mainly a long wall with outer gates. However as we entered the doorway into an inner courtyard, I began to sense the level of finely calibrated energy which was present. The courtyard contained a Buddhist rock garden, waterfalls, fountains, large swiveling mirror panels, apple trees, full size statues of ibises, and a large population of live white doves. It was absolutely stunning.

Inside was even more amazing. There were large glass pyramids, bathrooms with the walls and ceiling totally mirrored, big statues of Angels, mirrors everywhere. I could feel my energy begin to step up, adjusting itself to the frequency of the house. Ah, I thought, we have just entered a Starry Temple of Initiation.

This exquisite temple was located on the water with beautifully landscaped grounds. Overlooking the water was a large silver sphere on a pipe which rotated when you sat in it, which I did. Closing my eyes, I reopened them to discover that I was soaring over the water. There was a beautiful pyramid of mirror and glass tucked into the rocks and trees which could be entered by tapping on a mirror panel which opened up to reveal a hidden staircase into the upper chamber. I thought I had gone to Heaven, or that possibly, Heaven had finally descended here.

The entire place was endearingly familiar to me as if I had spent much time in the Starry Realms in a similar environment. It's quite something to go into the bathroom first thing in the morning with your toothbrush in hand, flick on the light, and find yourself reflected into infinity. Several aeons later you return, wondering what that strange object in your hand is.

The meditation room was my favorite. By the clever use of mirrors and lights in the octagonal ceiling and the careful placing of a glass pyramid on an octagonal mirror base in the center of the floor, a most unique effect was created which perfectly duplicated the Tower of Light of AN. One could look either upwards or downwards through a tower of White Light into infinity. It was truly amazing! And I realized that many of these effects could be simply created by anyone without major expense. Of course, you need the level of awareness to conceive them in the first place.

The owner of this house was a humble man of tremendous depth who ate only fruit which he kept inside a large glass pyramid in the living room. We enjoyed some powerful meditations together. And he seemed delighted to share the astounding energies of his house with us, saying that it was a secret place of healing and initiation for the spiritual leaders of the planet. And that it truly is.

Staying there for those two, magical nights was a tremendous gift. The energies were similar to those of my own house which is white, transparent, highly calibrated and starry, but much, more stepped up in frequency. It gave me tremendous insight into our new forms of architecture and interior design for our Islands of Light, allowing us to bring the Starry Temples onto the Earthplane. And it gave me hope that we could remain in form for as long as we can keep raising the vibrations of matter to match our continuous ascent into new realms of Light.

Next we were off to Oslo, Norway which I loved. There was a large talk, followed by a weekend workshop attended by a large group from all over Scandinavia. Oslo and our new friends there were delightful and we had lots of fun which was just what we needed before we headed for Egypt.

Egypt

We arrived in Egypt in the middle of the night. There were no more talks or workshops to give; we had five free days to make any needed inner or outer preparations for the 11:11 opening less than three months away. Passing through the deserted streets of Cairo, I was struck by the similarity of the backstreets of Cairo to the hidden alleys of Ra-Matah, capitol city of Rigel detailed in *EL*AN*RA*.

Our hotel in Giza was gorgeous, like an Arabian Palace. We sat numbly in the lobby while we were being registered, remembering that we had been in Oslo the previous morning. It was quite a switch of realities.

In the late morning we went out to our balcony and there they were! The Pyramids of Cheops and Chephron loomed before us with overwhelming power and majesty. Now I knew why this was a Master Grid Vortex! I'm rather used to powerful places, but this was definitely the most intense energy I've encountered.

Then it was time for room service and going back to bed in order to adjust my energies. As soon as I lay down, I started seeing things – colors, flashing lights, the usual stuff. Then an interesting thing happened. My body began flying through the air, going directly to the Great Pyramid. Without slowing down it passed right through the walls of the pyramid *(bypassing the entrance – for some experiences, you don't need a ticket.)* I gently landed inside the sarcophagus within the Kings Chamber.

High above me was a sphere of White Light and as I focused upon it, I felt myself being lifted upwards until I passed through the White Light. I was now lying upon on it, like resting on a cloud. Surrounding me was a delicate crystalline capstone constructed of pale, golden yellow transparent panels. The capstone shimmered with a pristine purity of Essence. Then it began to open outwards. . .

Rising ever higher, I noticed above me some beautiful iridescent clouds. Patches of these clouds began to open up, revealing an unspeakably brilliant sun of a vastness which boggled the imagination. This must be the Greater Central Sun, I realized with a sense of awe. I willed myself to ascend even higher, trying to enter the Sun. Although I rose higher, I could not go into the sun. *(Later I was grateful for this, for I would probably not still be in a body if I had gone into it then.)*

As it became apparent that I was not going to travel any further, I asked that I might receive the key for the next level of Starry Initiations so I could return with it to the planet and help others in their passage through the 11:11. Instantly I saw a large, rectangular, transparent tablet descend from the Sun and enter my head, fitting all the way down to my toes. My physical body resting on the bed now made a violent jerking motion as the tablet came inside. Then I slowly descended back into the crystalline capstone which is where I spent the next month. . .

Early on the following morning before it had opened to the public, three of us spent an hour inside the King's Chamber. All the lights had been turned off except for a small candle which we had brought with us. As I sat quietly in the darkness, I was surprised to see Thoth standing before me holding his famous scale. "Oh no, he's not going to measure the purity of my heart with a feather!" I thought to myself. And sure enough, that's what happened. At first, as my heart was placed upon the scale, it began to sink perilously lower and lower. Then I let go of my cynicism and breathed into my Starry Overself. Just in time, my heart began to rise until it reached the top of the scale.

Then Thoth himself smiled at me and began to laugh. "Don't worry, we're not going to test you anymore. You have already passed all your ancient initiations. We just thought you'd enjoy being weighed again and seeing that now your heart is even lighter than a feather!"

The Goddess Isis appeared, along with many others of the ancient Egyptian Pantheon of Gods. They were all so happy to see me! It was as if they had been expecting me for a long time, as if I was some visiting Queen of Heaven. *(Please understand, that I am not telling this story to exalt myself; this is merely what I experienced and I'm attempting to report it accurately.)*

I told them about the Doorway of the 11:11, and that the time of completion was near. Then I sat there in the silent vastness of the Great Pyramid and held open the Doorway so they could experience the energies from the other side. There was a feeling of tremendous love which radiated powerfully throughout the pyramid. The Gods and Goddesses showered me with their gratitude and support.

During the next few days I also had private visits inside the other two pyramids. In each of the internal chambers, I felt a great welcoming and all-encompassing Love. I held open the Doorway of the 11:11 and let those energies anchor deeply into the pyramids.

Solara with Ptah in Memphis.

One of the sweetest experiences I had was our visit to Memphis and the ancient Temple of Ptah. He had been one of my great teachers for many years during my awakening process, so I was terribly excited to revisit his Temple. Not much remains in terms of buildings, but the energy is still there. The grounds are littered with souvenir stands where after much searching, I bought three small statues of Ptah. Then I found an old part of the temple wall with a head of Ptah carved into it. Here I had my picture taken, an old family portrait, holding my statues, filled with joyous homecoming!

The next morning I was up at 4:00 am for an appointment with the Sphinx. It was a bit scary at first, scurrying along in darkness, being smuggled in by robed Egyptians carrying machine guns. But I pulled myself together by thinking it wasn't a bad place to die, seeing the headline in *The Starry Messenger*, "Solara Shot at Paws of Sphinx." My sense of humor miraculously returned as fear dissolved.

When I did arrive at his paws, I was surprised to discover a huge, black tablet between them. "When did they put that there?" I wondered. "It wasn't there before." I climbed up one of the paws and made my way behind the tablet to his chest. There I huddled against the breast of the Sphinx for over an hour, watching the arrival of the first light of a new day. It was indescribable, but I will try to put it into words. Love, profound love – tenderness, familiarity, recognition. . . No, more than that, it was intimate and sweet, like the bond between great lovers.

Finally, I assumed my vast, starry body and stood before the Sphinx. I activated his wings and they unfurled majestically. He was so magnificently handsome! Then I delicately sat on his back and he arose into fullest flight. Together we flew high up into the Heavens and soared right through the Doorway of the 11:11. It was one of the most exhilarating experiences of my life – no, of my entire cycle of earthly embodiments.

It was during these days in Giza that I was shown the place where we were supposed to hold the 11:11 Ceremony. It felt terribly wrong, like being mired in an energy null zone. So I asked internally to be shown the right place. I found it at the base of the Pyramid of Mycerinus, *the smallest of the three Great Pyramids,* in the ruins of a temple which I called the Courtyard of AN. The energies of AN were so strong there, even the stone casings on the pyramid were identical to the Inca walls I had known so well in Peru. The only potential problem was that everyone told me that it would be *impossible* to obtain permission to hold our ceremony there. But I simply knew, with that absolute sense of rightness, that it was the perfect and only place and somehow we would be there in January.

On my last morning in Egypt, it was time for my private visit to the Great Pyramid. Before I left the hotel at 6:00 am, I pulled a card from my homemade Angel Card deck to see what the keyword of my experience there would be. What I got was, surprisingly, *True Love.*

Entering the pyramid, I had about five minutes before the lights would be turned out and I would be locked inside for an hour all by myself. So I hurried up the long hallway to the King's Chamber, lit one tiny votive candle and jumped inside the sarcophagus. Just in time, for the lights were immediately extinguished! Lying down, I couldn't even see the light from my candle. It was completely dark. But once again, I felt surrounded and embraced by vast love.

A song came, an exquisite song of great purity about True Love. It had the most beautiful lyrics and melody which sung themselves through me without any thought at all. I could hear this sweet song traveling all the way to the Heart of Heaven. It was effortless and sublime. I was filled with the Essence of True Love. And even as I sang this most beautiful of songs, I knew that I would remember not one thread of it – for it was a gift of the eternal, manifest only in a fleeting moment of No-Time. And such perfection is not to be held onto, merely experienced freely.

Gliding back to the hotel, several Egyptians bowed respectfully, saying things like, "Good morning, my Queen." And as I have since discovered, the Egyptians are incredibly aware of spiritual energies. Indeed, throughout our gathering in January, they showed much respect, appreciation and understanding of what was truly taking place.

Home Again

Returning home, I found myself still within the delicate crystalline capstone of the Great Pyramid. It was difficult to ground myself, although I had always been very conscious to keep myself deeply rooted for balance. Everyday life appeared absolutely meaningless and flat. I went through our November Reunion in Natural Bridge, Virginia and the Whole Life Expo in Los Angeles in this state. I couldn't come back into my body – not just couldn't, but didn't want to. I had traveled too far. . .

Luckily, the next step was approaching. An extremely gifted healer named Ah Koo came to visit. He is an extraordinary being, a dolphin in human form who has been coming to Star-Borne once a month to help us align our physical bodies with our Angelic Bodies and lead us through various initiations. We have a deep bond, as if we've been working together for aeons.

When he began our session, I was still in the crystalline capstone. Soon it opened up and I flew out and upwards, flying higher and higher, further and further from the Earth. I tried to make myself return to the pyramid, but the vaster part of me refused, continually flying higher and further away.

126

Eventually, I arrived at another pyramid, circled its capstone, yet refused to enter. I flew onwards, going further
until finally encountering another pyramid. Again I tried
to make myself go inside the capstone, but would not. This
continued on until I reached the Eleventh Pyramid. Here
I allowed myself to put my feet inside the capstone while
the rest of my starry body remained outside and free. Then
Ah Koo made a circling motion at the base of my spine. It
was as if I was being reeled in on a fishing line. As I came
in, all the pyramids went inside of each other, until there
were eleven congruent pyramids all in One. The smallest
one being the Great Pyramid of Cheops.

This experience changed everything. Now I began undergoing a new level of Initiation known as the Eleven Pyramids which pertains to the Eleven Gates which we pass
through on our journey inside the Doorway of the 11:11. I
began to have major revelations decoding the 4- 7- 11- 22-
-44. I saw the patterning of the new star mandala to be
found in Octave Eleven. Although still not grounded, I
knew that the transparent tablet which I had received in
Egypt was now being deciphered.

Then a dear friend with the purest of energies came over
to meditate with me. I told him that I would be happy to
meditate, but that we would have to begin in the One Heart
inside the Eleventh Pyramid because that's where I was
presently located. With great ease he joined me there,
placing his hands in the air over mine in the old palms up
/palms down position. For twenty minutes or so, I felt this
powerful force pushing my energy downwards, deepwards.
I never left my position within the Eleventh Pyramid;
rather my base was being extended downwards by a
steady, unrelenting energy. Since then I have felt fully
grounded and balanced, but vastly larger.

The Abyss

There is one last step before we are ready to pass through the Doorway of the 11:11. It entails a courageous leap into the Unknown. This leap into freedom is achieved by embodying our full Presence, surrendering our fears and doubts, letting go of all past experiences, and serving our Higher Purpose with total commitment. Then we simply let go and jump gracefully over the abyss! This is the final abyss. It marks the completion of our cycle of Earthly initiations. After this has been mastered, we are free to move onwards into the New Octave. . .

It's much like taking a long climb up an imposing sacred mountain. We all know that it has been an arduous journey. Many times have we fallen and picked ourselves up to continue onwards. Many times we have simply given up and collapsed onto the ground, crying out in profound despair. We have known surges of impatience and frustration at the duration and difficulty of our long journey. We have experienced devastating loneliness which at times made each step painfully sad. Our fears of the Unknown raged within us uncontrollably. Sometimes we lost our way in the heavy fog of ignorance. We have been repeatedly battered and bruised by the obstacles encountered along the way. Often we were plagued by doubts as to why we were climbing this mountain at all. The journey appeared fruitless and meaningless. Maybe we would find nothing when we finally reached its elusive summit.

And yet, *always*, something impelled us onwards, upwards. We lifted ourselves up time and again, drying our tears, quieting our troubled minds, calming our pounding hearts, and focused our resolve to complete this sacred quest. And we did it! Each of us has arrived at the summit and here we stand in complete awe for in front of us stands the shimmering Doorway of the 11:11, beckoning to us our freedom.

So what happens when we reach the summit? At first, we experience a tremendous sense of exhilaration. We did it! We are finally here! Gazing at the open Doorway before us, our hearts fill with overwhelming joy. After we have fully explored the summit, our initial excitement begins to fade. We realize that there is something more which we must do. Our journey is not yet complete. Now we must go *through* the Doorway!

This is when we discover that in order to pass through the Doorway, we must first leap over the abyss. Just the very thought of it fills us with rising dread. Haven't we already done enough? Haven't we been thoroughly tested? Haven't we given our all time and again? Looking into the abyss, we experience a deep terror of the Unknown. Not knowing what is really down there, not knowing if we are going to crash and burn into annihilation, we step backwards with uncertainty. . .

Naturally, we're aware that we have wings as part of our Light Bodies, but how can we be certain that they will really enable us to fly? Our trust begins to waver. . .Then our logical mind steps into this gap, newly created by our fears. "Perhaps it would be a good time to pause for a while," it suggests seductively. "Great idea," we respond gratefully. Assuring ourselves that we are *definitely* going to jump over the abyss soon, *probably tomorrow morning,* we sit down to ponder our situation. . .

We decide that since we're going to be leaving the old behind, we might as well spend some time contemplating the vast scope of what we are letting go. So here comes the procession of past life memories, always a good way to fill up time. Of course, we realize that former embodiments are now quite irrelevant, *since they happened to only a small fragment of our being,* but there were lessons involved and we want to make sure we understand everything before we move on. . .

Months pass by and we are still camped out on the edge of the abyss. The open Doorway of the 11:11 ever stands before us, shimmering with promise. . . Others have joined us by now. As they arrive at the summit, the process is repeated time and again. . . Excitement, joy, awe, doubt, fear, terror and then ultimately, compromise. . . Let's stop for a while and think about it. . . Do we really want to let go of everything? What's in this Unknown anyway? Where's our safety net?

So quite an encampment has formed at the summit. We started out with tents and lean-tos, as we were here *only temporarily of course,* but after a while that began to change. We decided we might as well be comfortable, so houses were built of stone and wood. *They would last longer and after we move on, others could use them, we reasoned.* The same was true of our swimming pools and tennis courts, restaurants and post offices. In other words, our temporary shelter became quite elaborate. . .

But please don't think that we have forgotten why we came here. Don't you know that we have study groups several nights a week where we are taught how to step over the abyss? We have an abundance of books and videos available on the subject. Everyone reads them. And in our meditation group we simulate experiences of going through the Doorway. It's almost as real as if we really did it!

But sadly, in spite of all the talk and activities, no one is making the leap into the Unknown... Actually, that's not totally true. Once in a while a newcomer will arrive at the summit and immediately leap off the edge into the Unknown, disappearing from sight! Possibly you can imagine what a shocking occurrence this is. It disrupts all our activities and for a few minutes it shuffles around our sense of what is real. Suddenly there is the blinding flash of revelation – *Ah, this is why we are here! We are supposed to really do it, not just talk about it!* But then, it is time for our next study group – tonight we're going to actually peek through a window into the New Octave – so off we go. Besides how do we know, *where is the proof,* that this solitary soul actually made it through the Doorway? Maybe they just crashed on some sharp rocks far below or got eaten by crocodiles?

By now, you should get the picture. Do you see how much of "awakened" humanity has learned to accept second hand knowledge and live in a much diminished and compromised manner? The Greater Reality stands before us right now. It is available to everyone! We don't need a special password or to meditate for fifty years first. We can step into it at this very moment – or whenever we choose to. It is open and ready. What are we waiting for?

It is not scary. *It is far more frightening to remain on the edge of the abyss lost in illusion,* talking about beingness, rather than being. If we want to experience completion, freedom and fulfillment, we must take our leap!

And as one who lives much of her life on the other side of the Doorway, anchored in the Template of Oneness of the Greater Reality, I would like to convey to you that it is fine over here. It is far more than I can possibly begin to describe. It is safe, loving, joyous, remarkably easy in every way. It is the place where we have always yearned to be... It is our natural state... It is Home...

Trust yourself. Trust your own perceptions and inner promptings of your heart. You will not be led astray. Don't allow yourself to be held back anymore. We have all waited too long; we have all traveled too far to hold back now. It is so close, so accessible. The Doorway stands open before you. Take heart, bring forth your courage, spread your wings open wide, and make the leap!

The Doorway of
the 11:11

The Doorway of the 11:11

This can presently be perceived
as a crack between two worlds.

Δ

It is like a gap or abyss
which has the inherent potential
of linking together
two very different spheres of energy.

Δ

As we unite together as One,
bringing together our fragments of the key,
we not only create the key,
but we make visible the Doorway.

Δ

Thus the gap is currently functioning
as an invisible door
or a doorway into the Invisible.

The Map of the 11:11

**The Doorway of the 11:11 is
the Bridge between Two Spirals.**

This bridge is the channel for our mass ascension. The old spiral contains the patterning for dimensions one through six. These delineate the boundaries of our known dimensional universe. This is the spiral which we have traveled upon since our first Earthly experiences. Inherent within this patterning is the illusion of duality and separation.

Herein we have labored under the concept that we were individualized units of consciousness, separate from the One, stranded beings searching for God. Here we felt ourselves alone, abandoned perhaps, ever striving to remember something of vast importance which always resided just beyond the grasp of our conscious minds. Yet, a deep yearning to return Home has always been embedded within us, though we knew not where that magical place, or state of consciousness, might be found.

After we pass through the Doorway of the 11:11, we shall move onto a new spiral anchored on the Template of Oneness. The patterning found here is one of octaves. It contains Octaves Seven to Eleven. It is free of the dimensional framework and contains entirely new levels of awareness. Octave Seven is where the Earth shall reside. It is here that the new Dispensation will be revealed and fully manifested. This is where we shall experience the prophesied thousand years of peace.

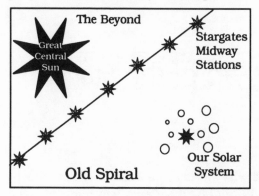

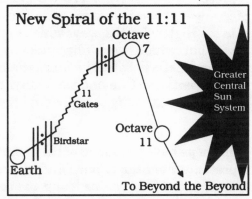

Most of the ones who will journey to Octave Seven shall remain there to build on the New. However, a small group of us shall choose to continue onwards to Octave Eleven. In Octave Eleven, another repatterning is possible, which leads to Beyond the Beyond.

On December 31, 2011, when the Doorway of the 11:11 finally closes, our journey between the two spirals of evolution shall be completed. This also signifies the completion of the ancient Mayan and Egyptian Calendars.

137

The Map of the Star

We are often asked why we use the symbol of the Star to represent the One. When I first began my public work as a Messenger, it was necessary to find new ways to communicate the Higher Truths, ways which were not only pure and fresh, but which were untainted by old religious and philosophical concepts. The Star is both symbolic and real. It represents the One and the Many. It graphically illustrates our positioning as individual rays or expressions of the One.

Many of us have the sound of RA in our Starry Names. RA represents the Star of our Unified Presence. Within the symbol of the Star can be found the complete map of our reawakening process. *The Star-Borne* contains diagrams which describe how we began as third dimensional fragments stranded on the tip of the ray of our Star, always looking outwards, feeling alone and separate. The reawakening process was described as turning around and facing inwards, towards the center of the Star. From this new perspective we can see that we have *always* been Home, and that we have never been separate from the rest of our Starry Family.

Now as increasing numbers of us step into our full Presence, it is time to reveal more of the Map of our Star:

The Zone of the Golden Solar Angels: (Diagram #1).
As we remember who we are, we begin facing inwards, towards the center of our Star. We embody our Golden, Solar Angel. By reclaiming our Angelic Presence, we are given our passport to travel the entire length of our ray of the Star of Oneness. In Diagram #1, you can see that the Zone of the Golden, Solar Angels encompasses the entire ray.

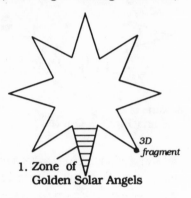

3D *fragment*

1. Zone of Golden Solar Angels

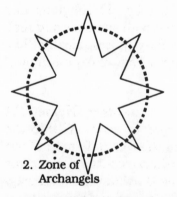

2. Zone of Archangels

The Zone of the Archangels: (Diagram #2).
Continually rising in consciousness and anchoring more of who we are in our physical bodies, we reach a frequency zone which encircles the rays of our Star. This band of energy is called the Zone of the Archangels. To reach this level of awareness, we have to become very large, freeing ourselves from the bonds of duality. All illusions of separation have dissolved and we have begun to unite with others in conscious Oneness. It is the union of our Angelic Presences which allows us to enter this band of energy.

Zone of the Starry Kings and Queens: (Diagram #3)

3. Zone of
Starry Kings & Queens

The next level we reach is a band of energy called the Zone of the Starry Kings and Queens. This is the highest level of empowerment we can reach in the Zone of the Golden, Solar Angels. Here we have fully reclaimed our Divine Birthright and Heritage. We have donned our starry robes and starry crowns. We are ready to step forward and serve with our full magnificence.

The Starry Overself: (Diagram #4)

As we rise into our Starry Overself, we take another quantum leap. We have transformed from one of the Many into true Oneness. At this level we cease to identify with ourselves as individualized units of consciousness. We become the hologram of the whole. Direct access is opened up into all parts of the Star. We have aligned ourselves with the All-Seeing Eye, thus activating our One Eye and our Greater Hearts have united with the One Heart

4. Starry Overself

The Council of One: (Diagram #5)

After we have activated our Starry Overselves, it is time to join together with others who are also embodying their Starry Overselves. Thus we enter what is known as the Council of One. Here we sit side by side as One in perfect love, trust, openness and respect. This is when the next level of work begins. It is from the Council of One that we will establish our Islands of Light and complete our ser-

5. Council of One

vice to humanity. This is the new bottom line of the Template of Oneness. It is not some long sought after, elusive goal, but is a level of consciousness which is obtainable now. It is where we need to anchor our beings to fulfill the next phase of our Divine Missions.

The Fully Awakened Starry Being: (Diagram #6)

6. Map of fully Awakened Being

This demonstrates the entire map of a fully awakened Star-Borne being. It also shows how the Star itself is transformed by our rising into full remembrance and empowerment. This is the shift in solar rulership or the movement into the Greater Central Sun System. It shows the completion of our Divine Missions and our return Home.

141

The Great Central Sun Systems

The movement through the Doorway of the 11:11 shifts the positional alignment from our current Great Central Sun System to what we term a Greater Central Sun System. We have been held into position with our Great Central Sun through a process of polarization. This has functioned as a magnetic attraction since our Central Sun has resided in Oneness and we on Earth in duality. In order to loosen ourselves from our old spiral of evolution, we must rise into our inherent Oneness. This frees us to move through the Doorway of the 11:11 into Octave Seven. Here we shall find ourselves aligned with a Greater Central Sun System.

In our old Great Central Sun System we were subject to the laws of duality. Our highest spiritual concept was that which we termed God – a vast, all powerful being who was separate from us. We could pray to God, ask for help and receive guidance. Although our prayers were often answered, God remained a separate entity. We knew that even though in some way we were a part of God, we could not *become* God. Whatever that state of consciousness represented, it remained unattainable in its totality.

In the new spiral of evolution anchored under the Template of Oneness, the concept of God as a distinct being has changed. *God has transformed from a personification of the One into the One.* We are all of the One. Together, our Unified Presence creates the One. The One is inclusive, embracing us all (the Many) in its wholeness. When you pray to the One, you are speaking to yourself, albeit your Greater Self. Nothing is separate or distinct from the One. The One includes everything in its vastness. Notice the difference here. See how the shift from our concept of a separate God to the all inclusive One marks a quantum leap into empowerment and mastery. Now each of us stands in direct alignment with the Central Pillar. We are all pristine emanations of the One.

There is another profound change which takes place as we move into the Greater Central Sun System. On the Template of Duality, our highest attainment was to reach the level of unconditional love. A good example of this is the phrase, I love you. I *(separate being)* love you *(separate from me)*. Although we could love each other totally, openly; we still identified ourselves as being distinct, individualized units of consciousness. In the Template of Oneness, unconditional love no longer exists for there is no more you and I.

This does not mean that we all merge into some indefinable, collective glob of wholeness. We do retain our individual forms and identities. However within our sense of uniqueness, *rooted* in the central core of our knowing, we know that all of us are of the One. Our primary identification with ourselves has shifted from being, for example: Solara a totally separate person, to Solara – an emanation of the One. I know that I come from the One. I know that everyone, all things, come from the One. Therefore that sense of inherent Oneness is woven into the very fabric of my being. First and foremost, I am of the One.

143

Our new bottom line in the Greater Central Sun System is all-encompassing love. Love simply is. We are all love. Love glues our Star of Oneness together. Love is the breath of the One. It is the underlying foundation of the New Octave. There is no more I, there is no more you; there is only the One. This all-encompassing love is composed in equal portions of Love, Wisdom & Power, well stirred together into the most potent of brews. This is what we live, eat, drink and breathe in the Template of Oneness.

The parameters of the Template of Duality are defined by the limitations of time and space. These formed the boundaries of our probable realities. In the Template of Oneness, we exist in a state of No-Time and No-Space. In No-Time we stop the illusory passage of time and expand it outwards into that eternal instant of forever. It contains past, present and future merged into Oneness. There is only the Now...Within No-Space all boundaries dissolve the physical, emotional, mental, spiritual; melding the patterning of dimensions, planes, octaves, realms, spheres into an undulating Oneness containing unlimited possibilities.

In the old spiral we learned to breathe in and out, over and over again, constantly, for that is what kept our physical forms alive. As we enter the new spiral, even though we are still wearing our physical forms, we move into a state of No-Breath. In No-Breath, we cease to breathe through our lungs and diaphragms in the old manner. There is no more out and in. Breathing slows down as we enter a state much like suspended animation. We begin to breathe effortlessly through our skin which covers all the surface area of our body, every molecule vibrating in gentle accord. Yogis in India have long practiced No-Breath. They achieve it by moving the seat of their consciousness to their third eye area. We do it by anchoring our beings in No-Time and by merging our physical bodies with our Starry Overself.

When first we enter our Greater Central Sun System, we will click into a new positional alignment. This is because our Sun System will be vibrating at an even greater degree of Oneness than what we have yet experienced. Rising up into this heightened resonance of Oneness will be our next challenge. And when that is finally achieved, we shall be ready to move onwards into the Beyond the Beyond.

In order to see the Invisible,

simply look where the visible used to be.

Now extend your parameters.

Look beyond.

Look l a r g e r.

The Invisible is to be found

on an infinitely vaster scale

than previously imagined.

The Map of
Overlapping Spirals

There is yet another map which details our journey through the 11:11. This map delineates our shift in spirals and how it affects our lives. The upper spiral represents the Invisible. It is the spiral of the New Octave. And the lower spiral is the spiral which we are in the process of completing, that which is anchored in duality. It shows the docking procedures that take place not only with the two Great Central Sun Systems, but within ourselves.

In Diagram #1, we see the two spirals are totally separate. Heaven and Earth, spirit and matter, Oneness and duality have yet to merge. At this point our entire being is anchored on the spiral of duality.

In Diagram #2, the spirals have started to interlock. We begin to move into the subtle realms of the Invisible. As we do, something interesting occurs. We discover that each time that we extend our beings into the Invisible, we are released from the hold of duality. This happens in measured increments called proportional adjustments. To use an Earthly analogy: If we travel three miles into the Unknown, then we also find that when we return to duality, there are three miles that we can't go back into.

In Diagram #3, the journey into the Invisible continues. We are becoming a blend of both spirals. Half of the old spiral of duality can't be returned to; it has totally dropped out of our reality pattern. It no 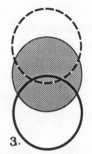 longer has any meaning in our lives.

In Diagram #4, the shift of spirals is nearly complete. Although we continue to live on the Earth, most of our being is anchored on the Template of Oneness. Third dimensional reality has lost its hold upon us. We have stepped into the Invisible, making known the Unknown.

In Diagram #5, our journey is complete. We have totally stepped into the New. The spiral of duality fades away into nothingness. The new Divine Dispensation is revealed.

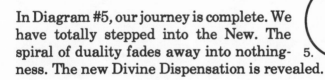

As we gradually move into the spiral of Oneness, we are going to continually experience a dissolving of duality as well as a loosening of the bonds of gravity. Sometimes this will be experienced as a process of dying, as the old continually falls away. This clearing is necessary so we can fully embrace the New. It is essential to our transformation into fully conscious Light Beings.

Each time that we travel further into the Unknown, we get a fresh infusion of Oneness; then every time that we return, we bring back that Oneness and anchor it into duality. It's a two way process with the energies traveling in both directions. Remember: A transfer is in position. As we move through the Zone of Overlap, it is helpful to remain focused on where we are going. Know that it is perfectly normal for large chunks of your previous reality to slip away each time you extend your being into the Greater Reality. Many of us are experiencing this, so please don't feel that there is anything wrong with you when this happens. This is simply how we make the journey.

The Opening
of the Doorway

The Doorway of the 11:11 opens once

and it closes once.

Δ

Only One may pass through.

This One is our Unified Presence,

The Many as One.

Δ

The 11:11 opens on January 11, 1992

and closes on December 31, 2011.

Numerology of January 11, 1992

This date can also be written as 1.11.1992.

Notice that it contains an 11:11

within the 1111992.

Together the numbers add up to 33

which is the master vibration number of

Universal Service. 1+11+21=33

Large doors require large keys.

Δ

The key which opened the doorway of the 11:11
was created by all of us joining together as One
on a scale never before experienced on Earth.

Δ

Each of us is a piece of the key.

Master Cylinders

There are two main grid systems which encircle our planet. These could be perceived as thin lines of energy, or *ley lines*, which form a lattice work of fine mesh. They conduct the distribution of energy throughout the Earth. The main grid system is called the B Grid. You can see this grid as a fine lattice of Light pulsations. Wherever two of these threads of Light intersect, a vortex is formed. Each vortex has its own keynote and focus. Some of them are already fully activated, while others still await their time.

Many of the activated B Grid Vortexes have become places of tremendous power and spiritual revelation, drawing to themselves seekers from all over the world. Examples of B Grid Vortexes include: Mt. Shasta, California; Glastonbury & Avebury in Britain; Uluru, Australia; Mt. Fuji, Japan; Mt. Cook & Lake Taupo, New Zealand; Sedona, Arizona; Lake Atitlan, Guatemala and Machu Picchu, Peru. There are myriad B Grid Vortexes scattered all over the Earth.

The Council of Nine

Underlying the B Grid is another grid system called the A Grid or Master Grid. The Master Grid has a much simpler mandalic pattern than the B Grid's elaborately complex interwoven latticework. Yet its matrix could be described as infinitely deeper, for not only is it located beneath the B Grid, but it contains the Master Coding for the entire planet. Access to this grid system is not open to everyone; perhaps it will never be. Entrance can only be obtained with an extremely subtle code which was imprinted in very few back when this planet was being created. They are known as the Council of the Nine.

The Council of the Nine is comprised of nine high initiates of the Starry Brotherhood of Og-Min called the Annuttara who have chosen planetary service through physical incarnation. This they are allowed to do for the span of one complete aeon, being required to incarnate at the very beginning of a spiral of evolution and remain until the next shift in templates. All of the Annuttara who choose to come to Earth, whether or not they serve on the Council of Nine, must undergo full immersion into matter, including compression into density and total forgetfulness. The Annuttara would be considered as the Elders of the Family of AN.

The Council of Nine works closely with their Starry Brethren in the Og-Min to maintain Earth's positional alignment on the Golden Beam until it is time for the shift in spirals. At that moment, the Pole Star will loosen its fastening with the Golden Beam allowing the Earth to shift its axis and move into alignment with a new Pole Star to be found in the Greater Central Sun System.

Delving into the inner workings of the Master Grid with access to the appropriate code, one is able to enter the Control Panels. These Master Control Panels regulate the flow of energy and calibration of vibratory frequencies within the evolutionary templates preselected for the Earth. It is here that the templates can be overlaid in such a manner as to create a Zone of Overlap which forms the bridge between two very different spirals of evolution. This is achieved within a preselected sequencing pattern which

157

adhers to predefined parameters. Access is limited to such a small number of beings. At various turbulent periods in the history of the planet, people have tried to usurp control of the Master Grid, but it is firmly, irrevocably protected by Divine Law and cannot be tampered with.

Inside the Control Panels of the Master Grid there is a map detailing the locations of the Master Grid Vortexes as well as a timetable for their activation. These Master Grid Vortexes differ greatly from the B Grid Vortexes. In times past there were only seven potential locations throughout the planet. Most of these sites are presently positioned over water, some where Lemuria and Atlantis used to be. Deactivated Master Grid Vortexes are located in the Takla Makan Basin and Antarctica. All physical traces of these vortexes have long disappeared. Possibly you may have memories of this.

As we are entering the patterning of the New Octave, we shall see the activation of eleven Master Grid Vortexes between now and the end of 2011. Some of them are located in: Egypt, New Zealand, Brazil, in the Pacific Ocean near Tahiti, China, Russia, the Azores, the Caribbean and Peru. Others are yet to be discovered. *(Possibly when the vortexes in the Pacific and Atlantic Oceans reach activation, this will signify the rising of Lemuria and Atlantis.)* Only two of these places have presently been activated.

In order for a Master Grid Vortex to be activated, an alignment must first take place between a potential A Grid Vortex and an existing, activated B Grid Vortex. This means that they must be located on a direct, vertical trajectory. Secondly, the Master Grid Vortex must receive activation before a Master Cylinder Vortex is created. This dual activation forms a double helix spiral which creates a channel for the anchoring of a formidable shaft of Light, called a Yod which emanates from the other side of the

Doorway of the 11:11. The anchored Yods form what is called a Pillar of Light. Each Pillar of Light is aligned with the Great Central Pillar and serves as a stabilization pinion to shift us into the New Octave.

The Great Pyramids

Up until April, 1991 there was only one activated Master Cylinder Vortex on the planet located at the Great Pyramids in Giza, Egypt. The Great Pyramids have long served us as a Beacon of Remembrance. The very shape of them has kept alive the Key of Triangulation as the means for completing duality. The Pyramids have served as resonating chambers for initiation into the Greater Reality. The scope of their potentiality far exceeds the levels of Earthly initiations into the spiritual realms as utilized by the ancient Egyptians, even though that civilization achieved a high level of spiritual evolution.

The three Pyramids, now ancient and weary like many First Wavers, are nearing their time of completion. The Opening of the Doorway of the 11:11, on January 11, 1992, marked the Completion of the Omega Point. When this happened, there was a powerful energy shift at the Great Pyramids. It could be perceived as an unscrewing of their outer casings which were recalled back into the Heavens. Many old energy patternings were removed from the planet at that time. The Great Pyramids will play a dramatically altered role in the twenty year period that the 11:11 is open. The Beacon of Remembrance shall shift into its new patterning and become a fully activated Beacon of AN. *(During our 11:11 Ceremony in January 1992, the ruined temple at the base of the third Pyramid of Mycerinus transformed itself into the Courtyard of AN.)*

This transformation of the Omega Point first took place within the Control Panels of the Master Grid. A recalibration was made which enabled the shift of evolutionary templates to manifest. The transformation of the Great Pyramids is directly aligned with the three stars of EL AN RA which are in the process of achieving triangulation. This realignment has long been awaited by the holders of the ancient Egyptian wisdom.

The great being known as the Sphinx is also an important part of this Master Grid Vortex. He has been serving for aeons as a Guardian of the ancient Mysteries. This Golden, Solar Lion now prepares to reveal the secrets of this encoded information to those who are anchored within the new evolutionary template. Serving as a Guardian throughout the long age just passed, he never left his post. However with the Completion of the Omega Point, the Sphinx has been released from his endless duty; he is now free to fly. So if you visit Egypt, you might see his old form of stone, but you won't find his spirit encased into it anymore. Look larger, *much larger*, and you just might catch a glimpse of his true vastness. And if you are truly blessed, he might take you for a ride into the New Octave!

The South Island

In April 1991, we experienced the activation of a new Master Cylinder Vortex. This one is located on the South Island of New Zealand. As it represents the Alpha Point for the planet and originates from the New Octave, it is of a much greater vastness than any previous Master Grid Vortex. Its shape is that of an inverted triangle and its outer points are loosely defined as the settlements of Queenstown, Te Anau and Milford Sound.

I was sent to the South Island of New Zealand in April, 1991 to locate and activate this vortex. This was a necessary preparation that had to be achieved before the 11:11 could be opened. I was given three days and three dedi-

cated companions to see this task to completion. Initially
it was quite perplexing, as we searched for its specific site.
That is because we were looking for something small, like
a lake or a mountain. In our desperation, we finally began
dowsing topographical maps with a pendulum which help-
fully told us that the elusive vortex was to be found
everywhere within the designated area! Finally, after
traveling to many special places which felt right and doing
activations in each of them, I began to understand what
was taking place. This Master Cylinder Vortex was enormous! It shouldn't have been such a surprise, because, *of
course*, everything is vastly larger in the New Octave.

While this new Master Cylinder Vortex received its pre-
liminary activation in April, 1991, its full, heightened
activation won't occur until 2011. This will happen over a
twenty year period in measured stages called proportional
adjustments. If it had received total activation all at once,
the planet would have experienced severe disturbances
especially apparent on geophysical levels. In other words,
Earth and humanity would have been fried by the influx
of such radically different, vastly heightened energies.

What we can expect over the next twenty years is to see the
South Island of New Zealand move into an even greater
purity. Visitors will find that they have been transformed
by their immersion into the subtle energies of the Template of Oneness. It is more than likely that the area will
increasingly experience powerful physical manifestations
of the Invisible.

The opening of the Doorway of the 11:11 was centered at
these two Master Grid Vortexes:The Alpha Point in New
Zealand, the Omega Point in Egypt. These two locations
formed the Master Cylinders for all the Wheels within
Wheels located throughout the planet. It was here that the
Unified Movements were performed continuously through-

out the entire thirty-eight hour period. The Movements began when the first time zone on the planet reached 11:11 am on January 11, 1992 and completed when the last time zone finished their 11:11 pm Movements.

The Master Cylinders were extremely important for the 11:11 opening for they served as anchoring points for the Great Central Pillars. Here the two mighty Yods imbedded themselves deeply into the planet, thus making possible the entrance of smaller Yods in various locations throughout the Earth. This is how together as One, we establish the foundation for the New Octave.

No-Time

No-Time is the measurement of the Greater Reality.

We are moving beyond the limitations of the time/space continuum. No-Time is that eternal instant of forever which ever expands outwards into limitlessness. It is available to all of us right now.

It is of utmost importance that we begin to live our lives in the enduring state of No-Time. This is quite easy to achieve. Anyone can learn how to do it. Living in No-Time will give us the needed sense of balance in the times to come. By embodying the state of No-Time, we further serve to anchor the Template of Oneness upon the Earth. This will greatly affect all of humanity, regardless of their present level of awareness.

Time is simply an energy; it is constantly moving and flowing like the wind. You could perceive it as a shifting mesh. Within the parameters of duality, time was frozen into measured segments which defined and limited what we were able to do and experience. However, this is one of the illusions of duality which we can now release. When we do, we can achieve true mastery, becoming Masters of Time. This is accomplished by moving our consciousness into the state of No-Time.

When we stop time and move into No-Time, we automatically move into the heightened awareness of the Greater Reality. We can still talk and walk and go about our daily tasks, but everything we do is imbued with a greater depth of consciousness. All of our conversations and actions reflect this. If just one of us lives in No-Time it affects everything around us. Imagine then the effect if thousands or millions of us resided in the state of No-Time! The harmonic resonance of Oneness would be magnified immeasurably. We would truly be grounding the New Octave into the Earth.

When we are in a state of No-Time, it doesn't mean that the clocks stop ticking; they don't. But time does stretch out into infinity. Here is an example: Often when I am traveling, I have little time to rest. Sometimes I can sneak in a half hour to lie down before my next speaking engagement. The first thing I do is to stop time. Then I dissolve my being, allowing my molecules to expand into limitlessness. *(It is often exhausting to hold our molecules together into form.)* Then I begin merging into myriad octaves of awareness, worlds which are impossible to describe. As I return to consciousness from these realms, my memories are instantly washed away, like wiping clean a blackboard.

After what appears to be the passage of aeons, I return to the present reality to check my watch and am amazed to discover that only five minutes have passed! Off I go again, dissolving my molecules to replenish my being. This is the secret of how to make the most of time by stretching it out. It's easy to become a Master of Time. All of us can do it. The technique to achieve this is one of our Unified Movements for the 11:11 and is explained later in this book.

No-Time also has practical ramifications in our everyday lives. It is most helpful when traveling for example. Have you ever been on a long car trip when you suddenly discover that you have traveled over a hundred miles in about five minutes? Many of us have experienced this.

Another interesting thing happens when we stop time. A crack opens up between the worlds. I always see this crack as a curved arch, but you might perceive it differently. You can flow up and through this crack with ease after you have entered the state of No-Time. Sometimes I swim through this crack with a pod of dolphins or fly through it while floating in the starwaves. Inside this crack is the vast Zone of Silence. It is a fascinating place to explore which contains endless potential.

Here is a simple story which I wish to share with you. By becoming a Sun-Watcher I learned how to enter the state of No-Time. . .

The Sun-Watchers

In a realm far, far distant, yet closer than you can imagine, was a simple land, undistinguished but for one remarkable fact. The landscape of this land was sprinkled with pyramids great and small. These pyramids were so ancient that the people remembered not whether they had been originally created by nature or by man. And indeed, upon looking at them closely, even the keenest observer could not discern this clearly.

Of course, there were the ancient myths which spoke of these pyramids, calling them the "Wam:Pa" which roughly translated means "Jumpers." These fragmentary tales revealed that the pyramids had been placed on the planet by the stars for remembrance. But few, if any, knew or cared what was to be remembered or even why it was important to remember.

Most of the people simply accepted the pyramids as a normal part of the landscape much like trees, rivers & hills and went about their daily life as usual, rarely giving the Wam:Pa a second glance. No one ever touched or climbed them, as this was strongly forbidden for unknown and mysterious reasons which had been long forgotten.

Now most of the people is not all, and you surely know that there are always a few, tucked in amongst the masses, who are quite different. They live their lives listening to another song, never quite fitting in with the rest. It was from this group, which we shall term *the others*, that the Sun-Watchers were chosen. Although to be truthful, they actually chose themselves.

It happened quite like this: One of *the others* would be struggling along attempting to fit in with the rest of the population. In spite of all their efforts, they never succeeded in extinguishing that secret, throbbing anthem which sang to their soul of remembrance. Then maybe they overheard whisperings about the Sun-Watchers and their hearts began to pound with wild excitement. Sometimes they were blessed to actually catch a glimpse of a Sun-Watcher passing by in blissful solitude. This did it! There were massive chills and a rising delight. Tears came quickly. Before long another one had left the world behind and set off quietly to become a Sun-Watcher.

The majority of the populace were aware of the existence of the golden robed Sun-Watchers, but paid them little mind. For the Sun-Watchers were very quiet and were seldom seen up close and certainly caused no obvious harm. Which was just as well, since everyone knew that the Sun-Watchers had extremely *strange eyes*. Other worldly eyes which could see through anything, piercing the veils of illusion. Just the thought of this made the people most uncomfortable. Not that anyone had really seen a Sun-Watchers' eyes up close, but the people had heard stories about persons whom someone else knew, who had once seen their eyes. So whenever any of them caught even a distant glimpse of a golden robed one, they averted their gaze immediately until they had safely passed by.

And who were these Sun-Watchers? Well, I shall tell you, for that is the purpose of this story. Their true name was "Way-Chen" which means, again by rough translation,

"Through the Crack" although no one ever referred to them by that name and many had never heard of it at all.

The Sun-Watchers lived scattered across the entire land tucked into hidden corners and remote valleys. Some of them lived perched onto the sides of mountains or by the edge of secret streams. All of them resided separately from the normal folk. They lived either in pairs or small groups sharing a cluster of tiny huts. The Sun-Watchers lived in simple isolation, growing small amounts of food, tilling the land with quiet song, rarely gathering together in large groups even with their distant golden robed brethren.

We mention the golden robes. Actually, these were simple squares of a hand-loomed pale golden yellow cotton which the Sun-Watchers wrapped themselves in and wore as clothing in a variety of ever-changing styles. They could be worn as sarongs or loincloths or meditation robes and served all manner of purposes and weather. Loose and comfortably flowing, their shape could be changed quickly to suit the situation, giving great freedom over the rigid clothing styles preferred by the rest of the population. Also, the golden cloths could be easily removed in order to serve as blankets and carrying cloths.

This is not to infer that the Sun-Watchers led an indolent life. It was merely a simple, quiet life with few worldly distractions. Keeping their material needs to a minimum, they were free to devote much time to the task of remembering. They knew not exactly what they must remember, but they all acknowledged the utmost reverence of that which had been long forgotten.

Sunset was their most sacred time. Each evening as the sun made its stately descent across the flaming sky, Sun-Watchers everywhere would complete whatever tasks they had been doing and quietly slip away in pairs to secret nooks and crannies hidden in the knolls and mountains. Here were their secret places for meditation. And here they would sit down, adjust their golden cloths accordingly and meditate side by side. With open eyes, they fixed their steady gazes upon the setting sun, watching as it descended behind one of the ancient pyramids.

It was during the precise moment when the sun passed behind the pyramid's edge, that something extraordinary happened. A pulsating burst of sunlight would outline the edge of the pyramid, lighting it up with a surge of electricity. The Wam:Pa would be activated as a Jumper causing a streak of brilliant reds, molten oranges, golden yellows, and vibrant magenta to flash together like lightning.

Then suddenly, as if it had been pre-ordained from On High, a crack opened up between the worlds... A deep, all pervading Silence could be felt. . . The Sun-Watchers ceased to breathe with worldly breaths. With No-Breath they moved into a state of pure beingness. . . .Time stopped. . . . . and simply ceased to be. . . . No-Time expanded outwards into limitlessness. . . . .

The Zone of Silence had been penetrated... For an instant or for an eternity, it mattered not, one could wander within it at will.

And in that timeless instant of No-Time, the memories flooded in and were remembered. . . . It was a taste, a grand and glorious taste of the Essence of the Greater Reality. . . . It was what we humans have strived for and yearned after for aeons, although few of us can yet give it a name. . . . It is the Source of our divine discontent, the grain of sand imbedded in the oyster of our beings which provokes our pearl of remembrance to expand and grow. The seed of our knowing which can only find true peace within the sanctuary of our Greater Hearts.

This eternal instant in which the crack between the worlds opens, revealing a sacred glimpse of the Zone of Silence, was what the Sun-Watchers lived and breathed for. . . Immersion into the Greater Reality was their God, their sacred Purpose, their hallowed shrine.

Then as this moment of total ecstasy, of pure beingness, came to its appointed completion, the crack closed itself up, once again sealing the Sun-Watchers within their present dimension.

As the sky slowly embraced itself with the deeper hues of night, the Sun-Watchers sat in hushed reverence, tenderly savoring their remembrances. They wrapped themselves tightly in their golden cloths to ward off the sudden chill of evening. Their starry brethren emerged from the depths of Heaven and smiled down upon them with loving encouragement. Then in the dark of night, one by one as One, the Sun-Watchers silently returned home.

Wheels Within Wheels

The series of Unified Movements
for Opening the Doorway of the 11:11

The 11:11 Activation is quite different than Harmonic Convergence. It is not merely a case of everyone going *somewhere* on January 11th, 1992 and doing their own thing. That will not open the door. What is required is Unified Focus or Focused Intent. We need to create *Wheels within Wheels*. This is how the key is formed and the door is unlocked.

There is a series of synchronized, Unified Movements which need to be done by all who are participating worldwide. We ask everyone to wear white, symbolizing the purity of our Unified Presence. And most importantly, we need to come together in groups, large and small, not as individuals, but as representatives of the One.

171

The Unified Movements

This is the series of Unified Movements which were performed worldwide on January 11, 1992 to open the Doorway of the 11:11. They are not included here merely for their historical significance. Rather they are a series of extremely powerful sacred movements containing major keys for transformation. Each small movement can be greatly expanded into an experience of heightened revelation. It is my hope that these movements will continue to be taught and delved into by the awakening Star-Borne. They are powerful and subtle tools for expanding your awareness into the New Octave.

The Origin of the Movements

I am frequently asked where these Unified Movements came from. Of course, the obvious answer is that they come from the One. But more specifically, when something comes to Earth from the One, there has to be a Messenger or Interpreter who communicates that which derives from On High. I wish to stress that these are not *my* movements, simply that I chose to be the vehicle which brought them to the attention of humanity.

The first movement I received was No-Time. For many years I have been aware of those magical moments when time stops and stretches outwards into infinity. They felt extremely blessed to me. Eventually, I learned how to stop time for myself. From that came the simple series of movements to enter the state of No-Time. The rest of the Unified Movements were brought through by me and other members of our staff at the Star-Borne Reunions that are held twice a year at various locations.

After we had received the complete set of movements, we set out to teach them to as many people as possible. Star-Borne Workshops and 11:11 Anchor Trainings were given throughout the United States and Canada. Members of the Star-Borne staff traveled to Russia and taught the movements there in the summer of 1991. I personally traveled to Australia, New Zealand, Brazil, Britain, and Norway as well as many cities in the States, leading groups through the Unified Movements and the Starry Procession. Star-Borne published a booklet entitled, *Wheels within Wheels* which along with our *11:11* booklet was translated into many languages. Finally, we also produced an instructional video.

This great work could not have been achieved by our efforts alone. Numerous people throughout the planet willingly took on the task of spreading the word. The news of the 11:11 was dispersed all over the planet and found a deep response. For this I shall ever be deeply grateful.

Although some people had resistance to doing the Unified Movements, many others discovered a great joy when they learned them. They are extremely simple, yet undeniably powerful! One interesting thing we discovered as reports of the 11:11 Ceremony filtered in from all over the planet is that those groups who participated in the Unified Movements experienced far greater ease in assimilating and grounding the incoming energies. And many groups brought through fascinating variations of the Unified

Movements, such as the point shifts of the Starry Processional in New Zealand or the double Sun-Moon circles used
in Brazil. This is exactly how it should be. We are aligned
in Oneness while at the same time we are free to add our
spark of originality to make our One even brighter.

Creating the Wheels within Wheels has never been achieved
on this planet before. Their accomplishment is in perfect
alignment with the numerous prophecies of Sun Dance
Circles turning and the activation of the plumed serpent
wheels. What is truly wondrous is that we finally did it! We
fulfilled the prophecies, joining together in perfect Oneness and we opened the Doorway of the 11:11.

Here are the instructions for the Unified Movements. They
are presented to you that you might continue to teach them
and lead ever larger numbers of our Starry Family through
the Doorway of the 11:11.

The Twelve Guardians

We began by asking for Twelve Guardians who serve as
embodiments of the Twelve Cosmic Rays. They are here to
anchor the Light and protect the sacredness of our ceremony at all times. The Twelve Guardians did not participate in the series of Unified Movements. They stood
outside the activities in the circle yet they held the foundation for all of us, serving as the stabilization pinions of the
newly anchored Template of Oneness. Standing in their
full Presence, they simply directed and anchored the
energies as they felt appropriate.

*In Egypt, our Twelve Guardians were truly magnificent.
Due to the 38 hour timespan of our Master Cylinder and the
difficult climatic conditions (sun, wind & cold), Guardians
were often replaced hourly. Throughout the ceremony we
had one person appointed to make constant rounds of our*

Twelve Guardians, checking to see who needed to be relieved. Announcements would be made on our sound system asking for the needed number of volunteers – and they would always come!

It was beautiful to watch the new Guardian take their position. First the two Guardians would face each other, do their mudras and announce their names. After bowing to one another, the fresh Guardian would get into position and the previous one was free to leave. Such an empowered changing of the guard.

During the early, early morning hours, when it was terribly cold in our Courtyard of AN, our Guardians stood with unspeakably magnificent dedication, with upraised arms, their white robes billowing in the wind. We shall never forget their shining starry eyes, their total radiance and unswerving commitment. And throughout our ceremony, our space felt safe, totally protected and blessed.

Wheels within Wheels

We begin the first series of our Unified Movements by forming two large circles. The outer Sun Circle faces inside while the inner Moon Circle faces outside. The Sun Circle represents the One, while the Moon Circle represents the reflection of the Light – much as we are all mirrored reflections of the One. Thus the two circles face each other, unifying all polarities, becoming the sacred union of Sun & Moon as embodied in the energies known as AN.

Inside the Sun & Moon Circles are smaller circles of eleven, known as the Inner Wheels. *(In Egypt we fluctuated from eight inner circles to one.)*

The sequence of the Wheels within Wheels is:
No-Time, No-Space, No-Duality, Antarion Conversion.

Remember: We are dealing with the subtle currents of the Invisible here, so please focus on the energies which are being moved rather than your physical movements.

No-Time

We begin by stopping time, for the state of No-Time is the measurement of the Greater Reality. To stop time, put your hands together in prayer position. Feel that time is in your hands. Now take your hands and slowly stretch them out, keeping your palms facing each other. As you stretch time out between your hands, concentrate on the energy which you are extending. When you feel time opened wide, turn your palms outward and stop time. Feel the difference between the states of time and No-Time. As you become increasingly familiar with No-Time, you can begin to live your life in this state.

1. Hold time in prayer position.

2. Pull time apart.

3. Stretch out time.

4. Turn palms forward – stop time.

No-Space

We shall move from No-Time into No-Space in one, continuous movement. Stretch your arms out sideways, palms facing forward, with your fingertips extending to the outer parameters of your being. Now slowly bring your hands together, arms outstretched in front of you, overlapping your hands with palms facing your heart. As your hands overlap, keep your thumbs up, touching them together to create a triangle. After you have triangulated your thumbs, carefully bring your hands into your heart, squeezing all outer space into your heart, making it very huge, filling it with infinite space. We have taken all outer space and moved it into inner space. Then move your elbows against your sides, completing the process of putting all outer space within your being.

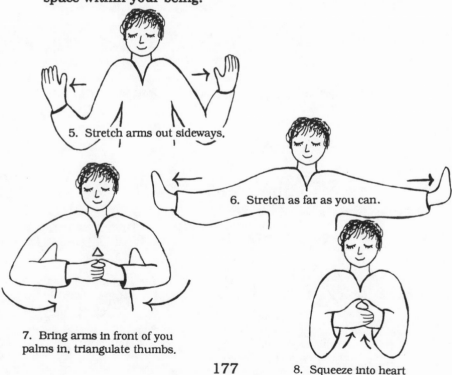

5. Stretch arms out sideways.

6. Stretch as far as you can.

7. Bring arms in front of you palms in, triangulate thumbs.

8. Squeeze into heart and elbows into sides.

177

No-Duality

Raise your right arm up and your left arm down. Stretch to the furthest extremes of your being, feeling the outer limits of your polarities. Now slowly, consciously, bring your palms together, keeping your arms straight in front of you. As your palms touch each other, feel the subtle energy uniting your polarities into Oneness. When your hands meet, bring them up into prayer position and very gently move them into your heart. You have now united all duality into Oneness and anchored it into your heart.

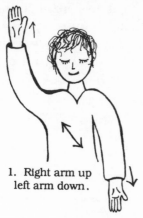

1. Right arm up left arm down.

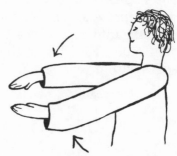

2. Bring hands together.

3. Bring hands into prayer position.

4. Into heart.

178

Antarion Conversion
Closing the Door of the Old & Opening the Door of the New

Begin by moving your left arm up and your right arm down in a diagonal positioning. Slowly bring your hands together in front of you, keeping your arms straight, consciously moving that energy. When your palms meet, your left hand faces down and right hand faces up, thus closing the Door of the Old. Now turn your hands over and let's open the Door of the New! Stretch your right arm up and left arm down. You may now step through the New Doorway you have created.

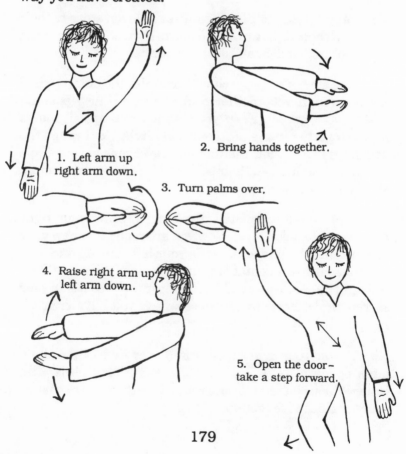

1. Left arm up right arm down.

2. Bring hands together.

3. Turn palms over.

4. Raise right arm up left arm down.

5. Open the door – take a step forward.

Activation of the Wheels within Wheels

The Inner Wheels of Eleven will take one giant step through this new doorway. As they do, their upraised right arms will meet, joining them together in the center of their sacred circles.

At the same time the Sun and Moon Circles will take hands and begin to turn towards their left in a clockwise manner. As they rotate, they shall look deeply into the eyes of those in the opposite circle, seeing the other members of their Starry Family as mirrored reflections of the One.

The Inner Wheels of Eleven now take eleven steps to their left, with their right arms held above their shoulders in the center of the circles, all touching hands.

After the eleven steps, each will go under the outstretched arms through yet another doorway into a new position within your wheel. Keep your right arms up, all hands linked together in the center of your circle. Go through the doorways in a random manner until everyone in your circle of eleven has changed their position. Now take eleven more steps in a clockwise motion.

When you have completed these steps, bring your right arms down to heart level. Now you are ready to renew your commitment to Oneness. Bring your left arm up and over your head into the center of your circle until it joins with all the right hands. You should be facing into the center of your sacred circle. Feel the Oneness which you have created. Breathe it in while you enter a sacred pause...

Now flower your arms up, out and over each other like a lotus opening its petals. See how beautiful this is. The Inner Wheels join hands and rotate in either a clockwise or counter-clockwise motion.

The Starry Processional

Whenever you do the Starry Processional or the Spiral, we highly recommend the wearing of white clothing, to symbolize the purity of our Unified Presence. These sacred movements emanate from the Starry Temples of Initiation and are newly brought to this Earth, for we are finally ready to receive them.

The Starry Processional is a very sacred dance. It symbolizes the realignment of our Star of Oneness. Whether you participate in it or watch it from afar, its effects are most powerful. For this movement we will form one large star. First get into a circle with everyone facing into the center. You now need to determine how many people are going to form a ray of the star. This will depend on the number of people in your group as well as the size of the space you are in. Now designate the inner and outer points of the star. These are key positions for anchoring the energies, and for keeping the individual rays in alignment with the whole.

Once all are in position, begin walking slowly around the room, keeping in your starry formation. The star will be turning clockwise, so some of you will be walking backwards. Please keep your rays nice and straight and remain very conscious of what you are doing. We are taking the sacred Star, the Star that together we are, the symbol of our Unified Presence, the One, and we are turning it, thus Realigning the Stars.

The Starry Processional is one of the most profound sacred practices that we have on the Earth today. Remember to hold the sanctity of the Star as you slowly revolve. We have a beautiful tape of music called *The Starry Processional* by Etherium which was specially created for this movement.

We have had some interesting experiences while participating in the Starry Processional at our Master Cylinders.
In Egypt, after the extremely powerful 11:11 pm GMT
series of Unified Movements, we knew the Door to be open.
Then the focus dramatically shifted from the Wheels
within Wheels to the Starry Processional. From then on,
each time when we did the Starry Processional we felt
ourselves to be spiraling upwards through the 11:11 into
the New Octave.

In New Zealand, the Starry Processional was much more
lively, as befitting the Alpha Point. They came up with
some exciting additions, such as point shifts when the
inner and outer points would change positions while rotat-
ing. They also had one person positioned in the center of
the Star to anchor the energies and direct the shifting of
the points.

Trying both forms of the Starry Processional, I made an interesting discovery. In the Egyptian form, we left the Template of Duality and entered the New Octave. The New Zealand form brings in the New and anchors it into the planet. The difference is quite remarkable. Both forms are profoundly effective and demonstrate the transfer of energy which takes place.

The Starry Processional is a wonderful practice to do on a continual basis. I have done it with as few as three people or as many as five hundred. You can also do it with smaller, concentric stars inside the outer star, if space is limited. It definitely gives you a continuous, heightened experience of moving through the Doorway of the 11:11.

The Spiral

The Spiral is a most sacred process which was presented as an optional movement for the 11:11. You will find it a profound experience. The Purpose of the Spiral is to form a spiral galaxy. Once it is turned, it is brought into full activation. It is a method of propulsion for moving through the Doorway. It is also excellent practice for forming the Merkabah of our Unified Presence. *(Interestingly enough, neither of the Master Cylinders did the Spiral, although that was not our initial intention. We both found that we were to do Wheels within Wheels and Starry Processional continuously throughout our thirty-eight hours.)*

Before you begin, two people, in addition to the facilitator, should be chosen. They will be the ones who will sit in the first and last positions. The one who goes first should be one of your purest, brightest beings, for they are upholding the sanctity of the Beam. But they also need to be able to remain focused and grounded while experiencing vast amounts of energy. The person who goes last serves as the

183

Gatekeeper; they are the one who closes the door of the Spiral. They also are the one who protects the sanctity of the Spiral, if need be. So choose someone who is strong and alert for this position.

Focus and silence should be observed as you get into the Spiral. First everyone will sit in a large circle. Explain to them that they should only get up when they feel a true Calling to get into the next available position. Sometimes there will be a space that no one steps forward to fill. Hopefully, someone in the group will eventually feel the need to serve and come forward to take this position so the Spiral can be completed.

Your facilitator will now go into the center of the circle and stand at the first position of the Spiral. They will designate with a simple arm gesture for the first person *(the one who was chosen beforehand)*, to come forward and claim their space. As each person chooses their place in the Spiral, they do their mudra and announce their Starry Name, "I am _____ ," prior to sitting down.

It is important that a small pathway into the center of the Spiral is kept clear so that your leader can come into the center once it is complete. Everyone should sit closely behind the one in front of them. As each position is filled, the leader moves to the next position and waits until someone comes forth for it. This continues on as the Spiral fans out clockwise. Remember: Do not get up until you feel a real Calling to a particular position. You are making a commitment to fulfill that place in our Unified Presence.

Once the last person *(the prearranged Doorkeeper)* takes their position at the end of the Spiral, your leader will walk through the Spiral on the path between the rows into the center and sit down.

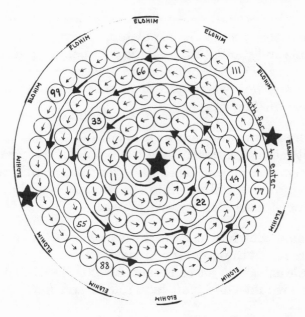

The leader now activates the Spiral. This is to be done very consciously. Your leader takes the right hand of the first person and squeezes it once, then the first person takes the hand of the next person in the Spiral, squeezes it once and this activation continues from one person to the next. Do not take the hand of the person behind you, until you have felt the activation from the person in front of you. This is a continuous movement until it reaches the last person in your sacred Spiral.

The Doorkeeper then gives a nod or a gesture to your leader signifying the activation has reached its completion. You will still be holding hands; this time you feel the squeeze from the person behind you, passing on the movement to the person in front. Don't let go of each others' hands and keep the movement flowing from one person to the next until it reaches your leader in the center of the Spiral.

185

When this process is completed, everyone should drop hands and stand. Now combine your personal sounds into the Song of One. While you are making your sounds, you may wish to do your mudra or other sacred gestures to help direct the flow of energy.

There are two different ways to unwind the Spiral. For the first method, you can take the hands of the persons on either side of you. Then the Doorkeeper will begin to unwind the Spiral back into a large circle. Now the celebration and music can begin!

Or as an alternative: Have the leader leave the spiral first, walking out the circular pathway with everyone following. While doing this you can chant, AN-NU-TA-RA HU. After you are unwound, you take hands and form one large circle.

New Movement

This is a new Unified Movement which was received in Egypt. It was not part of our Wheels within Wheels, but was utilized in our 11:11 Master Cylinder Ceremony once the Door was opened. What it does is open the Doorway, shift our probable realities onto an entirely new patterning, open another doorway and allow us to walk through. If done with concentrated focus, this can be a most powerful experience. It is shared with you now so you can teach it to others. This movement can be used effectively with a group when you are walking in a circle. The chant of AN-NUT-TA-RA HU coincides with this movement.

Step 1: Place your hands out to the sides with palms facing forward while making the sound of AN (*pronounced ON*). AN symbolizes the unification of our internal polarities, the completion of all duality and the union of Sun and Moon. This shows us moving through an open doorway being in our Unified Presence.

1. Palms forward
—stop time.

187

Step 2: Bring your hands parallel to your chest with wrists crossed, palms facing your chest. Your left hand should be on the inside. Make the sound of NUT while you are doing this gesture. *(NUT is pronounced NOOT)* NUT refers to the Moon, to the receptive side of our nature. This gesture represents our old set of probable realities.

2. Fold left arm into chest then right arm – palms face your body.

Step 3: Fold your hands in, down and outwards, so that you end up with your wrists still crossed, but your palms facing outwards, right hand in the outside position. At the same time make the sound of TA. This is the sound of creation for this part of the sacred movement is realigning the boundaries of our probable realities.

3. Fold hands in toward your body – down and forward – palms now face out.

Step 4: Return your arms to the same position as Step 1, with palms facing forwards. The sound for this is RA which symbolizes the Sun or the One. We are now stepping through a new doorway into expanded Oneness.

4. Bring arms out
to shoulders.

Step 5: Bring your arms down and outwards in a gesture of surrender while making the sound of HU. It is both the sound of surrender and the breath of the New. It is important while doing this part that you consciously make your surrender to moving into the New Octave.

After you have done this entire series of movements, you can keep on walking and repeating the process which

5. Lower arms to sides
– step forward.

becomes increasingly empowering. *We used this movement while making a long procession up and down the Avenue of the Sphinxes at the Temple of Luxor in Egypt. It was quite an experience!*

189

The Challenge of Oneness

When I first realized that the 11:11 Activation was to be a worldwide event entailing a mass mobilization of the Star-Borne, I was profoundly affected. My initial reaction was to go into a state of panic tinged with deep awe. How were we ever going to achieve this with so little time and such limited resources? Would I have the physical, mental and emotional endurance necessary in order to survive what lay ahead? Realizing that I could not achieve this single handed, I wondered if I would receive the necessary support.

After pondering these formidable questions, I resolved to see it through no matter what it entailed. Although still somewhat overwhelmed by the scope of what lay ahead, I gathered my energy and leapt into action, not knowing if I would find any response. But, I made my total commitment to give it my all.

Ever since I was young I've had the feeling that I had an important mission. Somewhere along the line a Great Work lay waiting for me. Whenever people asked me what I wanted to be when I grew up, I would reply, "a famous actress." "Why famous?" they would ask. "So people will listen to what I have to say," I said. "What are you going to say?" they asked. "I don't know yet, but it will be something important," I would answer confidently.

As my life progressed, nothing spectacular seemed to be happening. Yes, I was on a spiritual path from an early age, but most of my studies and practices seemed to be concerned with reactivating what I had already known and studied in other times. Increasingly I remembered who I was and had been in myriad incarnations, but nothing was new. I was still delving into old territory. In my twenties I gave up acting, although I had loved being involved in the theatre for it was one of the few *safe* outlets for expressing my power. But there were simply no plays which came from the level of consciousness I yearned to express.

As the years passed by, I contentedly resigned myself to a life as a partial recluse mixed with periods of intense public activity. There was no glimmer of a Great Work, but I was pursuing my spiritual path with full commitment. At times, I pondered whether the idea of achieving a Great Work was merely a childhood dream and felt no attachment to whether it happened or not. But the seed remained.

For years I watched those who stepped openly onto the front lines carrying the banner of the New. I gratefully observed how they served to open doorways into new levels of awareness for humanity, myself included. And I also noted how most of the time, their message ended up becoming distorted and misunderstood by others and how some of them ultimately got burned out and blown off course. This was a great learning process and not one to fill you with enthusiasm for stepping out openly with your Highest Truth.

Always there was the burning question: Is humanity ready for this? I wrestled with this question each time that I prepared to publish one of my books. Were people ready to understand? Would I be mocked, demeaned, or laughed at? Due to my own internal makeup, watering down the information in my books was not possible. I have always been compelled to put as much as I can into each book, whether or not people are ready to understand.

With *Invoking Your Celestial Guardians,* I came out and said that we were all Angels. Now at the time, people were becoming aware of Angels, but were still regarding them as beings separate from us. They *worked with* Angels, rather than realizing *that we are Angels.* There's a mighty difference there! Although many people loved the book, often I was tagged, "self-proclaimed Angel" which is not only silly, but inaccurate, since *we are all Angels.*

In *The Legend of Altazar,* I divulged information about AN and the Og-Min. This was extremely difficult as it was so sacred to me. I was afraid that people wouldn't understand. Instead, there was a tremendous response from those who also remembered their connections with AN & the Og-Min. I can't tell you how happy and relieved this made me. Then in *The Star-Borne,* I pulled out all the stops and tried to include everything I knew at the time. This book was really asking for it. But once again, I was deluged with letters thanking me for telling their story, from beings grateful to discover they were not alone.

Next came the challenge of *EL*AN*RA,* my simple intergalactic romance which took on the formidable task of healing Orion. I could already hear the impending criticism of my delving into the darkness of duality, yet knew that this story must be told and the healing of duality must take place before we were free to journey through the 11:11. And many have understood and felt their connection with the three star lineages of EL AN RA.

Miraculously, the resonance of Truth cuts through all illusion. Many people, although not everyone, understood what I had to say. They felt that I had written their Truth as well. Many began to awaken and remember as never before. But here was the Activation of the 11:11 which was different than anything we had ever experienced. Would people understand its vast scope? Would humanity be able to rise above their feelings of separation, of individuality, the delineations of their egos and truly unite into Oneness?

The answer is that some have and others have not. And I have learned to live with and accept the perfection of this, although at times it has severely challenged me. There has been a tremendous misunderstanding and distortion of what the 11:11 means. People often ask me what my next project is now that the 11:11 is complete. *It isn't finished; it has just begun!* Or they tell me about another stargate, just like the 11:11, which they are about to open. *The 11:11 isn't a stargate. It is our one and only bridge between two different templates of consciousness which we have been laboring aeons to open!* It emanates from an inconceivably vaster level than a stargate. This is like comparing a drop of liquid with the ocean.

I continually remind myself that it isn't important if everyone knows what the 11:11 is. Every major breakthrough on this planet was achieved by a mere handful of people, and already many have answered the Call, who know that the 11:11 is of tremendous importance.

The 11:11 has challenged us to our core. It has forced us to see where we choose to anchor our beings. It has pierced many of the veils of our illusions. It has questioned the depth of our commitment to fulfilling our Divine Missions on Earth. It has exposed many of the illusions of New Age spirituality. The integrity of our motivations has been put on the line. It has brought up the shadowy areas within ourselves which hold us back and keep us smaller.

Now it would have been a lot easier if the Activation of the 11:11 could have been achieved in the same manner as Harmonic Convergence – if all that was required was that we came together and did whatever we wished on January

11, 1992. But that would not have served the Purpose of opening the Door. We needed to come together in focused intent, wearing white to symbolize the purity of our Unified Presence and create the Wheels within Wheels. Do you realize how much trouble this caused?

"Why should we do *Solara's* movements?" "Who is she anyway?" "I'm not going to wear the same color as everyone else!" "The 11:11 is a scam." I tried to tell everyone that they were not my movements. Simply that since Unified Movements were necessary to open the Door, *someone* had to receive them. In this case, it was me, but it didn't have to be. I had chosen at some far distant time and place to receive the vision for the 11:11 and see it through to its successful conclusion. I was simply carrying out the task of fulfilling my part of our Divine Missions, the same as we were all asked to do.

On the Front Lines

It would be helpful to develop a greater understanding of what it entails to be on the front line, to be a pioneer in bringing in the New. At first glance it may appear as a glamourous lifestyle; but it is not. Much of the time, it's simply a lot of work, most of which never gets seen by anyone. Those few hours when you're onstage in front of an adoring audience are well balanced out by the endless days spent traveling, waiting in airports, staying by yourself in a succession of hotel rooms. When you're home, there are mountains of office work, full of boring details which are nevertheless important to complete.

The most challenging part of bringing in the New is the time spent alone traveling through distant realms and heightened levels of awareness. One of my tasks has been to find new doorways of consciousness, to move through them and fully experience them on every level of my being.

Once mastered, I communicate them to others, passing on the needed tools to help them move through. By the time this happens, it looks easy. The journey appears effortless. Now we can teach anyone to stop time or to look through the All-Seeing Eye of AN in just a few minutes. But it took me years of sometimes grueling, solitary work to master these things!

Another factor is that while you are in the midst of exploring these new levels of consciousness, it is often necessary to dismantle your being. This means functioning in a diminished capacity on the 3D so the rest of you can concentrate on inner work. It makes normal social conversations and activities practically impossible to participate in. Other times, at workshops for example, I am so busy anchoring the Beam and affecting a mass healing for the entire group, that people wonder why I appear aloof by eating my meals alone.

Sometimes I am judged harshly for this. Seeing me tired, sad, impatient or disheartened, they assume that I can't possibly be spiritual. This process is similar to what shamen undergo when they are seeking cures to various illnesses. Often they take the poison and let it work upon them with full force, *almost dying in the process,* until they find the cure which can then be used for the benefit of everyone.

Although I'm speaking for myself, I have watched this process happen to many. And I have gratefully received a tremendous amount of love, respect and support along the way. It's been pretty easy for me considering what happens to politicians and film stars. I'm filled with compassion for them now. Think of how many times we hear people saying, "Oh, I hate that person," about someone they don't even know and will probably never meet. Each time someone does that it bombards that person with a psychic barrage of negative energy. It's an old habit which we can easily clear from our beings. We must realize that everyone is doing the best that they can in each moment. And maybe that grouchy waitress was up all night with a sick child or just broke up with her boyfriend. Let's live with compassion for all our Starry Brothers and Sisters.

The 11:11 Finally Happens

What happened next was the Star-Borne staff geared up to working seven days a week. We printed hundreds of thousands of *11:11* Booklets, most of which we gave away for free or sold at cost, and we were inundated with requests for information from all over the planet. In December, 1991 alone, our postage bill was $12,000, paid for by the sales of my books and tapes. I put all of my income into this work. (Remember: I had resolved to give it my all.) I have spent the past four years devoting my life to the awakening of the Star-Borne, traveling indefatigably all over the planet, sacrificing any personal life. This has been the level of my commitment.

Then as more people jumped onto the bandwagon, tour companies began arranging 11:11 tours to various parts of the planet. Many of these were by groups who had no knowledge or desire to participate in the Unified Movements. People signed up thinking that they were part of our group. Articles began appearing in various publications with bylines by people I had never met, but the text of the article was written by me. Sometimes they mixed in their own interpretation of what the 11:11 meant, such as it was anchoring in the fourth dimension. *(Which it was not, as the Harmonic Convergence already did that in 1987.)* Then we had the springing up of Star-Borne Chapters all over the world by people we didn't know, who had never contacted our office. Articles critical of me, saying that the 11:11 was a scam appeared in publications, written by people whom I had never met. All of this was extremely challenging and a great lesson in letting go.

The funniest part came one morning during breakfast in a hotel in Los Angeles where we were doing the Whole Life Expo. The gentlemen at the table next to us leaned over and asked if we were part of the Solara Cult? Flabbergasted and highly amused, I managed to reply that I *was* Solara. They wanted to know where my church or my centre was located. "In the hearts of people all over the planet," I answered. The funny thing about being thought of as a cult is that it would make me a cult leader, and I certainly don't feel like one. I don't know, maybe other cult leaders also carry their own suitcases, iron their clothes, and clean their cat boxes, but I had certainly hoped that *they* at least, were enjoying a more glamourous lifestyle!

This has been my experience of the Challenge of Oneness. Remarkably, on January 11, 1992 enough of us did join together all over the planet and opened the Doorway of the 11:11. Together we did the Unified Movements, dressed in white, and it was totally beautiful, extremely powerful and it worked! The 11:11 opened for all of us. And I am exceedingly grateful to each one who participated.

There are many on the planet today who think that the 11:11 is over, but it is not, it has just begun. This is the big one which will lead us into freedom and mastery. This is our doorway to ascension.

Throughout our Master Cylinder Ceremony in Egypt I was filled with a deep sense of elation. I kept hearing the words, "Well done." I felt fulfilled as never before. And if you were to ask me would I do it again, I would have to answer, "Yes, of course," just for the memory of our magical time in the

Courtyard of AN and the energies which we have anchored into the Earth. I would like to pass on to you the words, "Well done."

So the Great Work continues. Although I will continue to serve in whatever ways possible, I can no longer achieve it on my own. Your help is needed as never before. We have a whole planet to awaken and prepare for ascension into the New Octave which awaits. Now let's rise above the Challenge of Oneness and get on with our homeward journey. . .

11:11 Experiences

Here are reports from some of the groups and individuals who participated in opening the Doorway of the 11:11...

Δ Master Cylinder:The Great Pyramids Δ

It is midnight at the Great Pyramids in Giza, Egypt. At the base of the third pyramid of Mycerinus there are ruins of an ancient temple. Uneven fragments of stone walls outline this huge, rectangular temple. It is whispered that the legendary city of AN rests beneath these ruins. The stars of EL AN RA shine brightly overhead, ever observing the activities on Earth. This sacred temple now transforms into the Courtyard of AN, revealing itself to be that which has long been preordained. Thousands of white candles flicker, placed upon ledges and niches within the temple walls, positioned around the many boulders and pits scattered over the temple floor. Memories of other times, other places, ancient doorways and other realms of consciousness begin to stir and reawaken...

We enter this sacred Courtyard of AN in silent reverence. White robed figures who have traveled far to converge upon this place at the same instant of No-Time at the beginning moments of January 11, 1992. There are five hundred of these timeless travelers, dressed in layers of white, coming from 32 countries. Each of us has heard the Call and chosen to answer with our full commitment. Although we speak many different languages, our One Heart resonates with the Song of One.

Two Guardians stand in silent vigil at the Outer Gates. Each one who approaches must first announce themselves with mudra and Starry Name. Then they enter the long corridor which serves as a birth canal leading to the Courtyard of AN. They pass by the Guardians of the Inner Gates who bow in silent acknowledgement.

Inside the temple walls the vast Circles of Sun and Moon are formed with eight inner wheels of eleven. The music begins and together as One, we begin the Wheels within Wheels. With fluid motions we move through No-Time, No-Space. The beauty of this is indescribable. It is beyond anything which we have previously experienced on Earth. All I can think of is that Shamballa has returned. We have truly anchored the Greater Reality into the planet.

No-Time expands into a deep hush. Never before have I felt it to be so powerful. As we move into the Starry Processional, a huge star is born; it is the Star of our Unified

Presence. It is finally here! As we begin to revolve, the Heavens themselves begin to turn in synchronicity.

Thus it was for thirty eight hours in the sacred Courtyard of AN at the base of the Pyramid of Mycerinus. The Unified Movements continued on ceaselessly throughout the long, cold night, through the day which followed, another long, cold night and up through the next afternoon. It was an experience which none of us shall ever forget, for it has been *seared* into the core of our beings. We have been transformed and will never, ever be the same. Such was the depth of the blessing we received by being there. We have seen what few human eyes will ever see. We have been immersed into the Greater Reality until the very fibers and cells of our beings were irrevocably realigned into the Template of Oneness.

There are small, precious memories which each of us carry like tiny jewels embedded into our hearts. The sight of the majestic Guardians standing so resolutely throughout our vigil, protecting the sanctity of our ceremony, anchoring the Cosmic Rays. Many served as Guardians throughout those long hours; each received a direct infusion of the Light of Oneness. During the dark hours of the night when a freezing wind penetrated through all our layers of clothes, Guardians would stand unflinchingly with arms outstretched. Sometimes it was so cold that we would have to replace the Guardians every half hour, but new volunteers would always respond to our Call.

The greatest challenge came in the early morning hours when it was the coldest and darkest. Our group dwindled to its smallest numbers. Yet the movements always continued on. . . I remember seeing ones passed out from exhaustion lying face down in the desert sand... And there were those who never left the temple complex, who served continuously with dedicated commitment, keeping the star turning for all. I will never forget the look in their shining, starry eyes; for they had truly broken through to that transcendent place of all-knowing, all-being. I honored you at that moment and I honor you now, for indeed you demonstrated your true magnificence at a time when it was truly needed.

Solara, Ramariel & Kumari in the Starry Processional

After our extremely powerful 11:11 pm GMT *(which was 1:11 am on January 12th in Egypt),* we knew that the Door had finally opened. A profound shift was felt. The crowd once again thinned out to the deeply committed ones and the emphasis moved to the Starry Processional which became ever more precious. I could feel us spiraling up and through the Doorway. Then came the miraculous new dawn, more beautiful than any we had seen. The first strands of light descended upon us and our energies lifted. Kumari, who had been serving with me as Mother of the Star, and I fed those in the Starry Processional with almonds, trail mix and squares of chocolate. Bottled water was passed out into cupped hands which gratefully received our humble gifts. All the while our star revolved...

As the day grew brighter, sunlight warmed our frozen bodies and we began to shed some of our layers of clothing. Our star became larger as more people returned. Kumari and I continued to dance inside the Starry Procession, moving in a slow, ceremonial step, holding open the Doorway of the 11:11. By mid-morning on January 12th, the energies began to intensify. We could feel the entrance of a penetrating beam of White Light, the Yod. It seared through my being like a laser, causing my body to jerk backwards and my legs to turn to liquid. If it hadn't been for Kumari's anchoring Presence, I would have fallen over. As the Procession continued, I could feel our entire, blessed star spiralling together up into the New Octave!

There is so much more to remember. Our amazing days of preparation in the palatial ballroom of our hotel. How easy it was to move into Oneness. What an extremely beautiful, pure and empowered group of starry beings from all over the world!. . . I remember our ride out in the desert overlooking the Pyramids on camels and horses which triggered the departure of the Celestial Caravan. How natural we looked riding camels while wearing long robes and halos!. . . The chants of camels and canoes which invigorated us with renewed energy. . .The exquisite Melchizedek Initiation brought to the planet for only the second time. . . The vast Love which surrounded and embraced everything. I honor each one who participated.

I must thank our staff who served so magnificently: Kumari for holding the sanctity of the Beam, Elariul & Kala*ai who took turns with me at the microphone leading the movements for 38 continuous hours, Etherium for his enthusiasm and inspired music, Aquataine for his powerful, fatherly Presence which was like a canopy of love and protection for us all, AArela for taking care of the 3D, Ramariel for his strength of Presence in the Starry Processional and on the Nile, Star Commander Albion for translating throughout the ceremony into three languages, Solar, Solaris, Nova, Urith-Ra-El, Aya, and Zaragusta.

And one thing that I must add: Our sacred ceremony in the Courtyard of AN continues. . .It is without end for it is anchored within the eternal moment of No-Time. It is the manifestation of the Greater Reality brought to Earth and is available to all. If you want to join us there, slip into something white and flowing, put on a tape of the *Starry Processional,* and together as One, we shall spiral into the New Octave!. . . *Solara Antara Amaa-Ra.*

△ △ △

Many on the Egypt trip had wonderful visions. But I'm sure that none were more splendid than mine. Words are inadequate to describe what I saw, but I'll do the best I can in the no-space allotted... I saw five hundred beautiful Angels walking freely and openly on the Earth. Their radiance outshone the third dimensional splendor of the opulent ballroom *(Was it built especially for us?)* with eleven large, gold leaf Moorish arches, huge crystal chandeliers and 11:11 woven into the pattern of the carpet.

The night that we started the movements was cold and clear. EL AN RA shone at the top of the Third Pyramid. At the foot of this pyramid stands a ruined temple which will hereafter be called the Courtyard of AN. The floor of this courtyard was uneven with pits and piles of rubble. Candles burned around the perimeter of the stone walls which were from 6 to 30 feet high. *(How Solara got permission to use this temple is a story in itself.)*

But here we were in this timeless scene continually doing the Unified Movements and Realigning the Stars. Sometimes, in the popular hours, large formations would turn as One, walking over rubble and down into holes. The points of the stars were One with their rays and those walking backwards, young and old, would not falter as they ceaselessly turned. In the wee small hours, precious little circles would turn as those truly committed Angels, bone weary, cold and shivering, would always go on for one more round. How can words describe the beauty of the commitment of those who stood as Guardians, backs and legs aching, hour after hour?

As long as we're talking about inadequate words, how, I ask you, do we begin to thank the woman who sacrificed her life to manifest this vision? When I think of Solara I remember a woman dragging hundred pound, book-filled suitcases through the Miami airport on her way to Brazil, with less than $200 in her pocket and no companion to help her. I think about a woman who has sacrificed personal life, family life and enjoys few of the small pleasures which you and I take for granted.

But mostly I see an impeccable Angel, the only one I know who could carry this Light and not falter, not give up when her very being ached. What words do I use to thank her for holding the Light long enough for ME to see it? There are no words... We can only adequately thank her by being fully empowered, all encompassing love. For that, Solara, you truly are. THANK YOU. . . *I am Aquataine.*

△ △ △

Periodically, Solara would announce the time and what countries we were connecting with. She talked about the Camel Caravan of the Old Template which was leaving and the Celestial Canoe of the New which was coming in. We chanted the Caravan: AN–NUT-TA–RA HU. It was a slow, restful chant; somewhat like bumping along on a camel. The Celestial Canoe was totally invigorating, AH AIEEEE HA WA, accompanied by strong arm movements as though one were pumping a boat swiftly along with purpose and new energy. The HA WA sound was a forceful expulsion of air. *(I sensed that it was a healthful release for the lack of air we had experienced in the long, intense initiation in the Kings Chamber of Cheops Pyramid earlier in our Egyptian adventure.)*

We had done many of the Unified Movements by then. The Wheels within Wheels, the Sun-Moon movements and the Starry Procession. I found myself moving backwards in the star more often than not. At one point, Aquataine saw that my footing was becoming shaky and gently took my hand, switching my position to one of forward motion. I was silently grateful.

After a sojourn at the hotel, I returned to the ceremony in the early morning. When I arrived, the starry circle had diminished considerably. It was a small group of about fifty tired looking beings. Solara was there flowing gracefully, eyes closed, barefoot, being gently led around the inside by a tall, dark haired maiden. She opened her eyes as I joined the circle and nodded a smile of gratitude and appreciation toward me. My heart was so full of the magnificence of what this event was bringing about, I felt my eyes well up with tears of emotion. More and more people started to join us now and the circle grew and grew . . . *Valoriel An Ra.*

Δ Δ Δ

My son and I were at the Great Pyramids for the 11:11. It was one of the greatest experiences in our lives and we are both very grateful because it changed our lives completely. Solara, it's more difficult to live in this third dimensional world right now; nothing will be the same – but we know this is our way!

I send you some pictures of a huge wall painting in my meditation room. Ar Mon Re, my son did it a short time after Egypt. He calls it, *The Celestial World.* It depicts a being on his way Home. . . *Ramra Sawi, from Sweden.*

Δ Master Cylinder: Queenstown, New Zealand Δ

On New Year's Eve I set off for the adventure of a lifetime to New Zealand with my favorite traveling companions Luna & Aztah. We set off bravely, not knowing what lay ahead, but feeling the anticipation of the new Doorway waiting to be opened.

Queenstown greeted us with towering snow capped peaks, crystal clear lakes and splendid forests. Although we were exhausted from our long journey around the world, we could not stay in our rooms, but had to explore the bounty which lay outside. New Zealand is truly the land of the new. For fun, people are either parachuting, windsurfing, or bungy jumping. Wherever you look in the sky, there are people flying by. No fear of gravity or the new!

By the second day we felt totally at home. We were interviewed on radio and by the local paper, and ate tons of delicious New Zealand food. When the rest of our group arrived, we felt like locals ourselves.

It was so great to reunite with those I already knew and to meet the others so dedicated as to travel around the world to open the Doorway of the 11:11. They spent the first night resting and exploring the streets of Queenstown. The next morning we all met and introduced ourselves. Slowly we began merging into Oneness. That evening when we reconvened, the closeness felt was similar to the last day of a Reunion. Matisha even wrote a new song inspired by the beautiful Angels present.

On January 9th, we met early for the long trip to Milford Sound. The Vortex in New Zealand is a huge triangular shaped area, and we traveled to the three points of the triangle: Queenstown, Te Anau & Milford Sound. The bus ride was long and the driver's jokes horrible, but the scenery was absolutely stunning. We stopped at Mirror Lakes and the Chasm and drank from a glacier-fed river. The steep mountains were streaming with countless waterfalls, I have never seen such untouched grandeur.

Once at Milford Sound, we boarded a boat and went clear out to the Tasman Sea. As we came around the last bend, we entered into the main vortex area. Silently the decks filled with Angels. We did our mudras, anchored a shaft of Light and merged with the tremendous energy.

Friday night we gave a public concert explaining the 11:11 & showing the Unified Movements. Matisha sang and

Grace shared poetry and stories. There was even a small earthquake while Grace spoke. It was so wonderful for us to be able to meet with all the local people. Truly New Zealand has been blessed by its inhabitants – the most clear, friendly, & alive people I have met.

The day of the 11th dawned auspiciously – bright & sunny. We began the Unified Movements promptly at 11:11 am. Time loomed ahead; there were still 38 more hours to go. Wheels started turning. *To the left of course.* I felt the slow churning. Each hour as we did the Starry Processional, it evolved, changing, mirroring the universe in its constant change. We took turns being at the center. It was so empowering and magical there that we wanted to share this experience. Our star was shifting, pulsating, joyful & alive. I have never had so much fun in my life. We truly moved & breathed as One, our vast body spinning, realigning the Heavens and anchoring it here in the physical.

Dusk fell, and the crowd dwindled. We still had around 50 people committed to going the distance. The energy in the room built up with each passing hour. Being a Guardian became more and more difficult – holding such high energy for so long. We kept the wheels turning each hour with renewed enthusiasm & joy through the delicate wee hours of the night. As dawn blushed the dark sky, it was like the first day was being born. We knew, despite swollen feet and sore muscles, we could make it all the way through. I have never seen such a glorious dawn, the birds singing brightly and the lake aglow with light.

Fresh people started to arrive and their energy fed us all. On and on the circle turned, always alive & new. Food was kept piled high on the tables, donated by anonymous sources to keep the circle well nourished. I give my thanks, appreciation and love to all who served so masterfully on every level. Everyone was there with total commitment and total love. We could not have done it without each person fully serving as they did.

By the evening of the second day, legs were swollen and backs crooked, but the wheels kept turning. *To the left of course.* Each time we did the movements they became more & more precious. The energy in the room escalated as the sun went down. Illuminated by candles, we spun up and up. By the last 3 or 4 movements I was no longer walking on the ground. The room no longer looked the same. The people inside became even dearer. And when finally the movements stopped, I felt as if another 38 hours were in order, although I could hardly walk.

The next morning a wild wind blew through the valley. A group of 60 gathered for a last good-bye. Everyone who had attended the movements, even just for a few hours, had transformed. Those that had been there for the full 38 hours glowed. Although we were bustling with last minute errands, they coaxed us into the group for a few last hugs and songs. They laid Aztah, Luna, Grace, Matisha & me on the floor, sang a beautiful song, and slowly lifted us over their heads. The New Zealanders were so full of love and appreciation for what we had accomplished. They now understood what responsibility they had taken on, living here in the land of the New. Fully empowered and activated, they began planning their next steps.

So we parted ways with beautiful Queenstown and all the new friends we had made there. Off we went to the new adventures awaiting on the other side of the Doorway. Kia Ora Aeotearoa!. . .*Elara Zacandra.*

Δ Δ Δ

People came to Queenstown from all over the world. It was a lovely mix. The leadership of the events was so well done. Those people really deserve a medal of some kind. They were unflagging and followed the energy with flexibility and sensitive receptivity. All the people there were willing to give, to serve the situation. There was a lot of joy, commitment, release, generosity, near exhaustion, and relief when the final hour arrived. So worthwhile, since it was participating in something much bigger than our usual life on Earth.

I particularily liked the linking up with various places around the world as each hourly cycle began. That gave a very clear conception of the spiral effect of the activation. As I tuned in on the morning of the 13th, I knew we had helped create a major shift of energies. . . *Omni Imlhara.*

Δ Findhorn, Scotland Δ

Dawn! Grandfather Sun creeping slowly and purposefully from behind the ancient mountain. He knows too. Seventy five miles down the valley and along the coast to the chosen place. The Universal Hall, half hidden by pines, waits like a womb to receive us. Light beings in white and gold prepare and more arrive. Quietly, reverently, they enter the space where they will fulfill their destiny. Their love shines in their greetings. The bond is strong.

Soon, the time is here. The energy is drawn and held. Each and all playing out their part, remembered through all the long journey. Silent joy spreads and fills. This is the way home. . . On the shore of Moray Firth the wet shingle reflects the sun with a new brilliance and the sky is a deeper shade of blue. The wind refreshes and tells of change. This is a beautiful, precious day.

We converged at the appointed times, consolidating, anchoring, opening the Door. Hearts grow. Separation dissolves. The planet shimmers with myriad points of light and the song is heard throughout the Cosmos.

This was the 11:11 at Findhorn. And that night a blue light shines above my bed. A Silent Watcher. Did I hear him say, "Well done!". . . *Epsirion.*

Δ From a Prison Cell in Japan Δ

On the 11th of January we transformed my cell into a temple. We are: Me physically and all the angels who visited me, bringing the vision of what is happening around the globe. My friends sent me many flowers which we may receive in our cells, so my altar was especially beautiful.

I had saved some white clothes for the occasion. Doing the steps described in *Wheels within Wheels* was truly awesome because I actually could achieve No-Time, No-Space, No-Duality, and at 11:11 GMT I felt you all so powerfully, and looked at your pictures in *the Starry Messenger.* I visualized you all in Egypt doing the movements and thus became a part of it.

In detention, it's bedtime, lights dim at 9:00 pm. The fluorescents are never totally off, just dimmed. I got permission from the guard to be woken up for 11:11 pm local time. Well I got up before the guard came to wake me and dressed, did the motions, prayed, meditated and joined you; but this time it was even better. I really felt the One and the many and also deep gratitude to the authorities for letting me pray at what is irregular to their routine. Then I held a little celebration in my temple and read some of Grace's amazing poetry. I dropped so many old, unnecessary burdens I didn't need anymore, forgave and was truly healed. . .*Solastar Qua-Y-El*

Δ Long Island, New York Δ

A new Holy Day was born... January 11th, 1992! It was powerful and ecstatic – so visionary and unified! Throughout the day I had visions. It started with a group of Angels in the celestial sky. Some Angels had very huge wings. I saw tall beings with folded hands, dressed in white, standing in space above the Earth and watching the events. I realized a few days later, that I saw so well because I was standing in space.

I saw the entire Earth from a distance. It had a lot of white-gold complex energy patterns moving over the surface and into the atmosphere. You could hardly see the water or the land. At one point, the Earth swirled through a huge doorway. As our gathering progressed, the energy intensified and while we were doing the movements, the built up energy exploded and started spiraling up into the sky and down into the Earth over and over again.

Towards the end of the day, I saw a strong, expansive beam of White Light shoot through space from the Great Central Sun and hit the entire Earth. There was a long pause, then another strong Beam of White Light. Thank you Solara, for showing us the way Home!. . . *Elohim Anarsim Rubyar*

Δ Vienna, Austria Δ

Our group met three times prior to the 11:11 to practice Unified Movements. At least nine groups met in the area

213

on January 11th. Now we are integrating the experiences of the 11:11 into our everyday lives, everybody in his own way... *Robert Unterluggauer*

Δ Toronto, Ontario, Canada Δ

In Toronto around 250 people from around the province gathered all day from 10:00 am to midnight. Everyone was dressed in their whites. We did the Unified Movements at all the key times. Our most powerful time was in the Sacred Spiral. As we unwound the Spiral, we made our celestial sounds. It was as if the entire galaxy was singing back to us. Then we went right into the 11:11 pm GMT session which was very potent and full of deep sacred space. A High Holy Day was most definitely experienced by all... *Elan Nanu & Le'eema Rheema.*

Δ Central Park, New York City Δ

It was a crisp, cold and exhilarating New York morning. Amidst the acres of austere leafless trees, the white winged pigeons glistened like stars as the new day's sun caught the tips of their wings. They were harbingers of what was to come as they nestled upon the serene angel overlooking Bethesda Fountain. Truly they looked like doves.

The circle of Angels gleaming in white grew larger and larger. The stark winter tones of nature served as a negative space to the brilliant sun-kissed white garb of our beloved Starry Family. The rocks seemed to hum and pulsate with a mutable energy that traveled upon the ice formed in its veins.

As Etherium's gorgeous *Starry Processional* melodically flowed into the wintry air, one need only turn and look up to the Dakota to feel John Lennon's incredibly peaceful presence weaving through the crowd. The dedication of

Sha-lin, Das Ra and Shandra that day was inspiring. You could see pure essence in their faces during the movements – the focus was so powerful.

The wafting scent of burning sage along with Wheels within Wheels harmoniously became a glorious tapestry, a celestial timepiece and all hands pointed to 11:11. . . *Eliana Raphaela Shamriel*

Δ With the dolphins at Kealakekua Bay, Hawaii Δ

Aloha to Solara, my Sacred Sister, the Messenger, Aloha to All of the Tribe of One. "I am Venusolari of AnRa-AnRat. I bring greetings from A-Qua-La A-Wa-La. We bring you peace, love and understanding." These are the words I was told to use as invocation each time I met with my Brothers/ Sisters, the Dolphins, in the months as we prepared for the 11:11. As I practiced the movements in the water, the dolphins would do them underneath me.

On the Sacred Day, we swam out into the Bay in silence. As we formed our triangle and did the movements in unison, our thoughts were also with Makua in a Circle of Eleven at Kilauea Crater, and EloRa at the Summit of Mauna Kea, with a large gathering of the Tribe. We were all part of a larger triangle.

The dolphins were below us doing the movements. From the time we entered the water they had been continuously toning. Their sounds were assisting in the realignment of the grid. Our bodies were half under the water and half above. We were acting as Conductors, passing the energy through. As we did the movements in the water, it gave us an unique perspective. We were actually able to feel and see the Shift, the Dove passing through the Open Door. When we left the water, the dolphins continued to tone.

215

We proceeded on our sacred journey by traveling to Honaunau, the next bay south on the Kona Coast. The water here was very active. It was majestic. We didn't speak of it until much later, but we all noticed that the Ocean was acting in a way that was unusual. The Ocean was being an active participant. As we performed the movements, the water also did the movements. As the Door was opening, the water gushed through.

As we left the Ocean for the second time that day, we felt a sense of Completion. We had fulfilled our role in the Drama of the Whole. Our next step was to go to Mauna Kea to meet with the rest of the Tribe, to join together for the Sacred Spiral. We were blessed to play our Role with the Ocean. . . *Venusolari.*

Δ Kilauea Crater, Hawai'i Δ

Aloha Solara and to the numerous 144,000 sovereign star lights that participated in altering the motion of time:

I would like to share with you a portion of our magical experience – how eleven of us, six feminine energies and five masculine energies plus a special guest from the land of *The Long White Cloud* of Aeotearoa made a commitment to the dedication of ourselves to the service of others and the loyalty to the One Infinite Creator, the Breath of Life, O Mauri Ora.

In the morning, at the break of dawn, we received our first acknowledgement from the stars. As the sun with its streaks of light breaking through the darkness and peeking over the horizon, a star fell and greeted us with its effervescence that seemed to illuminate the heavens for eternity and blossomed into a golden illumination that merged into the Keeper of the Dawn at KUMUKAHI, the First Source, The Ladder of The Sun.

All eleven of us and Maori Aotearoa, a special Pohaku given to the Council of Elders of Unification by the Elders of Taranaki of the majestic people of Whanga Nui, met at Halemaumau, *The House Always*, one of the twelve mysteries. At exactly 8:00 a.m. we stepped into the silence of Kilauea, the force that ushers in the world of light, on the island of Hawai'i, the most supreme living water, Divine Breath. The six woman entered into the silence from the northern gate of the crater; the gate of dreams and imagination. The five men entered into the silence from the southern gate, the opposite pole, the gate of integration, in the sea of chiefs, moving toward the gate of dreams. I announced our entry with my conch shell, Ku Keao Loa, the messenger. We received the music of three conch shells in return that heralded our gifts, ourselves.

The men and women were to come together and merge into the fiery feminine mana of Pele Hanau Moku, at the very center of the House Always. Its magnificence cannot be put into words; for where we sat was the very center, the bosom of Mother Nature bursting in raw energy, the potential of form – Pele the fire goddess.

There were many exchanges of aloha, not only between all of us there, but to every one extant on this beautiful foundation built and established in strength, that has been our source of learning within the law of confusion, our choices made in time; a place where we have grown spiritually to discover the greatest mystery in the universe – ourselves; to surpass our limitations placed on ourselves by ourselves, and breaking through the veil to become conscious in this great classroom for gods in training.

To the east stood the gate of birth and adjusting and to the west sat the gate of completion and perceiving where Hina would put to rest the completion of this cycle.

217

I called to the four corners of the universe to listen to my prayer and requests – that we come in service to others; that we are the assembly of the One; that we are the lineage of the One; that we are the perpetuation of the One; and the finest of the One's creations.

For we have refined all that was to be refined, lifetime after lifetime; evolving to completion; the attainment of our goal. All of us now will raise the Earth spiritually through the mouths of numerous star lights who find this day a duty, a privilege, and a responsibility to exercise that responsibility of just being; passing on to the Second Wavers our mana'o, mana'olana and kuli'a; thought, hope, confidence and the greatest desire to strive toward the One; by eating the cosmic fruit, Hua, of things to come and to be possessed by those things. Such was my request – to return freely to the ONE.

At our highest point, the point of no return, we each gave our own personal mudra and danced the dance of the eleventh house, the dance of Ho'oku'ikahi, Unification, unfettered by difficulty and in a state of free movement and intermingling of mana. We were unlimited like the winds of Kumukahi. Our emphasis was on our highest hopes for the Second Wavers to surpass limitations and reach for freedom not just for themselves, but for all.

Here we sit in the red sea of fire knowing that a group of star lights are sprinkling their star stuff with the Naia, *dolphins*, at Kealakekua Bay, the rising path to the Deity, the One. Another group of star lights are standing on the perch of Mauna Kea, all triangulating the Tau, the elements, and experiencing our own transcendence where to each seeker is revealed the transparent mana of discovering their god-stuff and star stuff that resonates to the music of lights within; allowing all of us to see through ourselves to the truth and find we were never apart.

At exactly thirty minutes after eleven we entered back into the world of sound. For three and one half hours we swam where all the mystics swim, in a space indescribable.

We had accepted the fishhook of Maui without struggle and allowed the heavens to pull us up into its bosom to listen to their music of light in the sea of lights within. We sang praises to those ancestors who walked before us and to those who have taken the challenge of things to come.

There is so much that each has experienced during and after and continuing. I want to say thank you to all who have participated in this completion, to all who heard the whisper, the call, who felt the urge to sing the song of Unification. To all: Mahalo Nui Loa.

Only once is this experience; it will never happen again, for all is memory now. The door, the gate, the window is open now. Don't forget your tickets and be prompt. To step through the doorway for the last time is to accept the challenge, a choice of free will to evolve from the love of the One Infinite Creator back into the light. See you all there..
Hono Ele Makua, Council of Elder, A me O Maori, Aotearoa

Δ Guatemala City, Guatemala Δ

It is with great joy that I inform you of our 11:11 Celebration in Guatemala. After receiving the information in *Wheels within Wheels* and *Invoking Your Celestial Guardians*, we started remembering our Angelic Names, sounds and mudras and were ready for that sacred day.

When doing our mandalas of the Wheels, we could see the Wheels being formed all around Terra, then the Door of the 11:11 was opened and the Dove formed by all the workers of Light. It was wonderful! From the very beginning we could see a dome of Light above us. Many received visions of what was going on at a planetary, local and personal level. There were many rays of Light in different colors around us. The following message was received: "This is the moment you have been waiting for thousands and thousands of years."

Two more groups were celebrating in our city and another two in different locations of our nation. Reports have reached us that people felt something special that day and many altars with white flowers were on the main road to the Pacific Ocean. Also, many people not connected with our group have been seeing and feeling changes in their lives. Thank you for what you and all the workers of Light around the world have done. . . *Aaiska An Ta Ra.*

Δ Phoenix, Arizona Δ

On January 11th, they came in peace and love, in numbers far exceeding anything we had anticipated. . . For the thousands who see 11:11 click onto the faces of their digital clocks and wonder why it creates a stirring within them, Star-Borne Lightworkers assisted in providing enlightenment. As the Starry Legions took their seats in chairs and on the floor, all clad in white, overcrowding the hall; immediate transformation began. Their faces curious and hopeful, expressions soon turned to wonderment. Some trembled, some cried, some came to be healed. Everyone's face glowed with love and renewal.

Organizers had expected 300, but over 600 had come to learn and share in the Light. In a time of turmoil, it was a day of peace. In a world shackled by hate, it was a day made free by the affirmation of love. In these days of disease and isolation, it was a passage of blessed unity. . . *Yolanda.*

Δ Rhayader, Wales, U.K. Δ

We anchored the Light and opened the Doorway in Mid-Wales. We were a small group of seven very dedicated

220

souls. Our event was held at the Kindergarten School Hall, set amongst beautiful grounds. The energy in the hall was quite something and shafts of Light were seen in the centre of our sacred circle. Following our final 11:11 Ceremony in the late evening, we departed into a clear starry night with a crisp frost glistening in the rolling hills and valleys, profoundly moved by the whole days activities. . . *Alta Ra & El Atar Amin Ra.*

Δ Vancouver, British Columbia, Canada Δ

We did it! We irrevocably anchored in a New Octave of Oneness. The higher frequency energies are affecting everyone. The Light of the One shines in people's hearts and eyes everywhere I look! Oh what bliss! The 11:11 here in Vancouver was amazing. We met in the Plaza of Nations where we were washed with astonishingly beautiful pulsations of Light energy all day. I am still in awe of the incredibly powerful magnitude and brilliance of the Light we anchored. I thank God for the chance to plant seeds of awakening to the Many. I know that this is only the beginning of the incredible journey home. I thank you Solara for your unshakeable commitment and for being the visionary of the 11:11. . . *Solarius Andradea Azatara.*

Δ Kingman, Arizona Δ

The entire 11:11 was truly out of this world! During the Ceremony while doing the Unified Movements, a brilliant Light was seen in the room which filled with Hosts of Angels! Afterwards, all had tears and seemed silent, smiling and stunned at the mystical/magical feeling of Oneness within a Power-House of Love!. . . *Asceremma.*

Δ Chitzen Itza, Mexico Δ

Over 1,500 people from many countries gathered together at the base of the Pyramid of Kukulcan to participate in

Ceremony. Around 80% of the people arriving were dressed in white clothing, even the children. Others came to witness, "We were told about this on the beach in Cancun yesterday and thought we'd come see what's happening."

It began as a gray, cloudy, overcast morning. We chanted Evan Maya, He Ma Ho thirty six times to move the rain. At 11:11 am, we gathered together to perform the Unified Movements. A group from Canada formed a circle on top of one of the ceremonial platforms. Most of us stood in a semi-circle at the base of the pyramid. The young man standing in front of me was blind, yet his mother stood behind him guiding him verbally in Spanish, and then blended her arms with his to show him the movements. As we stepped through the doorway, we experienced overflowing Love. All the participants were very serious, maintaining the silence and following the movements in unison.

My teacher Reinaldo Torres, spoke in English and Spanish. Next a Mayan Priest from Merida spoke to us. He said, "This day has been foretold in our history. I am deeply moved to see so many present here today from so many different corners of the world." He had us chant IN, the Mayan name for the Sun God eleven times and during this, the clouds parted, allowing the sun to shine through. Our sounds went to the Cosmos and this Priest gave us all his blessing. We had come home.

Hundreds came forward to receive hands on healing – lining up in front of the ministers, some who had just been ordained in Spirit. There were still lines present four hours later. As we traveled back to Cancun, it began to rain – and it had been raining all afternoon in Cancun, while the sun shone gloriously at Chitzen-Itza. . . *Geo-Ni Elohim.*

Δ Teotihuacan, Mexico Δ

Reports of one thousand people at the Pyramid of the Sun!

Δ Palenque, Mexico Δ

A few Americans and Europeans observed over three thousand Mayans participating in a ceremony at Palenque!

Δ Melbourne, Australia Δ

For us the weekend of January 11th has come but not gone. It has remained with us all and will continue to unfold. So many connections were made and so much took place on many levels. The weeks leading up to that time were hectic. The phone rang hot. La Re'el & I endeavored not to sound like the proverbial broken compact disc to people who made contact with 11:11 at the last minute. Namely, the person who rang at 11:45 pm the night before asking about 11:11. We now have an inkling of what life must be like at Star-Borne!

Here people have been great and so supportive. There were many groups in Victoria run by wonderful people. The love, bonding, focus and sincerity of the people we were with was extraordinary. Everybody actively participated to the fullness of their beings. We were One!

There is still a 3D world out there, but for thousands upon thousands of us across the Earth there has been a shift, the magnitude of which may be beyond our understanding. Things will never be the same again. I feel humble and grateful that I have taken part in this event that moved through groups across the planet and out into the universe. We truly are Wheels within Wheels!... *Aumanarius.*

Δ Δ Δ

I had no idea what to expect as a Guardian. I felt that perhaps I would focus energy, but what an energy and so remarkable! During the first set of movements my hands moved in various mudras, working through the group's chakras. I seemed to direct energy until every level was permeated with the colour and vibration of every other level. On reflection, what was achieved here was the subtle blending of all colours into an all pervading White Light. This Light was filled with beautiful rainbow colours inter-mingled into One. Then a sharp change of energy occurred and the room was flooded by the electric blue Light of the Archangel Mikael. This was a very powerful, clear energy and through this, the group was cleansed and protected. After that, the Wheels seemed to move with a very special unity and a sense of timelessness. All were moved by the warmth and love within the room.

The GMT movement was totally, amazingly remarkable. Aside from the quality, quantity and intensity of the energy, I will try to describe to you what I experienced: As the Wheels rotated and during the Starry Processional, I became aware of a golden disc of energy spinning and encompassing the entire group. I followed my inner promptings and was moved to grasp the sides of this disc in my hands, which I somehow did. As I turned the disc, the most astounding thing happened! The entire room seemed to shift dimensional focus as if being turned inside out. Suddenly we were not in a room, but hanging together in front of a vast magenta sphere called AN. This sphere expanded to encompass the entire field of vision. Everyone was there! The entire planet was there and a voice kept announcing, "You are the Family of AN." I was in tears at this stage, but the best was yet to come.

Archangel Mikael appeared, showering his love and bless-ings to all in a most tender manner. The feeling was indescribable. He rose to his full splendour and with a deep bow thanked all for being there and for all the work we have put in over the aeons. It was like a triumphant general addressing troops at their final moment. He then gave his mudra to all with immense love, tenderness and dignity.

The energy then changed to the most joyous, delightful warmth. Metatron and Archangel Uriel came with open arms, beckoning and welcoming all through the Doorway. Banks of Angels stood singing in exaltation. It was a song of joy, relief and union. Then the gathered Hosts poured incandescent, luminous Light downwards over the assembled multitude and enclosed all in a sphere of Golden White Light. All sang and danced as One.

At this point I looked at the faces of those present as they rotated in the Starry Processional and saw many beings uplifted in joy, wonder and Light. A voice kept repeating, "We are now responsible." I took this to mean that as individuals and as One, now that the Doorway is open, that it is in our hands to complete the remainder of the task, whatever that may be.

After the Ceremony was complete, I returned home feeling as if a huge weight had finally lifted. I can remember feeling that I had done at last the one thing that gave my life meaning. I still feel that way. How can we thank Solara for her vision and efforts? And all of Star-Borne for your guidance and the myriad others who joined us on that day. It was truly not only what we were given by the 11:11, but what we all gave. . . *La Re'el Iathraan.*

Δ Nambour, Queensland, Australia Δ

The day started with a report of an approaching cyclone, which brought an element of excitement and change into the air. . .The Spiral was very moving with a lot of people in tears, myself included. For the afternoon session we sat in a circle and tuned into all the other groups around the world, sharing what we experienced. The evening session was of a much higher essence. We met again on the 12th, performing the movements and aligning with the rest of the world. The energy this day was very special. I myself

225

saw it as love flowing in and out. I felt very connected to the One and was moved to tears by looking into people's eyes and seeing our Oneness. I saw the 11:11 Doorway open and lots of people crowding through all in white with starry halos... *Solara Itara.*

Δ Adelaide, Australia Δ

Well, 11:11 was totally magic in every way! Our Celebration was held in Botanic Park, a magnificent green place, central to everywhere. Nearly everyone wore white which looked spectacular, given that we were in a public park and had a big 11:11 sign which drew a bit of attention. But the energy was so simply enormous that people who may have felt to be disruptive simply melted into the scenery and watched (*dare I say reverently*), from a distance. As for me, it was like entering a great silence and a resting in the absolute knowledge that together we'll all make it back to ourselves... *Beylara Ra.*

Δ Montrose, Colorado Δ

A few days before January 11th, I was moved to a new Rest Home across town (*our old one was sold*). The transition was hard on us all – and right before the 11:11. But I set aside that day, fasted and anchored the Light. Here at the Home, it's like a mental institution as most are broken in body and mind. On that day they reacted in the negative. There were five accidents and the place was in chaos, yet it was finally turned to the Light.

I was indeed strong that day to deal with it all. My Father and Divine Spirit let me know: The New Grid Pattern is now activated upon the Earth. And I saw Twelve Great Beams of Light coming from the opened Doorway, anchoring great energy all over the planet. I also saw Twelve

Great Beams of Light activated over our universe. Now everything is happening quickly.

There is a great energy within me at this time. It affects all those near me. I feel that God lives in all my cells. I will not stay crippled or in this Rest Home for long or in this body of flesh. While I am still here, I'll be helping others to higher consciousness. It will be a great year for those of the Light and from beyond the Stars. I love you all. Keep on with the great work!. . . *Le Estria*

Δ Baton Rouge, Louisiana Δ

At 5:11 pm, *the 11:11 pm of GMT,* when groups all over the world were doing the Unified Movements, we felt a powerful, huge central column of Light anchor into the planet . . . *Mark Stupka.*

Δ Houston, Texas Δ

How do I begin to tell of the glorious event that unfolded in Houston? Countless hours, days, weeks and months of preparation, all for this one day, and what a day it was! The people came, so eager to be a part of something much greater than themselves. Some were not sure why they were there; they simply felt *drawn* to be there. Others had profound experiences with the numbers 11:11 and this day represented a dream that had come true.

Each of the three activations took on its own unique flavor. The 11:11 am activation was one of sweet simplicity and purity; 5:11 pm *(the 11:11 pm GMT)* represented the apex and carried a sense of great heightened spiritual energy and 11:11 pm had a more primal, physical feel of it. I so wished that everyone could see how beautiful the Wheels within Wheels movements were from my vantage point up on stage. Indeed, we had entered into a unified focus and our movements became as One!

Beloved Solara, my deepest love and heartfelt thanks to you for stepping forward in Divine Service once again, for holding the vision and making manifest this cosmic moment here on Earth. I am honored to be a member of our Starry Family... *Antara.*

Δ Charlottesville, Virginia Δ

Five of the starry Star-Borne Staff remained here to anchor the beam for the 11:11 and triangulate with Egypt and New Zealand. Of course, we were needed in the office also, to answer all the last minute requests for information. *(We were so busy, our FAX machine broke!)* We held a 38 hour vigil, anchoring the energy for those at the Master Cylinders. It was so intense; it felt as if we were right there with everyone. We sent our love, support, and laughter to help make the long, ceaseless movements a little easier.

On January 11th, over one hundred starry beings gathered at Swannanoa to turn the wheels and open the Doorway. Strangers became instant family as we were all brought into Oneness within the heightened energies. I was immersed in delicate powerful, joyful energy, saying over and over to myself, "We did it! We did it!" As I looked at each beautiful being, they would turn gold and then transparent as the new energies came in.

I am so grateful to have participated in this wonderous gathering, to have helped birth mankind into a new spiral of evolution. I want to thank the Star-Borne staff, Akiel, Elestariel, Elona and Garjon, for all the love and support they gave during this momentous event. But, most of all I want to thank Solara, for her unwavering dedication to her vision. You couldn't have done it alone, but we could never have done it without you!... *Paloma Antara Rameesh.*

Δ Dove Mountain, Tennessee Δ

Dove Mountain was wonderful beyond all our expectations. Nearly 200 people from twelve different states. Perfect weather, UFOs, Angels, Indian Spirits, Devas, signs, wonders, doorways, pyramids in the sky, powerful chants, dancing, Oneness and love!. . . *Medicine Bear.*

Δ Δ Δ

As a gathering mist upon the moors, like souls drew together. As I climbed the spiral pathway up the mound in the darkest hour just before dawn, the force of kindred thought, desires, and hopes pulled at me gently. Steadily approaching the flattened table of land atop Dove Mountain, anticipation grew in my heart. . .I stood silently for a moment, drinking in the sweet flavor of love in the air. My hand went out. Another met mine. I noticed that I wanted to hold on. The other's hand *(I know not whose)* held on firmly, refusing to be daunted by the desperate need.

As if calling the Sun, voices joined together, awaiting the fire to rise, to warm and brighten the day. Excitement heightened. My hand tightened. The circle slid upwards into the sky and into our hearts. From places afar we had gathered, but we were now here and One. From the dawn until the morrow we were One. The reclaimed Earth, the crisp cool air, the grass under our feet, the Moon at noon, the wink of a star from above. A thread of love ran through all those present.

I realized that I dearly missed this oneness of being. Have you ever felt a yearning but did not recognize your need? Then when it comes into view you say, "Ah! That's just what I needed." I relish the remembrance of togetherness. My soul was filled with the light of Oneness. The thread connecting us interwove a tapestry around the world, outside the world. We were not alone. The universe changed that day and night. I saw the skies shift... *Carol Bilbrey.*

Δ Δ Δ

I watched the cogs in the Great Cosmic Clock turn as men and women and children moved silently as Wheels within Wheels; I saw the Mind of God. I heard as God sang Himself into Divine Harmony, overtaking our voices and blending them into something so far beyond us that my head snapped back with the voltage, and my heart knew ecstasy again. And I loved being together with my brothers and sisters in this way, augmented by the multiple energies of level upon level of the Divine, more than I ever loved even the most noble moments of our humanness.

The Window of Ultimate Expansion opens; we walk through the door, but innocently, freshly, like children at play. The best job we ever did was done as we circled quietly, at play, in happy heartedness, which was graced with the frequencies of Divine Love and Joy. It is so easy that I laugh with delight!. . . *Dr. Louise Mallary-Elliot.*

Δ Philadelphia, Pennsylvania Δ

Independence Hall pulsated with power and Light on the morning of January 11th when nearly 200 people gathered to turn the wheels, open the Doorway and dance the starry mandala. As we stepped through the Doorway, we spoke in unison, E Pluribus Unum– In Many, One!

One visionary reported: "The sky was filled with thousands of Angels in golden gowns, creating yellow-pink wheels of love energy and directing them to the Earth." Another reported: "As the wheels turned, I saw the bright white of the Christ light in the center, with golden light moving around the circle." A third person described the experience: "I felt a repeating surge of energy of all the other groups throughout the world doing the movements too. I felt a river of love. What we did felt very real and very important to the planet."... *Aloyus Aretria.*

Δ São Paulo, Brazil Δ

The Door has really been activated! You wouldn't believe how great it was! It began with remarkable press coverage in the main newspaper and major TV stations. On January 11th, all the TV stations came to the auditorium where 3,000 people gathered, and broadcast LIVE our first set of Unified Movements to people all over BRASIL!! All day long TV stations throughout the country broadcast updates on our activities and invited everyone to join in from their homes! Three major papers also covered the event with cover stories and long articles.

To crown our wonderful day, the evening movements were again broadcast live on Goulart's program. *(He's the one who interviewed you when you were here and filmed your workshop.)* Goulart has been on TV for 36 years and everyone watches him! So people all over Brasil got to participate again from their homes. The 3,000 people, stayed from 9:30 am to 2 am, doing all the work. It was so powerful! We also had 516 11:11 Anchor Groups throughout Brasil, in ALL states. Pax. . . *Carmen Balhestero.*

Δ Joshua Tree, California Δ

11:11 was and is significant in many ways. The Angelic group-soul that Solara is a portion of is about to complete their Earth mission and return to their native lifewave and Universe-sector to make the progression into the next level of expression. They have sacrificed much to work on Terra as have all the volunteers here and are ready for a long, well-deserved rest and re-integration. Their work in strengthening the lines of attunement between the angelic and human lifewaves is invaluable for the Divine Plan. The reclamation of their Oneness greatly aids in the intensification of the One Unified Field of Love wherein barriers dissolve so that all may feel their Oneness.

On January 11th, thousands met around the planet to do a series of Unified Movements. The first step was to re-identify at a vaster level of embodiment and access the functional abilities at that level. Then with hand movements designed to direct energy flow, the center of each person wherein we are infinite, eternal and One was reached and expanded in focus. A null zone was created wherein the infinite field of unmanifest potential could be accessed and a new configuration brought forth. Then a major energy shift was established, reversing the overflow into the involutionary streams caused by the "Fall", redirecting the energies into the evolutionary current so that the force of the evolutionary flow is now dominant. This compensates for the ages of imbalance when the involutionary flow dominated The smaller inner circles then merged in oneness within each group and activated the internal restructuring process by repositioning themselves.

They then formed a Starry Processional. *(I experienced this as a repositioning in vibratory range of the planet and other spheres in the spinning galactic body.)* In addition to these activities, there was a very important spiral formed at the temporal midpoint, 5:11 pm in each locale. This was for their group ascension as One Being. *(For my part, I perceived the opening expand to the planetary circumference and Terra lift, each of Her Spherical Bodies rising successively higher into resonance with its correspondent vibratory range or dimension in the Galactic Mother's Body. I also experienced a filling and lifting of other collapsed dimensional spheres within the Galactic Mother until all was in balance.)*

As Solara has said in truth, "We are the instruments of Divine Intervention." Through our united invocation and intention and through the instrumentality of our vehicles on every level touching into the respective vehicles of the Earth Mother, our Divine Parents were enabled to lift, expand and realign Terra into vibrational ranges harmonious with the rest of Her Universe Family of Celestial Beings and restore the balance in the involutionary-evolutionary circulatory flows. I am told the evolutionary pathways are realigned, the evolutionary pull intensified and the templates of the New Heaven and New Earth are set. . . . *I Yin.*

Δ Pyramid Lake, Nevada Δ

Thirteen of us arrived at the lake on the evening of January 9th, promptly building a campfire which we gathered around seeking warmth. *(It was 10' F and dropped to below 0'.)* But we never noticed the cold for we were soon greeted by a magnificent rainbow around the Moon. We began at 11:11 am on January 10th with a Temple of Purification. All were smudged with sage and sweet grass, cleared by Tibetan bells and given 11:11 flower essence. We moved into a circle around the Pyramid Vortex, introduced ourselves and claimed our space. We were introduced to the Guardian of the Pyramid, AAh-Shee-Na and included her vibration in our Song of One. Everyone was so empowered.   233

Gathering around the fire, I annointed all through the Doorway of the 11:11 into the Order of Melchizedek, trinitizing with Metatron. We all knew that it was truly happening. I guided a journey to Beyond the Beyond into the Chambers of Creation. We traveled the intergalactic starway right into each Angel's origin as we melded with our Presence and received a gift, our personal contribution to the planet.

It was now 1:11 am and we observed two hours of silence in preparation for the first activation. At 3:00 am we began the Wheels within Wheels and finally a Spiral. At 11:00 am on the 11th, we began the next activation. Angelic Hosts were felt by all and the message was received: "You have done it! It has finished! It has begun! Thank you, thank you, thank you."

At 4:44 pm we spiraled again. As we unwound the Spiral into a circle, the Merkabah Vehicle of Light descended upon us as we ascended ever so high into the Starry Heavens. Thank God we were holding hands anchored in the Template of Oneness or none of us would be here to tell this story. How indescribable this feeling of One is!. . .*Ra.*

Δ Colombia Δ

Thousands of people participated in 17 cities throughout Colombia... *Maria Christina.*

Δ In the Dreamtime Δ

I read about the 11:11 and felt some sadness about not having been aware of it. That sadness quickly passed and I had the most unreasonable feeling that I *had* been aware of it and had even participated. Then I remembered a dream from some weeks before and ran to get my journal. Sure enough, January 11, 1992... I read the following:

I am alone on a mountain at night. My guide approaches me and points to a light which looks like the Aurora Borealis. He wants me to go there. I jump into the air and fly towards the light, skimming treetops. Then I see masses of people, all holding hands to form circles within circles. I want to join them, but feel my role is to observe. Spirals of light move skyward and I follow. Soon I am above the Earth. It is bathed in golden light, vibrating, healing, giving birth to something that I can't see. I awaken, phone a friend and tell him of my dream. He says he has had the same dream and I am shocked. *Then I wake up for real!* ... *Larry McKane, British Columbia, Canada.*

Δ Norway Δ

Many people gathered in Oslo for the 11:11. The energies were very strong and they felt connected with us in Egypt and felt the Doorway opening... A group did the Unified Movements on Tonsberg Tor which has a direct link with Glastonbury... In northern Norway, one person did the movements alone in the woods.. .*Lilina.*

235

∆ London, England ∆

The 11:11 Activation was, without any shadow of doubt, a great success. Interest started fairly slowly in December last year, in the usual British manner by which we are known throughout the world, disinterest-to-lukewarm response. As time unfolded closer to the date however, reaction had quickened to such an extent that a special telephone answering message was left to handle bookings and enquiries. We helped form groups in Germany, Holland, Belgium, France, Spain, Portugal, Italy, Monaco and the Channel Islands. A piece was put out on the Russian News Service of the BBC, in Russian on the morning of the 11th. A truly global link up of Lightworkers was created.

The great Doorway was well and truly opened fully in preparation for the emergence and grounding of the new energy dynamics, elevating Mother Earth, humanity and all other life forms on multiple dimensions in the establishment of the New Octaves of the coming era...*Philip Dawes.*

∆ Glastonbury, England ∆

Many were drawn here to the heart chakra of the planet with the knowingness in their own hearts of the Great Awakening – awaiting all who stepped through the Doorway of the 11:11. The great key was turned with the master vibration that is LOVE... *Antares Surya An Ra.*

∆ ∆ ∆

The 11:11 was the most inspiring experience I have come across to this day. The beauty and purity of the love energies made everyone feel like the Angels they truly are. As we walked the Spiral dance my heart opened to receive the Initiation for the One. The caring, nurturing and unconditional love filled the hearts of everyone present, gave me a feeling of pure bliss. As I looked into their eyes, their souls radiated pure magic and I am left with a feeling of true admiration for everyone there. I now know from the depth of my soul that the world can truly heal itself by the compassion and love of the One. . . *Solra Elania Sankara.*

The morning was crisp and clear and the magic began at once. As we climbed the Tor, the white Angels stood in the rising sun as the faint drum beats from the Tor called us upwards, filling us with joy. We waited, breathlessly, and filled ourselves with golden stars. All day we walked and circled, ceaselessly moving, filled with awesome Purpose and excited anticipation. The cold was unreal, but we kept each other warm with love.

The Spiral at 5:11 pm was overwhelming in the deep commitment shown by each Angel and some bystanders who had joined in. We sang our way through the circles and wheels and the final star was so huge that we encircled the entire Tor, including St. Michael's tower! The key turned, there was sound and movement, the sun set in a blaze of orange glory, sliding slowly into the darkened landscape, we knew the door was open!. . .*Mu-sindar Porfin Saar.*

Δ Δ Δ

It was a wonderful day which I enjoyed. When we were doing the circles and spirals it felt like all the Angels and the Tor were taking off. . . *Gabriell Sar Andar (age 9).*

Δ Δ Δ

I felt my heart aligned with our Mother Earth and the Great Central Sun. I stood on the Tor, joined by my Starry Family, and felt the power of the open Doorway pour into my heart. The remembrance of the Oneness once felt triggered my consciousness: I am a divine expression who came to this planet at this time to co-create Heaven on Earth. The bliss of January 11th is deeply anchored in my being. As I climbed on the Tor several days later. I found a white ray of light anchored and radiant in the center of Shambhala, the heart of Avalon. . . *Xeron.*

Δ Δ Δ

On the bright sunny morning just after dawn, there was a feeling of peace and tranquility as we climbed the Tor in silence, all dressed in white. There was no need for words. The mandala wheels turned all day, but just after sunset a truly sacred feeling came in. We wanted silence and the music ceased. We touched something infinite and divine deep within and the peace was felt from below our feet from the Earth, and above our heads from the Starry Heavens – the peace that passed all understanding. The Door is opened. Since then I have come home in Oneness and Love . . . *Mikael.*

Δ Puerto Rico Δ

Great news. . . wonderful news – the 11:11 activity in Puerto Rico was a success. About 300 persons attended in Isla de Cabras. Throughout the country there were many other groups doing the Unified Movements. It is impossible for me to describe what is indescribable. The day of the 11th the activation took place near the vortex of the Bermuda Triangle in an open space with nature. The sun was beautiful, it was like a dream; people were so happy and united. When we were doing the spiral, there was a Golden Light in the middle of the spiral, like a blessing from God. In the night a strange light appeared in the sky, like a merkabah or UFO. About thirty metaphysical groups united in love like ONE. There were many emotions; most people were crying of joy. That evening when the work was done, the people did not want to leave.

Since that date we are not the same, it is as if a new renovation has been implanted in the Earth. So many persons have told me so; people want more activities like that, but I doubted that one like this would ever happen again on this planet. I am anxious to hear news from other countries. IT WAS WRITTEN... IT WAS SEALED... AND IT WAS FULFILLED. . . *Luah An-Ra.*

239

Δ Brief Notes on the 11:11 Δ

Antarctica:
The 11:11 was anchored at two different sites.
Australia:
Orange lights hovering above **Sydney** were seen by thousands. The Wheels were performed throughout the country, from **Tasmania** to **Darwin.**
Ecuador:
Eleven people hiked for four days to the ancient Sacred Tiger Site deep in the rain forest to perform the Unified Movements.
Egypt:
Jean Houston led a group of 90 in the Unified Movements at the Temple of Karnak in **Luxor.**
Hungary:
Groups met throughout the country.
Malaysia:
A small group met on the Magick River near **Kuala Lumpur.**
New Zealand:
One lady went to **Mt. Cook** and a Maori saw a two story tall being in **Auckland.**
Nigeria:
A small group met in **Lagos.**
North Pole:
One person anchored the energy here.
Philippines:
Many thousands participated throughout the country.
United Kingdom:
180 people gathered together amidst the sacred stones in **Avebury.**
United States:
One person held the energy at the hidden vortex of the **Crystal Mountain** in **Arizona.**
There was a large group at **Haleakala Crater** in Maui, **Hawaii.** In **Washington D.C.** The Unified Movements were performed at the Washington Monument.

Many, many people have not shared their 11:11 Experiences with us yet. So please, take time and send them so they may be shared with our Starry Family.

The Silent Watchers

Throughout time, all the myriad activities within this Universe have been serenely observed by some special beings called The Silent Watchers. These Sentinels from On High see everything – nothing escapes their finely attuned Sight. Nothing is too small or insignificant nor too vast to pass by their finely calibrated scrutiny. The Silent Watchers are the Witnesses. Aeons pass by and they never leave their post. Silently watching as star systems are birthed and collapse, planets are created and reach their time of completion, great civilizations rise and fall....

The Silent Watchers miss nothing... They are aware when one pure heart on a tiny planet cries out with the pain of separation, of each flower which blooms, of every act of kindness or pettiness. The Silent Watchers ever observe those whom we term, The Vessels of Sweet Sorrow, the ones on each planet who cry the tears of the One. For there are always a certain number on any given day in each life zone or planetary body, who are crying for the Many that we may become One. *(If you serve as a Vessel of Sweet Sorrow, you will recognize those times when you are crying not for yourself, but for everyone. This is a great service that you are doing for all of humanity.)*

And although the Silent Watchers see everything, they are searching for just one sign. This is their sacred task. It is

241

similar to the earthly job of fire lookouts in the great forests, those who sit in their lookout towers, gazing out with binoculars watching for signs of smoke.

The Opening of the Doorway of the 11:11

Let us return to the 11:11 Ceremony. This time let's look at it from a different perspective, seeing it from the vantage point of the Silent Watchers. At 11:11 am on January 11, 1992, the Unified Movements begin. In Egypt and New Zealand, the two Master Cylinders activate. They remain in constant movement for the next thirty-eight hours. See them ever turning, going from Wheels within Wheels into the Starry Processional and back again, over and over until the last time zone on the planet completes its 11:11 pm movements.

As the Master Cylinders commence their series of movements, the first time zone on Earth to enter 11:11 am, *which happens to be in New Zealand,* begins its Wheels within Wheels. As each hour unfolds, a new time zone activates and performs the series of Unified Movements. If you watch this progression from On High, you will see that it is as if a mighty wing were sweeping across the planet. It is a wave of vast love created by our Unified Presence. At the same time, the two Master Cylinders continue to revolve, serving as Stabilization Pinions, anchoring the energies for the entire Earth.

When 11:11 pm in the New Zealand time zone arrives, the groups there start their second series of Unified Movements. Now is the time for the creation of the second wave. Two wings or a double wave simultaneously sweep across the planet, embracing it in all-encompassing love.

The third key time is 11:11 pm Greenwich Mean Time. This is the hour when all the groups throughout the planet perform the Unified Movements in perfect synchronicity, with focused intent. It is when the 11:11 is opened. Looking at this from our vantage point of On High, we can see myriad Wheels within Wheels, large and small, turning in unison, like the internal cylinders of a massive lock.

The Sign

It is said that when two wings sweep across a planet, when Wheels within Wheels are activated, that this symbolizes a life zone which is ready to move onto a new evolutionary template. This is the sign that the Silent Watchers have been waiting for. It signifies that our planet is ready to ascend into a Greater Central Sun System, to undergo a shift in spirals.

On January 11th, 1992, the awakened Star-Borne upon planet Earth joined together and manifested two wings, activated the Wheels within Wheels and sent the message that we are ready to move into the Template of Oneness. The Silent Watchers noted this with profound joy. They immediately made their report that we were ready to graduate into the New Octave of the Greater Reality. And the process has begun. . .

This is the scope of what we have achieved by coming together in conscious Oneness on that blessed day. It is the greatest deed we have ever accomplished here on Earth. From that moment forward, nothing will ever be the same, for we are now headed on an irrevocable journey into greater Oneness. Indeed, we have been truly blessed. The gratitude for a service well done is being showered upon us from On High. Please allow yourselves to feel this blessing, to honor yourselves for the completion you have achieved by serving as an Instrument of Divine Intervention. It is truly a time of greatness and fulfillment.

The Silent Watchers stand in position, silently waiting and watching, serenely happy that another solar system is ready to move on.

243

The Journey
Through

If you cannot see
the inherent perfection
in all things
and in all aspects of your life,

simply make yourself larger.

E x p a n d
your perspective
until the full perfection
of everything becomes visible.

Birdstar / Starbird

It has been stated that only one passes through the Door.
That one is our Unified Presence. It is created by leaving
behind our primary identifications with ourselves as individual units of consciousness and rising into a deep knowing and acceptance of our inherent Oneness. It is a realization that we are all rays, or direct emanations of One Star.

Once we know that we are One, our Unified Presence takes
the form of a vast white bird. This large white bird is
composed of myriad small white birds flying in formation
as One. It could be termed the Merkabah or the Birdstar.
It is our vehicle for mass ascension. *(This Birdstar is not a
spaceship. It is the expression of our Unified Presence!)* Our
white bird is so immensely vast that it shall take us the full
twenty years that the 11:11 is open to pass through its
portals into the new spiral of the Greater Central Sun
System.

Our Birdstar does not fly in from somewhere else. We
ourselves, create it. It is brought to birth from the inside
out, beginning in the heart. First we must unite with other
Star-Borne and merge together as One. As we create our
vast Unified Presence, we give birth to the heart of the
Birdstar. Originating from the heart, the energy flows

upwards and outwards, much like a fountain of Light, becoming ever larger as more of us unite. Thus by our coming together in increasing numbers, the entire body of the Birdstar is formed.

Each of us has our appointed position within the Birdstar. It is most helpful to go within and determine where you are located. From this information you can discern how to apply yourself to fulfilling your Divine Mission. And as you meet others who share your positioning within our Birdstar, a deep bond is formed with the realization that you will be working together.

As you look for your position in the Birdstar, try to be as specific as possible. If you are in the wing, for example, see which wing and where exactly you are located. There are three eyes which can be perceived within the Birdstar: the right eye, left eye and the one eye. If you are in the tail, you will be one of the last to move through the 11:11. In the tip of the tail, you will be responsible for closing the Door. The feet are interesting positions, for you are one of the last to be leaving and one of the first to land. You can learn much from your place in the Birdstar.

If you work with a group, a really fun thing to do is to gather everyone together in their positions, forming a vast bird. Now take your Birdstar for a test flight! This is a most exhilarating experience for everyone, guaranteed to fling open the doors of remembrance. You can easily see that when the beak of our Birdstar begins to move, that even the tail feathers are affected, for we are all woven together in the cloth of Oneness.

As we journey through the 11:11, our Birdstar travels on an irrevocable trajectory to Octave Seven. This is the final destination for most of us. There, the planet Earth will repose, liberated and transformed. Octave Seven is the paradise for all Second Wavers; it is here where they shall build on the New. During the thousand years of peace which shall ensue, Second Wavers will be busily creating the myriad new forms of the arts, communities, use of natural energy – of living and being together in conscious Oneness. Starchildren will have obtained their maturity and move into positions of leadership and guidance. In Octave Seven the 11:11 transforms into the 22.

Arriving in Octave Seven it will be time for all First Wavers to make new choices. Our old contract is complete; we have irrevocably anchored the New. Now we can choose whether we wish to remain in the joyous vibrations of Octave Seven and help to build upon the New or travel further...

Most First Wavers, once they discover that their weariness has totally dissolved, will choose to remain in Octave Seven. Yet there will be a few who will choose to journey onwards. These ones will gather together, tightly bundled into Oneness and undergo an inversion process which transforms what remains of the Birdstar into a Starbird. This process can best be described as turning the Birdstar inside out. This Starbird is the conveyance for those who wish to journey onwards to Octave Eleven.

Octave Eleven is the place of the Eleventh Pyramid. It is the completion of the initiation process within the New Octave. Here, the Eleven Ascending Pyramids and the Eleven Descending Pyramids interlock, forming a new star mandala. The 22 becomes a 44. Once this process of transfiguration is complete, we will be faced with yet another decision. Some of us will now choose to travel ever onwards, for Octave Eleven is the launching pad into the Beyond the Beyond.

As you can see, once we pass into this Greater Central Sun System, we shall be moving on to three predominant destinations. But this shifting cannot be perceived as any form of separation. It is impossible for us to separate since we all reside within the Template of Oneness. All the ones anchored within Octave Seven will have direct access to those within Octave Eleven, while the ones in Octave Eleven will maintain contact with the ones who have begun the journey into the Beyond the Beyond.

The Beyond the Beyond is a new template aligned with an even Greater, Great Central Sun. The full journey from the Template of Duality to Beyond the Beyond has never before been successfully completed. Some of us have been given fragments of the map of this journey. *(Part of the map is hidden in the book EL*AN*RA, waiting for those who might discover it.)* When it is time, our fragments shall be pieced together as a new Doorway is opened. Once opened, this Doorway to the Beyond the Beyond will be accessible to all those who are called to the next spiral of our Homeward Journey...

We have leaped across the final abyss.

Standing in the midst of ancient temple ruins,
we see an old stone pillar
covered with well worn Mayan glyphs.

As we approach the pillar,
we perceive an opening behind its base.
Entering into the opening,
we begin to climb down the pillar
which extends beyond infinity.

Nothingness,
except the open empty space of the deepest void
surrounds the pillar.

This pillar can lead you anywhere.
It can bend and revolve at will.
The glyphs are everchanging.
You have no control over what it does.

In order to successfully traverse the pillar
you have to change direction
by inverting your being
so the pillar leads upwards.

This is the next level of initiation.

The Zone of Overlap

Now that the 11:11 is open and we are beginning to move through the Doorway, we are traveling through the time of transition known as the Zone of Overlap. What this means is that the sceptres of responsibility are being prepared to be passed from First Wave to Second Wave.

First Wavers have long been the doers on this planet. They have served as the Pillars of Light, anchoring the remembrance of the Door Before as well as carrying the primary responsibility and vision for the 11:11. As they are now becoming imbued with energies from the New Octave, and increasingly moving deeper into the pristine realms of the Invisible, they are experiencing a vast shift of positional alignment. They are moving from the state of *Doing* to that of *Being*.

This is a profound and dramatic transformation affecting all levels of our beings as well as our daily lives. It begins to manifest in many ways. First, all that emanates from the Template of Duality starts to assume an air of unreality. Even the solidity of matter appears to dissolve before our very eyes. Old values, dreams and causes are seen as unimportant and meaningless. They are like puffs of smoke which disappear into nothingness.

We begin to enter a state of No-Mind – which means that our memories begin to slip away. Now although No-Mind is truly an advanced spiritual state, it is not really very enjoyable when you first start to enter it. Suddenly you cannot remember your own phone number or the name of your favorite Aunt or the capitol of Argentina! What's more you start to forget your past history – small details, like the story of your life. It all begins to appear irrelevant, such as the plot of some old film you watched twenty years ago. None of this really matters anymore. It's simply not of any importance to your present level of consciousness.

Now No-Mind is not really so bad when you let go of the concept that it is important to hold these old details in your mind. It's actually very freeing once you get past the initial stage of panic – which can last for a year or so, depending on how ready you are to embrace the New. We simply have to learn how to do things differently.

We need to find comfort in relaxing into No-Mind and moving from Doing into Being.

As we move through the Doorway of the 11:11, there is always a transfer of energies. In exchange for losing our Earthly memories and moving into No-Mind, we are gaining total access to the One. What this means is that anything which we really need to know or remember will be there when it is truly needed. It is no longer necessary to hold all that antiquated clutter in our conscious minds anymore. This total access to the One is unlimited – enabling us to retrieve anything from the Akashic Records, including third dimensional information which we never knew before, to complete understanding of the hologram of the New Octave.

Along with No-Mind we also find ourselves moving into a state of timeless serenity. That old sense of urgency is gone. Time appears meaningless. We now know it to be an illusion. So we are beginning to move through life differently than before. We are doing everything differently and slower, yet with renewed effectiveness. Everything is imbued in No-Time allowing time to stretch out endlessly. This expansion of time moves us into a totally new way of both Doing and Being. It makes us feel a lot freer. Form has lost all sense of confinement and limitation.

This brings up another point – that of formlessness within form. Merging our Starry Overselves with our physical bodies creates a new heightened sense of Self. The parameters of our beings are simply not located where they used to be before. We have become vast! So vast, in fact, that we now seem to encompass not only the entire planet and the starry galaxies, but we have become embodiments of the One and the Many. Now I know that this is a wonderful concept and it feels great most of the time, but try driving a car in this state! It can be quite a challenge. There are many of us driving by you on the various Earthly highways who are using our automatic pilots all the time!

Once again, there is no cause for alarm. It simply requires an internal adjustment to a new way of doing things with our fully awakened Self on board. After awhile it can become quite relaxing to glide through traffic effortlessly, filled with wonder that you can drive at all.

First Wavers who are moving through the Door are also finding themselves faced with an interesting paradox. Their level of knowingness and remembrance has reached an advanced state. They have much to share, more than ever before. Yet it is becoming increasingly difficult to speak. They are moving into the powerful realms of deepest Silence. Here nothing needs to be said for all is known. This is part of the transition from Doing into Being.

Writing this book is a good example of this state of consciousness. By anchoring my being on the other side of the Door, I have reached a place of full remembrance as well as clear insight into the New Octave. Yet I would rather sit in the depth of Silence moving through subtle realms filled with pulsations of Light and all-encompassing Love, than sit at my computer and write this down. It's not that I have lost my urge to share and serve, but rather that I am moving so rapidly into beingness that it is difficult to narrow my knowingness into the tiny segments that form the information shared within this book.

As we move through the Doorway, we are moving into the realms of the Unseen. What is happening is that all that was previously visible and real is fading away. At the same time, what was invisible to us before is now making itself visible. We are learning not to focus our attention on material objects but to look beyond – look larger. As an example, take a lamp; now instead of looking at the physical presence of the lamp, try focusing on the light which comes out from it and reflects on your wall or ceiling. This is the manifestation of the Unseen.

Our entire sense of perception is being transformed. Increasingly we will be setting our sights on the Invisible. The more we do this, the more shall be revealed. This opens up a whole new direction for the art of interior decorating as well. Our homes will become lighter, less cluttered and more starry, with objects such as furniture serving as triggers to make visible the Invisible. They are transforming into true Starry Temples with nothing to distract from the glorious manifestation of the Unseen – constantly changing with shifting patterns of light and color. Our homes are being enlivened with the Greater Reality.

Colors are also fading away as more of us surround ourselves with the purity of white, some gold and silver, as

259

well as lots of transparent and iridescent. This creates for us a blank canvas upon which we can better perceive the Invisible. It is less distracting, allowing us to move with greater ease into the subtle energies of the New Octave. In clothing, awakened First Wavers tend to wear lots of white with the occasional addition of some pale shades, awakened Second Wavers like bright colors and unawakened First Wavers & Second Wavers wear a lot of black and heavy Earth colors.

So this is what we can expect by being pioneers into the Unknown. There are myriad changes affecting every possible level of existence. Well, we are moving into a Greater Central Sun System. This is a rather big move and of course, everything is going to be different! That's why we wanted to come here in the first place. It's our time of graduation, remember. And if your attachments to the old template are too great, you can always choose to remain in duality where quantum leaps come relatively slow.

Passing the Sceptres

As you can see, the First Wavers are undergoing a tremendous transition, moving from *Doing* to *Being*. How does this affect the Second Wave? They too are experiencing the shift into No-Time and No-Mind. But for them it's not such a big jump, for they were never too immersed within the old patterning. For them it's a small shift, part of their exciting Earthly adventure!

Second Wavers are shifting from *Experiencing* to *Doing*. Many of them are quite thrilled over this concept. In fact they wish that the First Wavers would hurry up and relinquish control so they could get on with it. But like the wizened elders that they are, the First Wavers *though anxious to step out of Doing*, want to insure that the Second Wavers have a clear, grounded vision of what it entails to become Pillars of Light for an entire planet.

Although the First Wavers are well aware that there will be new ways of *Doing* in Octave Seven, they want to impart as much of their experience and vast storehouses of wisdom to the Second Wave before the sceptres of responsibility are totally passed on. They remember their own eagerness and impatience to fulfill their new roles when the last doorway opened ages ago. And they also remember how they were thoroughly taught, prepared and initiated by those who were about to ascend. The First Wavers want to complete their job here impeccably, sharing all they can with the Second Wavers before moving into full Beingness.

So we would encourage all of you Second Wavers to step forward now with your full commitment to serving the One. Positions of responsibility are waiting for you. The old Pillars are shaky and readying themselves to be replaced. This is the time for your full empowerment and initiation. Many of you are needed to come forth right now, because soon the First Wavers will be moving on. You need to get ready, for your time of leadership fast approaches.

And the funny thing – the more we move into the New Octave, the less difference we will find between First and Second Wavers. Embodying the One Heart, we will discover that we have all been both the in-going and the outgoing breath of our Star of Oneness.

The New Octave

Once we pass through the portals of the 11:11, we begin to enter the subtle realms of the New Octave. We are still traveling within the transitional zone wherein the Template of Duality and the Template of Oneness have merged in order to create the bridge to the Greater Central Sun. Although duality is still present, it begins to fade away as we move into the spiral of Oneness. Once again, sceptres are being passed. . .

This passageway will be open until December 31st, 2011. However, as our Unified Presence in the form of a Birdstar travels through the Zone of Overlap, we are being increasingly woven into the fabric of the Greater Reality. This new template could be perceived as a fine mesh composed of the many merged into One. The alignment into Oneness becomes ever deeper, more all-pervading as we move through the Eleven Gates within the Doorway of the 11:11. We are being transformed in every way imaginable.

We are traveling on an entirely new map. Everything is different than what we have known before, although our immersion into the New Octave takes place in a steady, gradual manner. In the old Template of Duality, we identified with ourselves as standing firmly planted on the Earth, as humans belonging to this planet, occasionally raising our sights to the stars. The starry Heavens became the focus for our aspirations, but the physical plane was our foundation, our predominant reality. If something did not manifest on the physical, it was not real.

In the new Template of Oneness, we are discovering that the physical is the last place where reality manifests. Our stance has shifted. We are no longer human beings having a spiritual experience, rather we have become spiritual beings having a human experience. We are existing on a far vaster landscape than before.

In the old template we could create anything we needed through thought. This is no longer necessary for we now exist in a template of such absolute perfection that effort and struggle are no longer required. The key here is Total Surrender. *(This is 100% surrender, 99% will not work.)* By totally surrendering into the cloth of Oneness, into the mesh of the Greater Reality, we are able to experience a new level of ease which has never before been possible. We need ask for nothing – all the doors are open before us. Abundance and perfection are present for everyone in limitless quantities. Everything you need is freely given.

With our newly found sense of Total Surrender, we can proceed with fulfilling both our Divine Missions and the purest desires of our Greater Hearts unhindered by obstacles, which were all an illusion in the first place. By simply being, by embodying our Highest Truth, fulfillment on all levels is readily available.

First Aid

While we are traveling through the transition zone into the New Octave there are a few heady challenges along the way. In order to help you survive this process, we have compiled a First Aid Kit which you may use whenever needed. Here are a few of the more common symptoms you may experience during your transition from duality into Oneness:

The Holy Roller Coaster

This one is just like it sounds. It is the last wild ride upon the ups and downs of duality. We get to travel on the Holy Roller Coaster when we have almost stepped free of duality. The good part is that if we survive our ride, we are finally free. So what do we experience? The only constant on this roller coaster is change; everything is subject to instant, unexpected change in any direction. One minute our lives are going fine; the next minute we are hemmed in by overwhelming obstacles. Yesterday we were happily in love; tomorrow we are alone. We are poor, then suddenly rich. You must be getting the picture by now. All the outer conditions of our lives are rapidly changing, *without warning*, totally out of control.

And that's not all! Can you feel your emotions transforming every five minutes until we become walking samplers of the full gamut of human emotions – and that was just in the last hour. Rising to the heights of happiness then plunging to the depths of despair, flashing with anger, then crying with sadness. We are serenely calm for a second, then bristling with impatience. This is how it feels to travel on the Holy Roller Coaster. It's as if we are trying to use up all our unspent human emotions because soon we won't need them any longer.

Have you noticed that even the weather is beginning to mirror this crazy ride? The day begins with a glorious, rosy dawn; then suddenly clouds appear out of nowhere and we are drenched with rain. But don't worry, in five minutes it will be sunny again. And on and on.

So how do we manage to survive the Holy Roller Coaster? The only way that I know of to get off, is to ride it through to the finish. In the meanwhile, we might as well buckle up our seatbelt so we won't fall out, relax and enjoy the thrills of this ride. It definitely isn't boring, is it? It really helps to remember where you are. If you know that you're on the final roller coaster of duality then you are less likely to take any of its wild gyrations personally. Just because your emotions are see-sawing all over the place is no reason to blame yourself or even your hormones for that matter. And on a positive note, since everything is changing so rapidly, you don't have time to get drawn into any of the details of what's flying around you. We're so busy just trying to survive that it's impossible to take anything too seriously.

Sit back, enjoy the thrills of a lifetime, *or rather an entire cycle of lifetimes.* Watch the blur of myriad shifting changes out of the corner of your eyes and remember that all roller coaster rides come to their appointed conclusion.

Sacred Pause Blues

Nothing happening in your life? Does everything feel like it's frozen and put on hold? Has life suddenly lost its meaning? Have you forgotten your Divine Mission? Then you must be experiencing the Sacred Pause Blues.

It goes sort of like this: *I woke up this morning feeling kind of sad. Wanted to stay in bed, but alarm clock's ringin' bad.* You know, the kinds of experiences that make you feel out of synch. As when you look in the mirror and a stranger stares back at you. And when you have much to do, but don't want to do anything. The Sacred Pause Blues goes on.

The Sacred Pause occurs in the moment, *which can last for weeks or months,* right before you are about to make a quantum breakthrough. The shift is already in position; it just hasn't manifested on the physical plane. You are absolutely sure that you have made all the necessary preparations, and it still doesn't happen! This can be quite frustrating if you have forgotten about the Sacred Pause.

Now what is the Purpose of the Sacred Pause? Truly, it's not just to bring added aggravation into your life. It's simply a time of assimilation and integration of all you have passed through in the last phase of your continuing process of evolution. It's also a time for clearing up anything that is incomplete and resolving old issues. Although it often appears as if nothing is happening *at all;* there is actually quite a lot going on. This time of the Sacred Pause is necessary so you can move cleanly into your next step.

So what can we do about it? There *are* alternatives to butting heads against the wall with our impatience and frustration. We can surrender to the Sacred Pause and work *with* it. First recognize that you are in the Sacred Pause. This should be encouraging, because it means that

266

Other Starry items ...

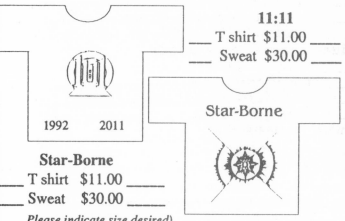

As You Walk Along Your Path –
Discover these gifts of the Star-Borne.

Books by Solara:

_____ 11:11 - Inside The Doorway..................$15.95 _____	
_____ EL◊AN◊RA: The Healing of Orion........$14.95 _____	
_____ The Star-Borne... ....$14.95 _____	
_____ The Legend of Altazar ....$12.95 _____	
_____ Invoking Your Celestial Guardians........$6.95 _____	

Meditation Tapes by Solara:

_____ Unifying The Polarities ....$10.00 _____	
_____ True Love / One Heart ....$10.00 _____	
_____ Temple Invisible ....$10.00 _____	
_____ The Angel You Truly Are ....$10.00 _____	
_____ The Star That We Are............................$10.00 _____	
_____ Remembering Your Story ....$10.00 _____	
_____ Star Alignments ....$10.00 _____	
_____ Archangel Mikael Empowerment...........$10.00 _____	
_____ Voyage on the Celestial Barge ....$10.00 _____	

Video Cassettes by Solara:

_____ Cosmology of the Beyond ....$25.00 _____	
_____ Entering the New Octave ....$25.00 _____	
_____ 11:11 Master Cylinder in Egypt ....$25.00 _____	
_____ Solara in Egypt ....$25.00 _____	

Music Tapes by Solara & Etherium:

_____ The Lotus of True Love ....$10.00 _____	
_____Through the Doorway ....$10.00 _____	

_____ Subscription to **The Starry Messenger** newsletter
$25. US, $30. Canada, $40. Foreign ....____

Sales Tax: _where applicable (Virginia residents add 5%)_
Shipping: _please add $3.50 for first item, 50¢ each addt'l item._
US FUNDS ONLY.
☐ Please add me to your mailing list.

Name:_____

Address:_____

City:_____ State:_____ ZIP:_____

Phone: (____)_____

you are close to your goal. Then give yourself the time to heal, purify, clear your being and complete your integration. Before you know it, the Sacred Pause will be over and you will be effortlessly progressing along your next step.

Prickly Peer Pressure

This has to do with the reactions of other people. Everyone seems to have an opinion about us and what we are doing with our lives. Some may think that we have gone off the deep end, while others may be threatened by our new sense of empowered freedom. Criticisms are in abundance: "You really think *you're* an Angel?" followed by derisive laughter. "When are you going to grow up and join the real world?" spoken with serious concern.

There are several ways that we can react to Prickly Peer Pressure. One is that we can stop seeing all these people and go off and become hermits. While admittedly effective, this path can be quite lonely. Another approach is to try to convince them through impassioned arguments that our path is a good one. While this has a small success rate, it is very time consuming; and who wants to waste their time trying to convince those who really aren't interested?

The most effective method of dealing with Prickly Peer Pressure is to stand firmly in our Beam and meet each person and every situation with an abundance of love and compassion. Then at least the people around us will get imbued with love. It's not necessary that they understand, although it is always preferable. And by embodying our Presence wherever we are, we will discover that many will be touched – for love always speaks louder than words.

Attack of the Dark Forces

This is another residue from the Template of Duality. We can feel the Legions of Darkness pressing around us, trying to thwart us, throwing obstacles in our path, hindering the fulfillment of our Missions, attacking us psychically. We just *know* that our efforts are being blocked by the Dark Forces. Hence we build up our defensive barriers to protect ourselves from the bad half of duality.

But wait a minute, did you forget that we're not anchored in duality anymore? Therefore we are not subject to its manifestations of light and dark. We are from the Great Light of the One which encompasses all the polarities into Unified Oneness. How can Dark Forces continue to exist? That's just it, they can't – and they will be gone as soon as you remember this.

Now, admittedly, there are times when the energy gets a little thick – like totally murky and intractable. When everything we attempt appears to be blocked. When we can barely breathe. We have all experienced such difficult times. And in the old patterning it was extremely convenient to blame this on the Dark Forces. But as they're simply not around in the New Octave, we're going to have to find a new way to deal with this.

The next time that we feel ourselves being barraged with negative energy, we can approach it with greater understanding. First we'll let go of the concept of Dark Forces since they don't exist. Now let's see what is really happening. Whenever there are *what appear to be* formidable obstructions in our path, it is a sign that something within us needs to shift. It's helpful at this time to do a little internal rearranging, what I call *Shedding Your Skin*. By peeling off another layer of our illusory selves, not only do we become clearer and more ourselves, but we find that all the obstacles have been removed along with the outmoded part of our beings.

The important thing is not to buy into duality and let yourself get pulled back into it. Life is full of many dubious situations and people which would happily polarize us into old levels of consciousness. But remember, we don't need to do this anymore.

Another helpful thing to do when there is heavy energy about: Try stretching your molecules, expanding your being into vastness. Then duality has nothing to attach itself to and simply passes quickly through you. This is also a most useful process when you are physically sick. By giving no resistance to the illness and making yourself into a hollow tube, the disease has no place to stick onto you.

And, if it is really important for you to keep the concept of Dark Forces alive, you might try another approach. This is the path of extreme friendliness. Greet the Dark Forces cheerfully. Compliment them on their truly scary looking presence. "Wow, those are great costumes! How did you ever create that realistic looking dripping blood? What fantastic sharp weapons you have!" After your initial friendly chitchat, you can now drop the bombshell. "Hey you guys, don't you know that duality is almost over and that we're all really One? Sooner or later we're going to merge into Oneness, so why don't you lay down your disguises and join us now?"

If this doesn't work, that's all right; you have planted an important seed within them. It's time to go to Plan B which is to notify them, that as cute as they are, Dark Forces are no longer an acceptable reality. Since they're not real, you just won't be able to play with them or take them seriously. Sometimes this is all you have to do and they will immediately dissolve before your very eyes. On other occasions you might have to stand your ground on the Template of Oneness, while you are tested. If you stay firmly in your Beam, they will soon disappear. You have hereby opened a large crack in the doorway to your freedom.

Starry Slug Syndrome

Do you feel mired in inertia? Don't want to get out of bed in the morning? Feel like you weigh five tons? Have you noticed the air around you feeling heavy and oppressive? Does even the smallest activity seem to be immensely exhausting to achieve? And do you want to eat copious quantities of food all the time? Congratulations, you have just encountered the Starry Slug Syndrome!

Are we really metamorphosing into slugs or is something else happening? You can relax, for there is a Higher Purpose behind this somewhat perplexing condition. Often when we are receiving massive doses of accelerated energy it is necessary to drastically slow down our physical responses. This occurs so we can give our full attention to the assimilation of these energies. Hence it appears as if we have no physical energy. As we are actually working very hard on other levels of consciousness, this is why we often have voracious appetites.

When we are experiencing Starry Slug Syndrome, the best thing to do is – *nothing!* That's right, whenever possible, do absolutely nothing. Take as many naps as you can sneak into your life and spend as much time as possible lying down. *(That is, when you're not eating!)* By giving ourselves the space to complete our assimilation process and do our work on the higher planes, we'll be working *with* Starry Slug, rather than against it. And before we know it, the Slug will be transformed into a butterfly. Off we'll go, with a burst of renewed energy, flying off to fulfill our Divine Missions.

There is never more than One.

Visions of the 11:11

#1 The Eleven interlocking Pyramids within my heart become increasingly smaller until they totally disappear. At the same time, I am growing infinitely larger and realize that I have become the entire map of the quadrant of the Greater Central Sun.

Δ Δ Δ

#2 A smooth, white egg appears in my solar plexus. It has a thick, creamy shell. Slowly, almost imperceptibly, the egg expands. Soon, my entire being is gently hovering inside it. This egg serves as our initiatory chamber into the New Octave, much like a cocoon does for a butterfly. Inside our egg, a lotus bud begins to grow. **This is the birth of the Template of True Love.**

Δ Δ Δ

#3 My heart is removed by a dolphin in human form. He simply reaches inside and takes it out, much like a Mayan sacrifice. There is no pain involved. *(I now understand what the Mayans were actually doing in this ceremony, back when it was still pure.)* **It is the removal of the smaller heart to make way for the Greater Heart.**

I feel a large hole where my heart used to be. It is very cold like white heat. *(Something that is so hot, it appears cold.)* It is empty. I wonder why I don't have a heart, then remember to look in a new place. *(In the new template, nothing is located where it was before. It is nearby, but much, much larger. You have to look bigger, vaster to find it.)* Outside the hole, there are several large concentric rings extending outside my body. They resemble flaring, solar coronas or flaming flowers. This is my Greater Heart.

Later, a pure, transparent drop of liquid appears in the empty hole in the center of my Greater Heart. It looks like a drop of dew. **My heart has now transfigured into the Template of True Love.** Whenever ones who have activated their Greater Hearts come together, their pure drops merge into Oneness.

Δ Δ Δ

#4 At the Pyramid Complex in Giza, Egypt, we must realign the three pyramids in such a way as to activate the Unseen. When this is achieved, a huge diamond full of dancing, iridescent Lights can be seen in the air above. This Diamond of the Unseen has been here all along, but has not been visible until the realignment of the pyramids.

Δ Δ Δ

#5 I am lying in a narrow crystal coffin in a state of suspended animation. On top of me instead of a lid are many square platelets. They appear to be made of glass or ceramic. Suddenly, they all blow away. For a minute I am exposed except for an invisible, transparent covering; then the platelets return, only now they are gold and silver. These plates are like scales of a fish – shiny and alive. Since I am in a state of suspended animation, I breathe through them. I can see them moving up and down with each breath, keeping me alive.

273

△ △ △

#6 I see many pilgrims walking through a rocky, moun-
tainous, barren desert. They are wearing simple, long
white robes. They come from all the directions. Some walk
alone, others in twos or threes, or groups of twenty or
thirty. As they encounter each other, they join together.
They are all converging on the same place. It is the end of
a long journey. **This signifies the Reunion at the
Completion of a Great Journey.**

△ △ △

#7 A Celestial Canoe is navigating through the starwaves
towards the Earth. It has come from an immeasurably vast
distance. In the prow, hanging on a lantern bracket is a
tiny, real star to light the way. This Celestial Canoe is
heading towards the Alpha Point in New Zealand.

△ △ △

#8 I see the Pyramid Complex in Egypt and begin to
understand the vast significance of the 11:11. A long point
of White Light penetrates into the center of the Complex.
This shaft of Light is immensely strong and brilliant; it has
a sharp point like a pin, penetrates like a laser and its
intensity of oscillation is unlike any beam of Light I have
ever encountered. **This Rod of Light or Yod has not
been on Earth before.**

Now it passes through my body from head to toe. It feels
like an intense pinpoint of searing Light skewered right
inside me. Finally I pull the Rod of Light out of me. As I
remove it, my body segments fall apart and drop to the
ground like discarded husks. Looking at my old, lifeless
body parts on the ground, I realize that they no longer

define who I am. Since I am not my body, I wonder what I am. Looking upwards, I realize that I am inside that long, pointed Yod of searing White Light. The Yod widens and becomes more transparent.

Δ Δ Δ

#9 After the Diamond of the Unseen is made visible above the Great Pyramid Complex, the outer casings or skins of the three pyramids are unscrewed and taken off. They have been recalled back up to the Heavens. The Celestial Caravan departs for the first and last time. **This is the Completion of the Omega Point.**

Δ Δ Δ

#10 The two interlocking sets of Eleven Pyramids forming an Antarion Conversion are joined by two more interlocking sets of Eleven Pyramids, thus forming the New Star Mandala of Octave Eleven and transforming the 22 into the 44. **This is the decoding of the 4 -7 -11 -22 -44.**

Δ Δ Δ

#11 There are Eleven Pyramids within the Doorway of the 11:11. Each one represents a level of Initiation and correspond with the Eleven Gates.

The First Light:

The story of the arrival of the first Celestial Canoe long, long ago.

Once long, long ago, at the creation of this planet, another Celestial Canoe came to the planet. This canoe brought the First Light to Haleakala Crater in Maui, Hawaii. Now that we are entering into the New Octave, it is time for the entrance of a new Celestial Canoe.

Δ   Δ Δ Δ   Δ

In the primordial darkness just before the Dawn of Creation... a tiny fragment of star, a spark of potential Light, AA-AA gently cascades down to Earth. The place of arrival is Haleakala Crater *(The House of the Rising Sun)* on the island of Maui in Hawaii.

Softly landing outside the rectangular temple of stone, the star fragment takes the form of a beautiful maiden, simply clad in the purity of white. She comes from the morning of time...

Two rows of beings await her arrival. Wearing feathered capes against the chill, bearing torches of pale, unearthly light to illuminate her path to temple's door, they beckon her inside with chants of welcome. "She has come. Soon it will be done."

Entering the sacred temple, the maiden sits in her appointed position upon a mat decorated with petals of flowers. The Kahuna Priest approaches in timeless reverence, preparing the sacred white paste of roots, and places delicate traceries upon her face. They begin a simple chant, *two sounds, a pause, two sounds*, awaiting the birth of the First Light.

Δ   Δ Δ   Δ

Across the vast, unlit sky there comes a Celestial Canoe bearing four royal brothers. In the prow sits RA-MU bearing the First Light of the new beginning. In the back is his brother RAMA who bears the gift of Leadership and Authority. On the outriggers sit MANU, with the gift of Cosmic Law, and MANI brings the gift of Healing. As the Celestial Canoe paddles through the starwaves it leaves behind as its wake, the First Light of the new Dawn.

A chant is sung by the four brothers, *two sounds, a pause, two sounds*. "The Sun has come!" "To birth the dawn." Behind them, the sky becomes steadily brighter. Ahead of them, darkness reigns in its final moments.

Δ   Δ Δ   Δ

The chants of both Heaven and Earth can be heard, though yet at a great distance from each other. They fit together in the place of pauses, interlocking into completeness. Slowly, yet steadily drawing closer together as the Celestial Canoe approaches the House of the Rising Sun. . .

Δ   Δ Δ   Δ

The maiden sits in silent purity within the temple. The Priest begins to intone his prayers to the One. These prayers are only spoken once, at the beginning of each new world, at the Dawn of the First Light.

Suddenly, a shaft of Light sears through the opened doorway of the temple, illuminating the maiden in its brilliant radiance. RA-MU stands in the portal, so bright that only the outline of his form can be perceived. The Sun has come!

Striding inside the temple, he positions himself next to the maiden on the mat. The two chants align themselves into one. "Oh Sun One, my loved One!" As the Kahuna chants his prayers of welcome, the sacred union takes place. Heaven and Earth are wedded into One.

Δ   Δ Δ   Δ

Thus it was as I remembered the arrival long, long ago of our first Celestial Canoe bringing the New Light at the Dawn of Time.

Celestial Caravan & Canoe

As the Doorway of the 11:11 opens, it signifies the completion of the Omega Point and the activation of the Alpha Point. We are closing the doorway of the Old and opening the Doorway of the New. The transfer is now in position and begins to activate. . .

The Celestial Caravan

From the Omega Point at the Great Pyramids, a Celestial Caravan prepares to depart the Earth for the very last time. Our weary travelers, composed of ancient First Wavers and the Egyptian Pantheon of Gods, mount their camels and horses. The animals are guided by the secret order of Starry Sufis, called the Al Ham'sa, who have returned to Earth to complete this final task. The Starry Sufis, still adhering to their ancient vow of silence, are led by Hasseif El Sharif, the Wandering Star Master of the Dawn. They are clad in simple white robes with white cloths wrapped around their heads so that only their piercing eyes can be seen.

Together everyone begins to chant, AN-NUT-TA-RA HU. Whenever they chant the HU, all of them raise their arms upward in surrender. With each plodding step, the Celestial Caravan rises higher. And as they do, a most miraculous wonder occurs. All of the profound weariness of the ancient ones begins to dissolve away forevermore! With rolling strides, the Celestial Caravan winds its way upwards into the Starry Heavens. The chanting, AN-NUT-TA-RA HU continues. . .

All are being transformed. Even the camels begin to lighten their steps and prance beside the horses with a renewed vigor. Around their necks are delicate crystal bells which ring out with pristine clarity. Striding effortlessly upon the starwaves, the Celestial Caravan mounts the heavenly pathway.

This Celestial Caravan only leaves the planet once. It marks the Completion of the Omega Point. The sceptres have been passed. . .

The Celestial Canoe

At the very same time as the Celestial Caravan begins its ascent, a Celestial Canoe navigates through the starwaves, coming ever closer towards the Earth. It has come from an immeasurably vast distance. In its upraised prow, hanging on a lantern bracket is a real star to light the way. This Celestial Canoe comes to the planet for the very first time. It brings the First Light of the New Octave.

Steadfastly paddling towards the Earth with focused intent, we can hear the vigorous chanting of AH-AIEEEE HA-WA. The AH is accompanied by a firm stroke of the paddle through the Celestial Seas. On the AIEEEE the paddle is lifted into the air and instead of drops of water dripping off the paddle, there are tiny sparkling stars, bringing the illumination of the First Light. The HA WA are sounded like deep breaths, again with firm strokes of the paddle. This chant is totally invigorating, bringing a fresh energy which moves the canoe swiftly along its journey. It is headed towards the Alpha Point on the South Island of New Zealand. This is the Activation of the Alpha Point.

The Diamond of the Unseen

As the Celestial Canoe descends and the Celestial Caravan ascends, there comes the time when they both enter the edge of the Zone of Overlap in the center of the Antarion Conversion. They approach from opposite sides and their moment of arrival is 11:11 am on January 11, 1992. It takes the Canoe and Caravan nine and one half hours to reach the two apexes of the Zone of Overlap. Here is experienced the first Shift in Trajectory. As they continue to traverse the inner perimeters of the Zone of Overlap, two more Shifts in Trajectory are accomplished. Finally, thirty eight hours after the 11:11 Ceremony has begun, the camels and canoe reach the place where they first entered the Zone of Overlap. This coincides with the completion of the last 11:11 pm on the planet.

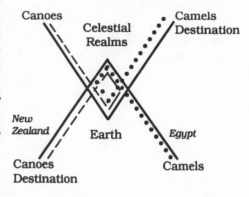

By traversing the inner perimeters of the Zone of Overlap, they activate the Diamond of the Unseen which now makes itself visible for the first time within the center of the Antarion Conversion. This marks the completion of the Template of Duality and the anchoring of the Template of Oneness. The Doorway of the 11:11 is fully open. . .

281

Each of us is traveling upon both the Celestial Caravan and the Celestial Canoe. On December 31, 2011 when the 11:11 closes, it will mark the arrival of the Celestial Canoe in New Zealand and of the Celestial Caravan in the Greater Central Sun System of the New Octave. The two templates will move into their final separation. The Great Work has been accomplished!

In order to see the Invisible,
simply look where the visible used to be.
Now extend your parameters.
Look beyond.
Look l a r g e r.
The Invisible is to be found
on an infinitely larger scale
than we have previously imagined.

Beyond the Physical

As we move into the New Octave, there is going to be a tremendous shift in perception. We will still be wearing our physical bodies, but they will feel considerably different. Even our very identification with these bodies is undergoing a vast transformation. Firstly, our physical bodies will have merged with all our larger bodies – those which we term the Angelic Presence, our Light Body and lastly, our Starry Overself. This extends the parameters of our beings until the physical body is no longer the solid casing of matter that it used to be.

Some people are concerned as to whether we shall be ascending in our physical bodies. Our bodies will be coming along, but they will be like the tip of a fingernail compared to the vastness of our Starry Overself. We will no longer primarily identify with ourselves as physical beings. The delineations of the physical will not define the parameters of who we are. They will be part of us, but not the whole.

Even the grounding of our physical body shall be different. We will no longer feel anchored on the Earth in the old manner. Our heavy sense of gravity and mass will disappear. This doesn't mean that we are going to start bobbing up into the air, but as our bottom line raises, we are going to experience a new level of grounding. With this comes a sensation of floating, like being gently suspended in the womb – *a hovering above the solidity of matter.* If you can tune into this feeling of floating, of suspension *beyond* matter, then you will move with greater ease into the New Octave.

Entering the realms of the Invisible, one of the first things that we notice is the total change in the quality of the space around us. It becomes more liquid, assuming many of the qualities of water, like an aqueous substance. We can see and feel fluid currents of subtle energies in the air. As any form of energy, such as a person, emotion, or sound, passes through this space, we can feel the repercussions of this movement in the shifting currents of subtle energies. This is much like throwing a pebble into a still lake; it creates a shift in vibration which causes ripples of energy to spread outwards in concentric rings.

The New Chakras

Our chakra system is also undergoing a powerful transformation. After spending much time discovering, cleansing and activating our Seven, *and sometimes Eight,* Chakras while we were anchored in the Template of Duality, we are now discovering that the chakras themselves are changing drastically. This is because the old chakra system was formulated for our passage through the old spiral. Remember: We are moving onto an entirely new map. Hence we are being given a totally different chakra system to work with.

As we move into the subtle currents of the Template of Oneness, we will become increasingly aware that our chakras have transformed into a new patterning. Here are some fragments of the map:

The Lotus: First, Second & Third Chakras

The first change is discernible in the area of our First, Second and Third Chakras. They no longer exist in their previous form, but have united into one Chakra. The thousand petaled lotus of our old Crown Chakra has now become our new bottom line. From our old Root Chakra, the lotus's roots descend deep into the watery depths of the subtle currents, weaving themselves into Oneness with lotus roots of other awakened ones.

The base of our lotus flower is located where the Second Chakra used to be. This symbolizes the unification of our inner polarities. And the petals of our lotus are superimposed over our old Solar Plexus Chakra, signifying the alignment of our will with purest love. Thus do our First, Second and Third Chakras irrevocably align themselves with the Template of True Love, marking the final completion of the illusory division between spirit and matter.

A lot of people are concerned that as we move into the Invisible, we will no longer be able to experience the joys of sexual union. Instead, what we will find is that sexual union is no longer confined to the physical body. It extends all the way to the Starry Overself. Once we have experienced this level of total union, it is hard to return to the rather dull limitations of the old form. Making love just with the physical body is like uniting with only one tiny fragment of your being. In the Template of True Love, we bring our full Starry Selves into play, merging into previously unimaginable levels of Oneness.

The Greater Heart: Fourth Chakra

As we transform our smaller hearts into our Greater Heart, our Heart Chakra shifts onto a vaster template. This Greater Heart can be observed *beyond* the area where your smaller heart used to be. It is much, much larger, resembling concentric rings of solar coronas emanating outwards from the physical body. *(Much like the cover of*

The Star-Borne.) The center of our Greater Heart appears empty, but if you look closely you will discover that it contains one pure drop, which is the Essence of the One. Whenever two people who have activated their Greater Hearts encounter each other, their pure drops merge together into what is known as the One Heart.

The One Eye: Sixth Chakra

In the Template of Duality, our Third Eye was opened in order to activate our psychic senses and awaken our intuition. This expanded our perceptions beyond the purely physical realms. However, we now see that the levels of awareness which emanated from our Third Eye were limited. As we move into the New Octave, a triangulation occurs between our Third Eye and our two physical eyes. This creates a state of heightened perception which is termed the Activation of the One Eye. This One Eye represents the alignment between the All-Seeing Eye of AN and the All-Seeing Eye of God. When our One Eye is fully activated, we receive direct access into the One. Thereby we are able to see or know anything. All we need to do is focus our attention in a certain area and the perception is freely given.

The Yod: Seventh Chakra

The most profound change of all has occurred to our old Crown Chakra. It has merged with our Eighth and Ninth Chakras and transformed into the Yod. This penetrating shaft of Light is the direct emanation from our Star of One. When this is activated we become living, breathing Pillars of Light in perfect alignment with the Great Central Pillar. This astonishing Beam of Light floods our entire being. It is the capstone of our Starry Overself. We now embody the Greater Reality in every molecule, in each timeless instant of No-Time.

The Missing Chakra: Sixth Chakra

You might have noticed that we have omitted the Sixth Chakra. This is because its functions have been taken over by the new chakras. We now communicate with our Greater Hearts, through the Love from our activated Lotus, aligned with the understanding of Oneness emanating from our One Eye.

The Subtle Currents

Moving deeper into the subtle currents, we notice that our area of focus has changed. We no longer direct our attention towards objects which are solidified in matter. Instead, we find ourselves looking *beyond,* into what was previously unseen. A good example of this is found in the shifting lights that sunlight brings into our houses. These manifestations of the Unseen assume a much greater importance in our lives. Even when we are out driving our cars, we will feel more connected with the band of energy which we are traveling upon rather than the myriad details of what we are passing by.

As we become increasingly aware of these powerful, subtle energies, the shifting currents of the Invisible will be made visible. Not only will we be able to see and feel them, but we will find ourselves aligning our beings to them. They will become a more predominant part of our everyday reality. The solidity of physical matter will begin to fade away. We will be able to see matter, but it will become increasingly unreal and transparent.

Contrary to what some might assume, this doesn't make us feel spaced out and disoriented. Rather, it gives us a heightened sense of the Greater Reality. There is a new found sense of serenity. We feel more alive, more connected than ever before. We see the strands of Oneness which link

288

everything together, knowing that we are an integral part of the One. And an incredible sense of freedom and lightness of being begins to fill us as never before!

How does this translate into the sensations of the physical body? Even though we no longer identify ourselves with the limited definition of our old parameters, we are totally present. Our new heightened awareness reaches outwards and embraces the totality of the One. *This means that we feel more, not less.* There is a deep sensitivity to all the underlying vibrational currents. This is totally different than our old form of sensitivity which we experienced during our awakening process when we were touchy and jumpy when disruptive energies were present. Instead, we now discover that we can flow smoothly through many different levels of energy without being negatively affected by them, merely by aligning ourselves to the Template of Oneness.

In the subtle realms much more can be achieved with considerably less effort. A mere glance can convey volumes of knowledge; entire histories can be exchanged in a look. A slight touch of your finger can heal, empower, stop time or trigger massive shifts in levels of awareness. A profound revelation or emotion can be instantly felt by many. We tend to move slower, but achieve more without any struggle at all. And resting in the heart of the Great Silence, with direct access to the One, we realize that we have deciphered the hologram of All-Knowing. Therefore, we have nothing more to prove to anyone and it is hardly necessary to speak unless we choose to.

Remember: We are becoming vastly larger.

We have expanded the boundaries of our probable realities.

We are moving into a Greater Central Sun System.

There is nothing to fear about our immersion into the Unknown. It is much like the story of the first time that I went swimming at age four. I was at my Grandmother's cottage at a mountain lake in California. There was much excitement that morning since I was finally going to swim in the lake. We went down to the dock and they put a life jacket on me. Up until that point I was thrilled; then the fear of the Unknown hit me. I looked at the deep waters of the lake and was terrified. Screaming and crying, I tried to return to the house, but they wouldn't let me. I was thrashing about wildly as they picked me up and threw me into the water. Hitting the water, I submerged for an instant, then bobbed back up to the surface, discovering that I *loved* being in the lake and never wanted to get out. Since then I haven't been afraid to explore new realms of consciousness...

The Unknown is not scary; *but it is totally different* than anything we have experienced in a long time. The funny thing is that once we make the leap, we quickly discover how familiar it is, how comforting. It feels wonderfully refreshing to move into the subtle currents of the Greater Reality. And for those of us ready to make the homeward journey, this is the next step.

On the Celestial Barge

Further Initiations in Egypt

Following the completion of our 11:11 Ceremony at the Pyramid Complex, we returned to our hotel in Giza. An hour later we were on our way to the Cairo Airport. Arriving that evening in Luxor, our extremely weary, but *glowing* group of Starry Family, boarded yet another bus which took us to our Nile Cruise Boat called the Cheops.

While totally exhausted, *(I had but few hours sleep in three nights)*, I felt quite excited to be on our boat which we had all to ourselves. Soon Matisha's song, *The Family of AN* and Elariul's delightful harp music could be heard over the ship's intercom! We felt quite at home. What was truly remarkable was that each time that the boat began to move on the floating currents of the Nile, there was a quickening of our passage through the Doorway. . .

It felt as if we were gently floating inside an egg, much like suspended animation. This was similar both to being inside the womb and inter-dimensional travel. Everything felt sublimely delicate and shimmering. My voice became almost a whisper and I could only move in slow motion. The air itself became liquid, filled with subtle currents. We

291

were hovering, floating in the most heightened sense of No-Time I have ever experienced. We were traveling on the Celestial Barge, the heavenly boat which was taking us through unbelievably exquisite and subtle realms of Light!

In the morning we visited our first temple. It was funny, for most of my life I had desperately longed to visit Egypt, to experience once again the many sacred places where I had spent numerous lifetimes. Now I was finally here and it didn't matter. I no longer identified strongly with my past lives, knowing that they had occurred to only a small fragment of my being. At first, it felt as if our only task was to set these ancient energies free. But, I soon discovered that they still had much to teach me.

Luxor

It was dusk when we arrived at the Temple of Luxor. We began with a long procession up and down the Avenue of the Sphinxes. Over a hundred of us, many dressed in long, flowing Egyptian robes or Star-Borne sweatshirts, chanting "AN-NU-TA-RA HU" combined with our newest unified movement of expanding our probable realities. It felt wonderful to openly be ourselves, to return to these sacred temples in full remembrance!

We discovered a huge 11:11 designed into the front of the Temple. It had been set into the stone itself to serve as a pre-encoded trigger. So the ancient Egyptians had known about it all along! Then I laughed to myself, realizing that *they* were really *us*. *We* had built these temples. We had served in times past as the Gods. And we were still here on Earth in human embodiment, finally preparing for our time of completion. The homeward journey had just begun!

Entering the Inner Sanctum, we somehow managed to compress our entire group inside. I knew this to be the site of the Temple of Ascension of Seraphis Bey which has long served as the place of final preparations and initiation for ascension within the old template. The real ascension chamber was located in the etheric above the physical one. As our chanting continued within this holy Inner Sanctum, I realized that we were helping the Ascension Temple to ascend. Now was its time of freedom and sweet release. I saw the entire Ascension Temple moving through the 11:11. Our ceremony was completed by another joyous passage up and down the Avenue of the Sphinxes.

Our experience at Luxor felt good, but I regarded it as just another service which we were doing for the planet, nothing that really involved me personally. We were simply freeing the old energies to move on. Then came Abydos...

Temple of Osiris at Abydos

I was awake early in the morning long before the dawn, consciously savoring my experiences of traveling deeper and deeper into the New Octave while our boat cruised up the Nile. Delicately floating in the center of my egg, I could hear the chanting of the Celestial Barge. This new chant was softer, sweeter, ever more subtle. Letting it sing inside me, my journey through the New Octave became totally focused and effortless. Finally I sank back into sleep. In the morning, I was dismayed to discover that I had forgotten the new chant. I could feel its resonance inside me, but I could not bring forth its sounds.

Later that morning I connected with two very special beings, Kumari and Ramariel, who were also traveling with me in the tip of the beak of our Birdstar. Our deep bonding began while dancing in the Starry Processional. Without a word, the three of us had aligned into Oneness, forging an irrevocable, silent understanding while we danced through those long hours.

I saw Kumari first. She had heard the new chant in a dream and remembered the sounds, but not the melody. They were "AH-TA SA-RA." As soon as she spoke, I knew it was the same that I had heard. Next we encountered Ramariel, who had heard it too and remembered the melody! From this point onwards, this chant has been everpresent with all three of us, with endless subtle repetitions and delicate variations, as we continue to move deeper into new realms of Light.

As we journeyed on the bus to Abydos, I was in a continuous unfolding of revelation. I saw that we were undergoing a deep process of initiation, that within our eggs was the seed of a lotus. The Purpose of our journey was to give birth to the lotus of True Love. This was happening not only to each of us, but we were doing it for the entire planet. For once any of us is able to experience True Love, it opens the door for all – for truly we are One!

At the Temple of Osiris we experienced four levels of initiation. In the first temple where Osiris had been killed, we felt the separation of all the fragments of our beings. As I began to speak about this, some of our group began to sob. This was the final completion of the process of separation.

Next we entered the small Temple of Isis. Somehow our large group managed to squash ourselves inside. *(It helps when you all know that you're One!).* Here we focused on the aspect of Isis which is called Isis in Search. She is searching for all the fragments of her True Love Osiris, which have been scattered all over Egypt. Isis calls to Osiris to return to her on the Boat of a Million of Years. Then I led our group in the Meditation to Call Forth your True Love. It was very powerful. I felt my True Love and I walking towards each other along a brilliant channel of Light. We both had a sureness of Purpose and focused intent. We were both ready to encounter one another.

Entering the Temple of Horus, we began calling all the fragments of our beings to reunite within us. The chant of "Netula, Natala, Ima Botek" powerfully resonated within the small chamber. We could feel all the scattered pieces of ourselves returning into Oneness. We brought back all the parts we had left behind during our myriad incarnations, as well as our intergalactic and Angelic Selves, anchoring all our fragments into our vast Starry Overself.

Now we were ready for the Temple of Osiris. It was time to fertilize our eggs. Together we made one, mighty sound. It was "HU" which brought down a brilliant shaft of white Light, a Yod which penetrated deeply into the central core of our eggs, impregnating the seed of our internal lotus.

We completed our visit by going to the small Temple where the head of Osiris is said to be buried. The water around this Temple is the softest green, the color of Osiris. Kumari, Ramariel and I reentered the Temple, softly singing "AH-TA SA-RA," walking three abreast in a sacred step. A Temple Guardian approached, gesturing for us to circumnavigate the entire inner walls of the Temple, leading us on wordlessly, as if all of this had been preordained.

That night on the boat, we discovered that many of us had become sick, mainly with intestinal disorders. Very few made it to dinner that night. Truly it felt as if we were all dying. And indeed we were, for it was now time for our passage through the deep, hidden realms of the underworld ruled by Osiris. Our boat felt like one of those phantom ships from pirate days in which the entire crew had died from some terrible disease, drifting aimlessly from current to current wherever the winds might take us. But as I reminded the few of us who gathered together in the lounge that evening, we all need to die in order to be reborn. And the bigger the death, the bigger the rebirth!

We were undergoing this death process in order to be reborn as the arisen Phoenixes.

Horus at Edfu

The following morning many of us were miraculously up again, this time traveling by horse and carriage to the Temple of Horus at Edfu. Horus is the son of Iris and Osiris; he represents the merged polarities within us all. In Egyptian mythology, he also represents the reborn God, who returns to bring the final victory in the battle between dark and light. Or another way of saying this would be that Horus returns to *complete duality* and moves humanity beyond into a new Template of Oneness.

The Temple of Horus was huge and imposing. It felt more alive and vibrant than the others we had visited. It has a huge 11:11 built into the front of it just like at Luxor. The temple was bristling with hundreds of tourists. I had no idea just what we were to do, so we gathered our group together in a large circle, feeling our expansive Oneness. We had received a new movement for the Celestial Barge, so this was taught to the people.

Then without forethought, the procession began. Going single file, we formed one long line, doing the new delicate mudra and chanting, "AH-TA SA-RA." Entering the portals of the Temple, we began to encircle the inner perimeters of the outer courtyard, all the while singing and doing our new mudra. It must have been pretty impressive, because tourists began to scatter everywhere! We were filmed by many as we made our steady march in ceremonial step towards the inner doorway. Sometimes large tour groups stood blocking our path, but our pace never slackened. We continued on like one unified Celestial Barge, right into the Inner Sanctum of Horus.

The Egyptian Temple Guardians were in awe; some of them had tears in their eyes. Somehow they knew that we were the returned Gods. They bowed respectfully as we passed by. Our Egyptian tour guide later said that he had never been so moved in his entire life! Many of the Egyptians present knew that this was real, recognizing the fulfillment of their ancient prophecies. In the Inner Sanctum of Horus, our chant grew in resonance, finally evolving into the Song of One which reverberated powerfully throughout the Temple Complex.

There was one final long procession, circumnavigating the perimeters of the Temple in the narrow space between the inner and outer walls. The walls were covered with massive bas reliefs and hieroglyphs which I only glimpsed out of the corners of my eyes, for leading the procession took my total focus. The energy was extremely intense; it took tremendous concentration not to fall over. I was greatly aided by the strong focus of those behind me. And I knew on that day that we had truly returned to set all people free, to announce the completion of duality.

The Locks

Our journey up the Nile continued. We finally arrived at the locks which we had to pass through before we could go to Aswan. Since many boats had arrived before us, we had a long wait. Late that night, as I was finally drifting off into sleep, I heard a great commotion outside. Looking out my window I saw that we had entered into the locks. Our boat was confined in narrow walls with many dangling ropes wielded by robed Egyptians yelling frantically in Arabic. I was seized with a tremendous sense of excitement, though I could not discern why going through the locks was so exhilarating. Jumping out of bed, I ran about in my room, going from window to window, filled with joy, even exclaiming outloud to myself how excited I was! This was most unusual behavior for me, since little brings that level of excitement into my life anymore. And what was so thrilling about ugly concrete walls confining our ship?

Nayada & Etherium sitting on the docks of Philae.

What I now understand is that the experience of going through the locks is very similar to that of moving through the eleven stepping up stations within the Doorway of the 11:11. Somehow this had triggered my remembrance of the Eleven Gates which correspond with the Eleven Pyramids. As we emerged from the locks there was a powerful shift in energies. The scenery itself became softer, more feminine. Suddenly we could sense the powerful Presence of Isis. . .

Temple of Isis at Philae

It was the final day of our Nile Cruise and still ahead of us was a visit to the Temple of Isis on the island of Philae. Many regard it as the most exquisite Temple of them all. I had long known that this was the most important Temple for me; indeed it was the only one which I had felt that I needed personally to visit. So it was with a rising sense of expectancy and wondrous anticipation that I carefully dressed myself in an Egyptian robe of white and silver, even donning my starry crown or halo.

We traveled first by bus, then by motor launch out to the island. The Temple itself had been moved from its original island due to the flooding of the Nile created by the Aswan Dam. But I knew that its energies would be intact. I had remembered many past lifetimes at this Temple, yet understood that this was not the Purpose of our visit. It was here that our internal lotuses would bloom as we anchored the Template of True Love.

What actually happened came about so easily and effortlessly, with such stunning familiarity, that it felt as if we had done this many times before. Perhaps, parts of it had occurred during previous incarnations, but even then it was only for the Purpose of keeping alive fragments of remembrance which originated from the Greater Reality itself.

299

Again without forethought, we formed a Procession chanting a new, even softer version of "AH-TA SA-RA." Our hands were upraised in the symbol for the open Doorway of the 11:11. This time we walked two abreast, though until we reached the outer portals of the Temple, I was slightly ahead of my partner. Leading the Procession, I discovered that our old ceremonial step would no longer do. We had to walk even slower in a step-close manner. I no longer felt myself to be who I had thought I was, for I now embodied Isis, returning to her Temple with her True Love.

As with our visits to the other temples, this one was filled with hundreds of tourists who quickly and respectfully moved from our path. The Temple Guardians bowed in conscious recognition of the sacredness of our ceremony. At the portal to the outer Temple, I paused to let my partner catch up, for I knew that the rest of this journey had to be completed together. Without a sideways glance, our hand movements changed in unison. Our outer hands still forming the 11:11, while our inner hands pointed down towards each other, forming a deep V.

Passing through the inside courtyard, we entered the Inner Sanctum. The Temple Guardians had rushed on ahead of us and shooed all the tourists out. They closed the gates of the Temple behind us so that we could remain undisturbed. Again, none of this was prearranged; it simply unfolded in the midst of our doing and being.

Something extraordinary happened near the end of the ceremony. We were doing a mudra which was raining the blessings of Heaven down to all of humanity when I realized that this was a marriage ceremony. And my partner in the Procession and I had just gotten married! I couldn't break the focus to look at him and see how he was responding, whether he was aware that we had been united in a most sacred manner. I had the brief thought that if he didn't share my feelings, we could simply regard this as a symbolic union bringing together all True Loves, for that was also true.

Our Procession moved through the outer courtyard. There my partner and I stood on either side of the doorway, bowing to the others as they passed through. Lastly, we bowed to each other in deep gratitude. At this very moment, a Temple Guardian appeared out of nowhere, gesturing the two of us to follow him quickly, which we did – instantly disappearing from sight.

We were taken to a most hidden, holy place, the location of which we were sworn not to reveal – the secret chamber of Isis. The Guardian checked to make sure that no one had followed. The three of us sat upon my magenta burnoose of AN, and began to meditate. Then, with a radiant smile, the Guardian left us alone in the hidden chamber. My partner and I faced each other with wonder, declared our love and dedication, sealed with a kiss of purest True Love. Thus was the Template of True Love anchored for all. . .

There is much more to this story, but I will let it rest for now. It is so unspeakably delicate and sublime. . . I have experienced the embodiment of True Love. I feel my beloved merged into every fiber and cell of my being.

But as I write these words, and possibly the reason why I cannot conclude this story, I am awaiting the return of my True Love. And while I wait, my Greater Heart calls out to his, like Isis did to Osiris long ago, giving wings to my yearning, clearing the pathway between us, resting in the stillness of the sacred pause before the final union.

The Template of True Love

There is nothing more powerful on Earth than fully embodied True Love. Its resonance dissolves all illusion and melts the veils of separation. Its purity heals all past experiences and deep sorrows of the heart.

Now that the Template of True Love has been fully anchored, we shall increasingly find ourselves drawn together with our True Partners. There is no search involved, no effort required, no advance planning needed. Once we have anchored our beings in the New Octave, our coming together is as irrevocable as the rising sun, as natural as life itself.

Nothing can hinder the full expression of these sacred unions. For truly now is the time. Your True Love doth approach, already wedded to you in every molecule and cell, throughout every dimensional universe of space/time and No-Time, anchored firmly within the Template of One. Fulfillment and freedom are at hand. The long time of loneliness is past.

Once you encounter each other, an alignment is made, much like putting two plugs into a single socket, melding you both into position. This new positioning was not previously possible for either of you as individuals within the old patterning of duality.

The Template of True Love
has hereby been activated.

To recognize your True Love is not a matter of personal preference. There is simply a harmonic resonance of immeasurable purity and symmetry of Essence which irrevocably draws you together until you align into position. The power of this resonance is unquestionable.

No words need be spoken.
No looks need pass between you.
No histories need be exchanged.

A totally new unit is hereby created. Two complete wholes have united and transformed into a greater whole. Together you embody the Pyramid of AN. Aligned as one perfect, pristine unit, you now see with One Eye. The lotus begins to unfold its petals and blossom. Your Greater Hearts merge together and unite, sending waves of massive, concentric rings of solar flares outwards.

It is the creation of a new form of energy, fueled by your synchronicity, by your perfect alignment of Purpose, by your effortless shifting into a synergised focused intent.

Your bodies of Light transform into a new being of total Oneness. You now form one invincible forcefield of Light, radiating the purest Essence of True Love. This is the full activation of the Beacon of AN. All whom you encounter shall be blessed and transformed.

This newly created embodiment of True Love which you represent is one of the most powerful forces on the planet for anchoring the New Octave and leading humanity through the Doorway of the 11:11.

True Love

One of the major effects of the opening of the 11:11 was the anchoring of the Template of True Love. Following a series of preparatory initiations in Egypt, the Lotus of True Love was finally ready to flower. This occurred at the Temple of Isis on the Island of Philae on January 17, 1992. A symbolic marriage ceremony took place between Isis/Osiris and Solana/Soluna. *(For those of you not familiar with the latter two, they appear in "The Legend of Altazar" and represent Twin Flames who are each whole and complete within themselves. It is said that they only encounter one another during the beginning and endings of major cycles.)* This ceremony represented the sacred union between each of us and our True Loves.

The state of True Love is quite different than that which we have known as romantic love throughout our passage within the Template of Duality. Rather than focusing our attention and our emotions on another person, True Love is a level of consciousness wherein we anchor our beings. It could be perceived as a band of energy with which we align ourselves. This is the frequency of All-encompassing Love which forms the bottom line of the New Octave.

Reuniting with our True Loves on the physical plane is one of our final completions. It is what many of us have awaited throughout our cycle of embodiments on Earth. It symbolizes that our inner work of union has been accomplished. We are now whole and complete within ourselves.

When we experience True Love, we are imbued with the harmonic resonance of All-encompassing Love. Our Greater Hearts have activated and are now ready to align with others in a state of perfect Oneness known as the One Heart. As increasing numbers of awakened Star-Borne make this alignment, our One Heart grows steadily larger. Eventually we will all unite in perfect Oneness.

Partnerships

One of the ways in which we can reach the state of One Heartedness is through a relationship with your True Love. Coming together in partnership with another is not a prerequisite for entering the New Octave, however it does provide a fertile ground for experiencing True Love. For those of us who choose this path, we must be prepared to fully surrender our beings to utterly new forms of living and loving. These new relationships will be unlike anything we have known before! We will be creating a new map of relating in Oneness with another.

The unification of partners is the first stage in fully embodying the Template of True Love. This process has already begun and shall continue for the next few years. It is available to all who enter the Doorway of the 11:11 and anchor their beings on the Template of Oneness.

And how do we meet our elusive True Loves, who have been so difficult to find for what appeared to be aeons? The answer is effortlessly, quickly and when you least expect it. There is no search required, for we are all traveling on an irrevocable trajectory towards total, perfect union. This is woven into the inner fabric of the Template of True Love.

After consciously choosing to experience True Love with a partner, we must focus our intent by openly expressing our yearning. Allowing ourselves to give wings to the deep yearning for union which emanates from the core of our beings serves to clear the path. After we have done that, now we simply let go. Surrender and know that what is truly yours will come to you. And your True Love is already on their way right now!

Now we enter the phase called the Sacred Pause. We might consider this as a time of waiting. But it is not waiting in the old sense of the word, waiting while uncertain whether it will happen or not. Rather it's waiting with the absolute sureness of its outcome – that your True Love definitely approaches. This Sacred Pause is a most important time.

While you are experiencing the Sacred Pause, there are many preparations to be done. First you can tune into the vibrations of your True Love, feeling the purity of love between you. Then the sacred union starts to activate. This begins on the highest spiritual levels and works downwards until it finally manifests into the physical. So until you encounter each other in your physical bodies, know that your sacred union has already begun. You are together on the higher planes and ever coming closer.

During this time you may experience some important dreams and insights. You will definitely feel a great stirring and shifting on deep levels of your being. It's important that you allow yourself to feel the activation of your Greater Heart as it further aligns with the Template of True Love. Often, a tremendous amount of clearing will take place as you release old concepts of love and relationships. Although this can be intense, there will be a powerful inner healing as you shed your old hurts and disappointments and get in touch with the depth of your yearnings to unite with your True Love.

307

The next step is to become an embodiment of True Love. This is necessary before your new partner arrives. See everyone in the world as your True Love. Feel your inherent Oneness with whomever you encounter. Treat them all with tenderness and respect. If you can do this, you will be amazed at the amount of love which will be directed at you. You will become a Beacon of Love. Now you are ready to encounter your True Love...

And please remember that there is more than one potential True Love for each of us. In truth, we are all potential True Loves. So don't focus on a specific person, for your True Love is the embodiment of an Essence, and it is the Essence which you seek. Whatever person you align with in a True Love relationship simply embodies the One Heart within us all. We may experience the state of True Love with many people, but there is one only who is approaching to stand beside you as your partner.

Even the way we recognize our True Love shall be different. Personal preferences and prejudices are dissolving as we move into all-pervading Oneness. So prepare to set aside any preconceived notions you might have on what your partner will be like, or even of how you would like them to be. This union is not going to originate on a personality level. What there *will* be is an unquestionable alignment of Essence between you. Neither of you needs to extend any effort to make this happen. It will simply be there, ready to be acknowledged.

Remember: In the New Template, these sacred unions are going to come about in unusual ways. It may be with someone you have known for years and never thought of as a potential partner or it may be with a total stranger. You might be involved in a ceremony and discover afterwards that you have been married! *Now that's an interesting way to start a relationship...* The best thing that we can do is to expect the unexpected and flow gracefully with however it chooses to manifest. One thing is certain, there will be no question of should we or shouldn't we; is this it or not? You recognize quite soon that you are True Loves.

What happens once we are finally together? We will certainly not be focusing our energy and attention on our partner, nor they on us in the old way. Instead, each of us being already whole and complete, we shall simply align our Greater Hearts into the One Heart and embody True Love. And there is nothing on Earth more powerful than fully embodied True Love! You don't form a self contained unit like the 3D relationships with their endless processing, adjustments and compromise between the partners. You radiate your state of True Love to everyone, lifting the level of harmonic resonance for the entire planet. You fulfill your Divine Purpose united together as one unit, like two eyes of the same being.

This does not mean that you are inseparable. It is important that you each give yourselves time to be alone and that you stand in your full empowered Presence at all times. Your two beams of the One Star are going to join together to form one beam, but this can only happen after each of you are irrevocably merged with your own beam. Established roles found in the old kind of relationships are going to disappear as you step into a new form of total equality and balance.

Already established relationships

Perhaps you are already involved in a relationship, one which appears to be happy and successful. How do you transform it into a True Love partnership? First, both partners must make their commitment to anchor their beings in Oneness. Each of you has to choose to make this journey through the Doorway. It is impossible *and unwise,* to try to drag or coerce another through the Door. You each have to be in full support of the other and have a unified focused intent. Your relationship is like a team of horses, both the horses have to want to go in the same direction. And your reason for doing this must be because it is in alignment with the highest Truth of your individual beings, not merely for following your partner in order to stay together. Remember: These are equal partnerships!

The next step is to move your relationship onto ever higher levels of awareness. You can do this by fully embodying who you really are and supporting your partner in openly expressing who they are. It will help greatly if you are able to call each other by your Starry Names, for this evokes your full Presence. The biggest challenge is to let go of the third dimensional trappings of your relationship. This means dropping all those old roles, habits, and ways of relating to each other which are anchored in duality. See why it is important that you both make your commitment to undergo this process! You might even want to have a new marriage ceremony between your two Starry Selves, symbolizing your union on greater depths of consciousness. As you increasingly step into your Greater Selves, you will find your union growing in wondrous ways you never imagined possible.

True Love without a relationship

Some will choose to experience True Love without being in a partnership. This is fine too, and will certainly not hinder your progress. If you choose this path, it is important that you focus on the fact that everyone presently incarnate on Earth is an aspect of your True Love. It doesn't matter if they are male, female, young, old, beautiful, ugly. We are all mirrored reflections of the One! Let your love and tenderness be expressed. Dare to be intimate, by expressing your True Self with whomever you encounter. By doing this you will soon experience an abundance of the Essence of True Love coming your way. You will feel truly supported and nourished by many.

You can also develop an extremely gratifying relationship with your True Love on the inner planes. Feel their Presence with you at all times. Feel yourself being embraced with their love. Have silent conversations with your True Love and make them a real part of your life.

And all of us, whether we choose the path of a new True Love relationship, heighten an existing relationship to the level of True Love, or stand alone as an embodiment of True Love, will serve in anchoring and activating the Template of True Love for all of humanity. This is how we move into the New Octave. This is how we bring the New Octave here to the Earth. This is how we all fulfill our Divine Missions.

Meditation for Calling Forth Your True Love

1. Begin by visualizing the Star of our Unified Presence above you. As you focus on the Star, see it activate. As it activates, it grows evermore radiant, sending forth iridescent pulsations of Light frequencies.

2. Now call forth a beam of Light from our Star. Let it shine down upon you, much like a searchlight, caressing you in its steady beam. You are now in your full empowered Presence.

3. See spread out in front of you all of humanity presently incarnate on planet Earth. Feel the presence of these multitudes extended before you. Everyone is here.

4. Now call to the Star above to send down another beam to encircle your True Love. See this beam pick out one person from all of humanity, choosing the perfect partner for you. Your True Love stands illuminated by the Light of the twin beam of our Star of Oneness. *(Often you will see your True Love begin to slowly move about, as if they were waking from a long slumber.)*

5. Focus on the Star above, seeing its twin beams encircling both of you with Love from Above.

6. It is now time for the triangulation of energies. Watch as a clear pathway of Light opens up between you. By directing an increased flow of Light from the Star above through you both, the pathway can be cleared and strengthened, making it an invincible runway of Light.

7. Slowly walk along this pathway, each step bringing you closer to your True Love. At the same time, see your True Love walking steadily towards you. Pay careful attention to the sacredness of your feelings at this time.

8. You and your True Love will now come together in the middle of the path of Light. Feel the joyous recognition between you, the exquisite purity of your love. Freely express your gratitude, your yearnings. Then stand together in the Silence and allow the total alignment between you to take place.

I have three new audio cassettes featuring the music of Etherium which are highly recommended for this process. "Unifying the Polarities" heals and unites your inner male and female. "True Love / One Heart" contains this meditation and powerfully moves you into the One Heart, and "Lotus of True Love" evokes True Love through a musical reenactment of the legend of Isis and Osiris.

The Eleven Gates

The Doorway of the 11:11 is open for twenty years. During this time we will be passing through Eleven Energy Gates. These Gates are stepping-up stations to new plateaus of awareness. They are very similar to locks in a canal. When traveling through a canal you are at a certain, consistent level of energy until you reach a lock. Here within this narrow passageway, you are raised up to a new level of vibratory frequency. Then you proceed on the next phase of your journey along that band of energy until you reach the subsequent lock which once again steps you up to a yet more accelerated frequency patterning.

This is the patterning sequence of how we move from the Template of Duality into the Template of Oneness *with the totality of our beings*. It takes the full twenty years that the 11:11 is open to complete this process. Remember we are traveling from our present Great Central Sun System to a Greater Central Sun System. This requires a tremendous shift within our beings as we move from carbon based bodies to silica based bodies. Our new bodies shall be composed of free flowing *liquid* Light!

Now in order to make this vast journey, we need to transform in metered increments called proportional adjustments. Each of the Eleven Gates represents our entrance into a new phase or level of awareness, bringing us closer to the desired level of transformation. The Eleven Gates also correspond with the Eleven Pyramids which represent the keynote of mastery or Starry Initiation available at each level of experience.

As we pass through each Gate, we are stunningly transfigured. This process is irreversible, which means that once we go through a Gate, we can't drop back down to our old level. As soon as we pass through the new Gate, we experience such a dramatic shift in consciousness that the previous level immediately loses all sense of reality, quickly becoming like a dream., *(This is what the Starry Brotherhood of the Og-Min mean by "No-Down, No-Return.")*

The First Gate

When we opened the 11:11, we entered the zone of the First Gate. Some of us have begun our passage through this gate. For those of us who did, we noticed an immediate and profound difference. This manifests not only as vast changes in our inner beings, but also in a quantum shift of our perceptions of what we had previously regarded as reality.

Remember: We are moving onto an entirely new evolutionary template.
On our new map, nothing is where it used to be;
nothing is the same as before.

Even the most exalted parameters of our highest spiritual awareness have turned themselves inside out and transformed. What used to be regarded as *enlightenment* is now our new bottom line. Looking back down upon our old lives, we can't help experiencing a new sense of detachment. We do feel a deep love, more profound and all encompassing than we have ever felt before, but the old patterning no longer has any energy to draw us into accepting it as real.

One of the tasks before us is to help our Starry Family move through the First Gate so they can anchor their beings in the new template. The deep sense of serenity and ability to flow by aligning oneself to these new bands of energy will be most helpful in these chaotic times of transition. It is necessary for our successful passage through the Doorway. In order to facilitate this process, Star-Borne is repatterning our workshop and Reunion programs so that we may bring as many as possible through the First Gate.

We have already described our movement into the subtle realms, how space becomes flowing and alive like water, how our very chakra system has transformed. You can understand how when you pass through the First Gate, you feel totally different than you were before and that you are moving into an entirely new set of probable realities.

Now this becomes quite interesting when you see what the effects of this are upon humanity as a whole. Already we have some who are making their transition through the First Gate and are operating at a very altered level of awareness, quite unique from the rest of humanity. Then we have the ones in the process of entering the 11:11, or making their first tentative steps through the First Gate, but not yet fully anchored there. They are stepping into the Unknown. They are the ones who find it easiest to relate to the experiences of those of us who have already passed through the First Gate. Then there are the multitudes still anchored in duality.

So you see, humanity is no longer spread out along one frequency band anymore. Some have already passed through the first stepping-up station. This is going to have far reaching effects in the times to come. What is going to happen when some of us move through the Second Gate and humanity becomes stretched out on three separate bands of energy? It might become increasingly difficult for the ones inside the Second Gate to communicate with those in duality. This is part of how we move into invisibility, shifting templates, and of how our two temporarily over-lapping spirals begin to separate themselves.

Eventually over the next twenty years, we shall find portions of humanity strung out within each of the Eleven Gates. A few will have already completed their journey through the 11:11 to Octave Seven while many others will choose to remain in Duality. As we spread out through the Eleven Gates we may discover that our boundaries of communication will be mainly limited to those passing through the Gates immediately before and after us.

As for the ramifications of this on a practical level, I would say that the ones of us inside the First Gate only have until the middle of 1993 to help awaken those anchored in duality. After that we will be moving on through the Second Gate wherein we will experience another quantum shift in consciousness.

Although the Doorway of the 11:11 doesn't close until the end of 2011, you don't have the full time period to make your decision to journey through. As you can see by the succession of Gates or stepping-up stations, you need to choose soon and begin the necessary preparations. You can't just leap from duality directly into Octave Seven without passing through the proportional adjustments of the Eleven Gates and the levels of initiation of the Eleven Pyramids.

In the Tip of the Beak

Those of us who travel in the tip of the beak of the Birdstar are in the process of clearing the channel through the First

Gate. What we are experiencing is that most of the third dimensional realities have become unreal. There is nothing in this state of unreality to hold our attention. This is why many of us are discovering that there is little in our old life patterns that interests us anymore.

Before we can totally pass through the First Gate, we must travel through a colorless, dream world called No-Reality. It is like a swiftly moving current, overwhelming in its force, which pushes us onward, washing away all vestiges of the unreality of the third dimension. No-Reality is not the Greater Reality; it is more like a null zone in which the only constant is being immersed in a rushing torrent where there is nothing to hold onto. The Greater Reality forms the banks of the river of No-Reality. For the moment, the Greater Reality has frozen, No-Time has stopped. We can feel its Presence close by, but cannot enter into it.

Fortunately, while we are passing through No-Reality, we are given touchstones of the Greater Reality to remind us of our destination. *(For me, they were the pictures of our 11:11 Master Cylinder in Egypt which are alive with energy.)* This time is to be utilized for integration and assimilation of energies we were infused with when we opened the 11:11. I am still in the process of decoding the transparent tablet I received during my first visit to Egypt.

While we travel through the First Gate, there is important work to do. We must activate the whales, those great beings who hold encoded within them the Divine Blueprint for our journey through the 11:11. Whales are our guides through the Eleven Gates. They will also help us to fully activate the Template of True Love. This is the great completion of their cycle of service upon the planet. It is their most important task. However they will not be able to serve in this capacity and fulfill their Divine Missions until they are activated. This is the task before us.

We are also experiencing tremendous changes within our bodies as we move into our new internal grid patterning.

Our old chakra system transforms into a new energy alignment. There is an activation of our subtle channels. Vortexes of energy open up and expand in the palms of our hands, our temples, the sides of our face, inside our elbows and knees, and on the bottoms of our feet. You may experience rods of energy protruding from these places. They act as *extenders*, enlongating your being. Sometimes it feels as if you are walking on stilts. This is all part of the mammoth transformation we are undergoing.

The First Gate is an aqueous substance of flowing liquid Light. It might be said that we are to swim through the subtle currents of this gate. The gate itself resembles a quiet, semi-circular bay. Once we climb out of the water of No-Reality onto the pink sand beach of the Greater Reality, we discover that the air itself is a form of liquid. The sky is aqua and combined with the pink sand, the two colors signify the Completion of the Isis and Osiris Legend. When the time comes to travel onwards, we will again reimmerse ourselves in the bay, journey on a strong, underwater current which will finally deposit us at a hidden grotto, which represents the Second Gate.

The Second Gate

Information is already being received about the Activation of the Second Gate which will take place on June 5, 1993. *(Please note how the date makes an eleven, 6 + 5, and a twenty two, 1993 = 22. This adds up to thirty three, the number of Universal Service!)* Once again we will issue the Call for our Starry Family to gather together worldwide that, together as One, we shall move through this Gate. A new series of Unified Movements will be done, forming the Wheels within Wheels. And within the Starry Processional we will continue to realign the stars and spiral upwards through the 11:11.

This activation will be centered in Brazil as well as at the two planetary Master Grid Vortexes in Egypt and New Zealand with participation throughout the planet. Further information on the specific locations of the Master Cylinders will be forthcoming as appropriate. 11:11 Anchors worldwide will receive all the latest updates and be asked to organize events in their areas. This will provide us with another magnificent opportunity to join together in conscious Oneness.

The Second Gate differs greatly from the First Gate. One must enter the First Gate alone, by swimming through the river of No-Reality, empowered in your own beam. This is the first in our series of Starry Initiations. Passing through the First Gate, we transform from the many into the One. We have thoroughly anchored our beings in the subtle realms.

For the initiation into the Second Gate, we enter in twos. Here the twos become the One. This is directly aligned with the anchoring of the Template of True Love. It is also why most of our True Loves are going to be manifesting in our lives before June 1993. (*And again I will stress that you don't have to be in a relationship to go through this door. But you will need a partner with whom you feel an Essence connection for the 11:11 Ceremony itself.*)

This Second Gate Activation is going to be extremely powerful. The levels of participation will be even stronger than for the opening of the 11:11. Many who missed out before will step forward this time. The embodiment of our Unified Presence will flower across the entire planet. And together, as One, we will move through another stepping-up station on our journey homeward.

The New Starry Grid

Each of the Eleven Gates holds key points for the activation of the new Starry Grid Network. Once activated, this Grid will supersede any of our previous Earthly grid systems. The patterning of this Starry Grid will be determined by three main factors. These are: the locations of the Master Cylinders for the Eleven Gates, the locations of the Islands of Light and the locations of the ones of us who have fully anchored our beings into the Template of Oneness.

You could perceive this Starry Grid as a mandala of fine pinpoints of Light stretching across the planet. The Light patterns will shift and reform whenever and wherever the awakened Star-Borne move about the Earth's surface. This movement is the triggering mechanism for activating pulsating currents of Light frequencies. As each new Gateway is approached and passed through, the mandala transforms, constantly recreating our Starry Grid until it completely matches the Template of Oneness.

The effect of this activation upon the planet will be profound. This is how Earth will experience her own Starry Initiation through the Eleven Gateways, enabling her to fully anchor herself into Octave Seven. It is most helpful if you can tune into the Starry Grid and watch it being formed.

Into the One

We have truly embarked on a most unique and exciting journey. The vastness of this endeavor is presently unimaginable. Our new map is slowly being revealed. We have courageously set off into the uncharted realms of the Unknown. Each day we are brought together into greater Oneness – our Unified Presence ever growing more precious and magnificent.

As we go deeper into the New Octave, we find ourselves traveling through totally new levels of awareness. Each level is a band of energy. As we enter the next frequency zone, we add another color to our visible spectrum and a whole new area of experience and knowledge opens up. This is why much of the information in my books is quite different from that found elsewhere. It is being retrieved from new bands of energy, originating from the *as yet,* undiscovered colors in our complete spectrum.

Astronomers have stated that everything we see in space is defined by our limited spectrum of colors. And that we are able to see only a tiny part of the whole spectrum. There are infinite worlds and levels of consciousness waiting to be discovered beyond our small visible sector of the spectrum. This is a scientific fact! It is similar to the many sounds which our human ears cannot hear, but other species can.

321

These new levels of energy have been there all along; they simply were not visible to us before. The ability to perceive them is directly related to the degree of our reawakening. As increasing numbers of the Star-Borne awaken and move through the Doorway, the previously unseen shall be revealed. We are all explorers into the Unknown.

And to view us from On High, to see what we are truly achieving on Earth, is quite remarkable. Watching our dedication, courage, commitment, perseverance and love in action is profoundly touching. Never before has there been a time on this planet so sweet and inspiring, so focused and powerful. We are all extremely blessed to be given the opportunity to participate in this great transformation. And that is why we chose to come here in the first place. This is the Purpose behind all those endless incarnations.

The Great Work has truly begun. And, as always, there is much more to achieve. We shall be continuing our process of remembrance, anchoring more of our Starry Overselves into the physical, establishing our Islands of Light, integrating each new level of accelerated awareness, and helping our Starry Family move through the Eleven Gates. All the while, remaining delicately balanced in Oneness, watching the out-going tide of duality continually fade away into nothingness.

During the next twenty years we are going to experience immeasurably vast changes on all possible levels. As we move beyond the physical into the subtle currents of the New Octave, all that we have previously known to be real is going to turn itself inside out. Many of the Starry Councils who served us during our passage through duality are going to be disbanded. The hierarchies are being realigned. The evolutionary timetables within the Master

Control Panels are being recalibrated. Nothing will remain the same. We are going Home!

The challenges before us are great, yet we have tasted the Greater Reality and already been transformed beyond all previous boundaries. This direct infusion of our ultimate goal serves as a touchstone to impell us forwards into the Greater Reality. This goal is obtainable as never before. The Doorway of the 11:11 is open to all who choose to pass through. This we have already achieved by rising into our Unified Presence.

Our Great Work is hereby revealed. Our Divine Missions are being fullfilled. We are doing what we came here to do. Completion and freedom are at hand. And again, I pass on to you the message from On High:

"Beloved Ones of the One, Well done!"

The Temple Invisible

Discourses from the New Octave

TEMPLE INVISIBLE #1

This is a deep Essence connection which originates from Beyond the Beyond. There is a harmonic resonance which travels to the depths of your beings, something you have rarely experienced on this plane. Hence you supply profound levels of nourishment and triggering of inspiration to one another. The mere fact of the existence of the others brings tremendous reassurance & support. You are true allies...

There is something you must discover for you are called upon to journey together into the Unknown for the purpose of initiation. Each of you individually holds part of the key. It must be put together in order to enter the portal. This key is iridescent in appearance. It is not a crystal key, for you have already passed through that doorway. This portal leads into the starry realms of the Invisible. Its Essence may be perceived as an iridescent sheen overlaying emptiness.

Together, you are being called to see what cannot be seen, to hear what cannot be heard, to experience the unknown.

No effort is required from you in order to achieve this initiation. It has already begun. The harmonic resonance has been activated. The veils of the Invisible have been penetrated and dissolve at this very moment in No-Time. This is taking place within the core of your beings, resulting in a shifting of your internal grid overlays.

A new star mandala is being created which shall greatly serve you in the times to come. This mandala is a template for future endeavors. It cannot be created by an individualized unit of consciousness, but must be created by a combination of individual energies united as One. You are moving into a new blueprint of combined energies. Hence, this is a necessary step for the fulfillment of the New Octave of the great work which beckons.

This initiation into the Temple Invisible shall move you into Octave Seven, fully anchoring the core of your beings into the frequency patternings of the New Octave. From there, you shall expand your circle in order to journey into Octave Eleven.

TEMPLE INVISIBLE #2

The point of contact between you could be termed a transference zone. Here, there is a great deal of electro-magnetic force which at the present moment is acting somewhat as a magnet. Not only is it drawing you together from the most subtle levels to the physical plane, but it signals that there is some important work to be done...

The keyword is Transfer. An activation is already in effect.

As has been mentioned before, all of you hold parts of the key. When this key is placed together, the activation shall be heightened. The door to the Invisible shall be made visible, birthing a New Octave of awareness. It takes a most rare combination of energies in order to create this zone of transfer. This is inherent within the core of your Essences, hence the state of harmonic resonance.

This resonance has already become an overriding factor within your lives. It is continuous, unending – becoming ever stronger. Originating in No-Time, it permeates all states of consciousness. It cannot be ignored, for you have journeyed too far towards the completion of this initiation. The point of transfer is in position, awaiting its full activation. In the meantime, there is work to be done in the releasing of old patterns, concepts & perceptions, for this initiation must be approached in an entirely new manner than anything you have before experienced.

The transfer could not take place until the channel was in position. This channel is like a line of energy linking your individual spheres. Your combination of energies has set up this channel. Thus the activation of the transfer has already begun. The channel is created and sustained by the state of harmonic resonance, but the transfer is of different units of vibrancy pulses. These units of energy have long lay dormant within your cellular patternings, awaiting the moment of transfer in order to be fully activated.

When these separate frequency pulsations meet in the channel, they form a unit which creates the proper conditions for the transfer. When the transfer takes place, there is a shift in position, as what is moved back and forth is vastly transformed, opening the vortex into a different spiral formation. So in fact, there is a shifting of spirals. The vortex is the ticket which conveys you into the Unknown. This ticket entitles you on a conveyance to continue your journey by another route.

One form of power is changed into another. This is the kind of power that will open the doors and clear the path. From that moment on, one carries and sustains that power. This sets up a heightened state of resonance which enables others to increasingly pass through that portal. You stand at the threshold now.

TEMPLE INVISIBLE #3

We are here to fling open the doors into the Temple Invisible, thereby calling forth and setting free the fullest manifestation of the Unseen.

We came into matter, not to be imprisoned by it, but to utilize it as a showcase to make visible the Invisible.

How else can the Unseen be seen? Only through our eyes, for we are the eyes of God. Thus do we serve as an extension of the Greater Reality, stretching into and beyond all previously perceived limitations and barriers as time is mastered and dissolved.

Time is an imposition on the Greater Reality, but it also serves a Purpose. To recreate the Greater Reality while living in the midst of the illusion of time is our challenge.

Time and space can be perceived as a fine mesh which has been created to sift and filter formless Essence. This sifting of formless Essence through the mesh of time and space separates the elements which are predestined to be joined together.

When formless Essence passes through the mesh of time and space and experiences the illusion of separation, there is created a heightened yearning to return to Oneness.

This yearning causes a quickening within the individualized units of consciousness which leads to profound transformation.

Inevitably, the separate units are drawn ever closer until they reunite as One. However, since they have experienced the painful illusion of separation, this serves as their triggering mechanism to breakthroughs in consciousness. Hence when they reunite, they come together in a transformed state of heightened awareness.

The Star has finally been glued back together. The formless Essence has reformed itself. Yet, there has been a shift, the Star itself is different. Red Sun has been transformed into White Star! This shift in solar rulership signifies an entrance into New Octaves of awareness beyond our present imagining.

Passing through the Doorway of the 11:11 enables you to bypass all previously established patterns of progression.

In Octave Seven – the Birdstar transforms itself into a Starbird by turning itself *inside out* through a process of inversion.

In Octave Eleven – there is a repatterning into a new star mandala which is then projected into Beyond the Beyond.

TEMPLE INVISIBLE #4

Standing within the inner sanctum of the Temple Invisible, the walls begin to fold outwards, like petals of a flower. In the center is revealed yet another inner sanctum, previously unknown to us. Here we enter and as we do, the walls fold outwards forming yet more petals to the flower. And once more a new inner sanctum stands waiting for us to enter within the center of our flower.

This continues on and on, ever entering more inner sanctums while we feel the layers of our beings open and dissolve. Going inwards from the sacred core to realms within realms never before explored. It is so easy and natural, an enduring movement of unfolding and revelation beyond all known experience.

We have merged our Essences to create the iridescent key to the Temple Invisible. All the portals, doors within doors, are open to us. And with silent reverence we enter them one by one as One. The timeless moment of sacred initiation has come!

We are being transformed – opened outwards from the core of our beings, extended beyond all previous limits and depths, that we may become embodiments of new levels of consciousness, heretofore unknown. Thus may we serve as living portals of the Unseen, making visible that which has been Invisible. Bringing to Earth a new harmonic resonance enabling us to travel beyond the known. This sound of resonance is truly a Divine breath, the central bellows of God.

Sound is breath. This breath must be taken in and sent forth in one continuous, spiraling movement of duration. It is eternal as are we. It is the expression of both the manifest and the unmanifest, united as One. It is the timeless instant of No-Time which is the Essence of the Greater Reality – the force behind all energy, the silence behind all stillness, which permeates everything. It is our spark of life, our flame of Divinity, our eternal connection to the All That Is.

And it Calls to us, ever louder, faster, softly, with great power, penetrating all the layers of our beings until we have no choice but to listen, to step forth, and to follow it wherever it may lead us. This we do, being drawn ever closer together, merging into One, until we no longer know any vestige of separation.

The petals ever open, new inner sanctums are entered, going deeper and deeper. Our flower becomes ever larger, more radiant, fuller – as our beings expand into greater vastness.

Hereby we are preparing the way for the journey into Octave Eleven. For some of us must ever go further, discovering new realms, that we may bring back with us, *merged into us,* the sacred resonance to this Earth, this life, that it may be truly heard.

Once fully opened, our precious flower shall serve as the template for the new star mandala which leads us Home.

TEMPLE INVISIBLE #5

Silently we enter... The inner sanctums of our beings have already opened. The outside layers have unfolded and flowered. Nothing remains save the sacred center which now opens wide in exquisite surrender.

Here we sit, you and I, awaiting the merger into One. And thus has it begun. Waves upon waves, vibrations of purest Love penetrate into the core of our beings. Traveling effortlessly ever beyond, into realms yet unexplored. The inner sanctum unfolds, revealing yet another and another, endlessly, eternally. And with one unified, enduring breath we silently enter...

Our eyes meet in a silent sealing of union. The subtle channels activate and expand, calling forth new levels of energy never before experienced. Our beings dissolve into the merged Essence of pure Love. We are imbued with a sublime ecstasy which transcends everything that we have known before.

Long have we yearned for this, for there have always been glimpses that this was possible. These led us ever onward on our solitary quests, bringing us yet closer, though we knew it not. And here it is, the most precious of gifts, the most natural way to be, given to us today. And silently we enter. . .

We are gently anchored within the Greater Reality. An eternal moment within the state of No-Time which shall endure forever. Yet always there is more, greater depths to be revealed and explored. But now it is irrevocably different, we are transformed beyond return to past conditions.

Our cores have expanded, moving ever outwards. New inner sanctums wait to be revealed. The flower of our unified being grows more petals, becoming ever more beautiful and full. This bliss is our natural state, easy and effortless. The initiation has just begun and shall continue until we have reached the fullest expansion into One.

And together, as One, silently we enter. . .

TEMPLE INVISIBLE #6

Triangulation is the key for reunification of the Star. Undergoing the process of triangulation creates a lattice-work or grid restructurization which forms the central skeleton of the Star.

These triangles of merged Essence become the underlying mesh which holds the Star together. Triangles are constantly being formed and reformed by the merger of different combinations of individual energies. These triangles overlap in myriad patternings creating a complex structure of overlapping merged Essence. Thereby is the One strengthened and brought ever closer into completion.

As we serve on both an individual and a group basis in the formation of the triangles, our coming together is essential to the process of triangulation. We do not merely lend our energies to the creation of one static triangle, rather we are constantly forming and reforming into new levels of patterning, always leading to a greater sense of wholeness.

The lattice system that is hereby activated could be perceived as lines of interlocked and overlapping energy, similar to Golden Threads, which link us together in conscious Oneness. The Star is being rewoven into its new higher vibratory patterning, creating a vast mandala of Golden Light.

This star mandala is our template for our future journey into Beyond the Beyond. It heralds the completion of our experiences on dimensions three & four as well as our inherent movement beyond the sphere of Octave Four, which contains dimensions one through six.

To fully create and activate our star mandala we must first form into our preordained star pattern of the Birdstar which is the vehicle to take us on our journey through the doorway of the 11:11 into Octave Seven. The Birdstar is the transitional vehicle into the Beyond the Beyond.

At the point where the Birdstar inverts into a Starbird we are finally free to make our choice as to the distance of our journey, for there are many stopping places along the way. Very few of us shall choose to see this journey through into its fullest completion. Nor is this necessary for everyone. Even if one small portion of us chooses to go the entire distance, it shall have a profound effect on all.

Thus is the perfection of the Higher Plan revealed. All the doorways stand open. The time of hindrance is finally past. Completion and freedom beckon.

TEMPLE INVISIBLE #7

As you prepare for your full entrance and immersion into the New Octave which awaits, you begin to see the completion of the long roads you have traveled to this destination. Looking backwards, the journey appears endless, such a deep passage through realms of sleep and ignorance. Yet, note well how this has served you. The process of awakening was a necessary part of your full emergence.

You are nearing completion of the first spiral. You have entered the transitional zone to the next. In this transitional zone, there is a restructuring or repatterning of some of the key components of your beings. The bonds of separation have been loosened and fall away at this very moment. The illusion of limitation has dissolved with the realization of who you truly are. The cycle of earthly initiations is now complete. You have passed through all the portals that were available while you identified with yourselves as individualized units of consciousness.

Indeed, the level of completion which you have achieved is vast. You are very close to achieving true mastery over time, space & matter – closer than you presently realize. What is there left to do?

As you emerge into the New Octave, which could be termed the Octave of One, you will begin to perceive new doorways of initiation. However, these new portals cannot be entered by you in your old state of being as separate individualized consciousness. Here you must pause and reconnect yourselves with others, merging your Essence into One. Thus do you put together the necessary keys to unlock the new portals into the Unseen.

The first gateways can be unlocked by two functioning as One. As they are activated and passed through, they create a heightened resonance which will enable others to follow. Thus is the way made clear for many.

As the journey homeward progresses, the portals become ever vaster, requiring increasingly larger numbers of beings to merge together as One in order to enter. Thus is the iridescent Pathway which leads to the Greater Central Sun made more visible.

TEMPLE INVISIBLE #8

A Directive on the New:

Create the key in geometric patternings of overlapping triangles within triangles. Thus the door opens and the new spiral is made visible.

The New cannot be found within the old patterning nor upon the old spiral. A shift in spirals is necessary here.

You have reached the completion of the old spiral. Now you must make the shift. This entails a leap across the abyss which shall launch you into the New.

This abyss which represents the gap between the known & the unknown, the visible & the invisible, is different from any abyss that you have previously experienced. All bonds within the third and fourth dimensional patternings of duality must be loosened in order to free yourself to make this leap. You must obtain a true lightness of being.

This does not mean that you shall be unable to function within the world. However, be prepared to experience the world differently than before. Much of what you have known and held sacred shall fall away as irrelevant and unimportant. You shall crave different kinds of nourishment than before and will willingly release old habits, conditionings, preferences & desires as their sense of appropriateness diminishes.

At the same time, you will experience an increasing sense of ease as the New ushers in a beautiful octave of abundance, purity, sureness of Purpose, power & all-encompassing Love. All weariness will drop away as you make this shift into the Greater Reality.

The new spiral stands before you – shimmering with promise. You can almost touch it, but if you did, your physical hand would pass right through it. It is nearly invisible, so subtle, yet stronger than anything existing within the world of matter.

You are Called forth to make this leap into the Unknown, into the New – for all else has reached the point of completion.

341

TEMPLE INVISIBLE #9

The gap is the invisible door into the Invisible.
It can be referred to as the crack between the worlds.

To arrive at the gap, which is also an abyss, you must first rise through the entire spiral patterning of dimensions one through six, thereby completing the cycles of 1 through 9. The nine of completion could be perceived as a large, still pool. In the center of the pool of nine you enter the Zone of Silence. Here in the heart of Silence as your being fills with the vastness of pure Silence, the gap can finally be perceived.

The 11:11 cannot yet be seen because the doorway is merely inherent potential until the key is created. The key is formed by uniting the myriad fragments of key which each of you hold. This can only be achieved after you have released the illusion of separation, that you are individualized units of consciousness. When your primary identification with yourselves is that you are of the One, then your fragments of the key are ready to be joined together.

Within the Invisible you receive your first glimpse of the new spiral which contains Octaves Seven & Eleven. Now you must unite your fragments of the key. This is done by coming together into your pre-ordained star patterning. As this starry mandala is activated it begins to turn, birthing a new spiral galaxy. This process opens the doorway.

In truth there shall be many spirals, large and small, forming upon the Earth – each one spinning in harmonic resonance. They will appear as wheels within wheels within wheels. Together, spiraling as One, they form one vast, interconnected spiral. It is this grand spiral, containing all the spirals, which is the key. This is the One and the Many.

As the Doorway of the 11:11 opens, the newly birthed large white bird shall rise up and begin its twenty year journey through the passage into Octave Seven. At the end of the year 2011 the 11:11 will close, instantly disappearing back into the Invisible, never to appear again.

TEMPLE INVISIBLE #10

As Heaven descends and Earth ascends, a state of fusion is created. This sacred merger shall occur both within you and within the Earth as a whole. This could be termed an Antarion Conversion Effect.

What you will initially experience is compression. Sometimes the pressure upon you will be so great, that physical activity will be difficult. Remember that the Earth is constantly rising ever higher while the Heavens are steadily descending into perfect, total union with the Earth. This is also happening inside of you.

The keyword is Fusion.

This fusion creates one pure drop of Essence, far different than what you have held within you up until now.

Remember that at your initial descent into matter, your DNA coding was embedded deep within your fragment of the One or Starseed. Now, after undergoing the process of fusion, your Starseed is transformed into a new star patterning. This is the pure drop.

This pure drop is like a crystalline elixir which nourishes the flower of your being, thus causing the unfoldment of inner sanctum upon inner sanctum within you. The flower ever opens wider, becoming larger and larger as new layers of your being are exposed until all vestiges of individuality and separation disappear. You have reached the desired state of Oneness.

Now you are ready to create the channel by focusing your intent. The myriad beams of focused intent call forth the channels. These channels meet and interlock in the center forming a new unit within the zone of overlap. This unit is the womb for the heart of the Birdstar.

The heart of the Birdstar is birthed by activating the channels once the womb is in position. The energy moves back and forth, the drops of the One join together and thus the realm of the Invisible has been penetrated and quickened.

This shining vehicle of our Unified Presence is brought to birth from the heart outwards – like waves of Light folding outwards unto themselves. Our Birdstar does not fly here from somewhere else. It is created by our efforts in birthing the heart of the Birdstar. This we are in the process of doing.

TEMPLE INVISIBLE #11

Each of us is an invisible thread, vibrating with pulsations of Light frequencies. We are like long, thin strands of Light. As we reawaken and as our cellular memory banks are reactivated, the Light frequencies of the threads of our beings become more finely calibrated. We begin to resonate in accord with ever higher patternings of energy. The vibrations of our individual threads quicken and refine. This acceleration continues until we have reached a certain level of oscillation pitch frequency.

Once this is achieved, we begin to enter a new patterning. Our strands of Light are drawn together with the others who resonate at the same level. We experience a heightened yearning to reunite with our kindred threads, for although we may yet appear separate on the outside, there is no longer any illusion of separation on the inner. We now know that we are One.

Choice enters here. This is where we may stop and choose to maintain the illusion of separation, attempting to hold onto the known, the familiar – that which has already been experienced by us again and again. Or we may choose to proceed onward on our mystical journey into the Unknown. This is the path which leads us into the Greater Reality.

As we make the commitment to follow this Call, our strands of Light are led further Beyond the Beyond, drawing closer together with the other threads. We are traveling along an irrevocable trajectory into reunion. As we approach each other, a state of triangulation is acti-

346

vated and our strands begin to reweave themselves into the fabric of the Greater Reality. We hereby create the body of our vast white bird.

Those who have rewoven themselves into the fabric of the One will gradually become transparent to the ones who have chosen to remain anchored in duality. They shall appear increasingly invisible to the world of matter. Yet the fabric of the One will be evermore radiant and complete.

As the Doorway of the 11:11 prepares to close, when the moment of the final separation arrives, there shall be felt a mighty stirring of the dragon wind. This wind is created by the combined presence of dragons of the air, dragons of the waters, dragons of fire and dragons of earth. They have united together in alchemical sacred union, their elements have merged into one magnificent, churning, billowing wind never felt before. The dragons spiral throughout the heavens with immeasurable power and grace until nothing within this solar system is left untouched.

Everything that has not been woven together into the fabric of the Greater Reality shall blow away – carried off to begin anew. And this separation shall be quick, invincible and so immensely powerful that it will painlessly take place in an instant. This is how the vast white bird of our Unified Presence begins to fly. It travels not, yet all else is blown away. Hence do we arrive at our appointed destination of Octave Seven aligned with an ever Greater Central Sun System.

TEMPLE INVISIBLE #12

Already an energy transfer has begun. As we enter the portals of the Temple Invisible, the threads of our beings are woven into the Cloth of One. Returning once again to the old Template of Duality, we carry within us, *merged into us*, the vibrational coding of the One. This serves to dissolve the rigidity of the old patterning, what is termed the Visible.

Increasingly, as we journey in consciousness back and forth through the doorway, we aid in strengthening the passage between the two spirals of evolution. This enlarges the scope of the opening enabling many more to pass through.

The transfer is activated. The Unseen is made visible in increasing increments called proportional adjustments. We, ourselves become living embodiments of the Invisible, pillars of the Great Light incarnate. There is a gradual shift in alignment from our present Great Central Sun System to an ever Greater Central Sun.

This further serves to melt away the calcification of the Visible. Thus the Visible slowly dissappears from the sight of those who choose to see. Hence the sceptre is passed from the seen to the unseen. What has previously been veiled is revealed, while what was the foundation of our perceptions can no longer be perceived.

The two templates move away from each other into their final separation. This is achieved through a process of fusion into the chosen reality patterning. It is the irrevocable parting of the ways, each moving effortlessly into their new positional alignment.

The Great Mystery is revealed in its perfect simplicity of Purpose. A fragment of our totality undergoes separation from the whole in order to transform the whole into an even greater Oneness. The Template of Duality is triangulated and reaches its appointed completion by turning itself inside out.

TEMPLE INVISIBLE #13

Passing through the portals of the Temple Invisible there is a significant shift in perception.

As we move deeper into the subtle realms, our parameters of perception expand, thus creating a transformed field of heightened resonance. Here all is seen differently than before.

One can easily perceive the unifying threads connecting everything together within the Greater Reality. The interconnectedness of these threads form delicate, crystalline mandalas of living, liquid Light. These mandalas are the formless forms of the New Octave.

Birthing the formless into the world of form, bringing limitlessness into limitation, anchoring Oneness into the Template of Duality requires an exchange of consciousness between two, very different, spirals of evolution.

In order to do this, one must become the bridge between Great Central Sun Systems. This bridge is the Doorway of the 11:11. To function as living embodiments of the doorway, one must be able to encompass within the parameters of their being not only the entirety of the present dimensional universe, but the hologram of the New Octave.

The transfer is complete when your being is clothed in the fabric of the Greater Reality which is woven of the One and the Many.

Now the real work begins. This task entails birthing the New into the old patterning thus transforming the whole. The birth is achieved by the emitting of the previously mentioned mandalas of liquid Light. Once brought into manifestation, these mandalas can be traveled on and expanded upon. They are the new star waves of the Greater Reality.

The pace of the journey accelerates as each of us becomes a Celestial Navigator, riding upon the delicate beams of liquid Light, embracing the vast, all-pervading Silence with our even greater Vastness. Freedom and mastery have been obtained. We have fully anchored our beings beyond the realms of duality and are no longer subject to the illusory limitations of time, space and matter.

In serenely perfect stillness we glide upon the Celestial Star Waves, weaving them into our tapestry of Oneness. Thus ever newer galaxies are birthed into the New Octave adding to our starry mandala which is the template of One.

TEMPLE INVISIBLE #14

Sitting serenely, high above, overseeing everything from a vantage point of tremendous vastness, I sit like a great central pillar. My central pillar is the tree of life, it is the staff of creation, it is the direct beam from the Greatest Central Sun. It emanates from Beyond the Beyond and keeps me in perfect alignment with my Source, my Home, the One.

The skirts of my robes fall gently around me. Woven into them are the stories of you and of me, of all peoples and all times. Woven into them are the complete histories of planet Earth and this entire dimensional universe. But there is even more than that, for my robes contain the threads of the new woven together with the old, the Known unified at last with the Unknown.

And if one were to listen very carefully, they might hear emanating from the cloth of my robe, a sound. Listening more closely, the sound intensifies into an anthem both stirring and sweet. It is the Song of One, the one sound composed of all. Each one singing the unique Truth of their Being, adding their voice to the Song of All There Is.

Some of the threads of my robe are so ancient and frayed, it feels as if they shall dissolve away from sheer weariness. Others are new and shiny, composed of other worldly metals finely spun and immeasurably strong. The myriad threads embrace each other, sharing their gifts of softness and shininess, of knowledge and energy, united together in focused resolve, committed to their sacred union. The combination of so many different types of threads merged together in love causes the colors of my cloth to melt into a transparent iridescence, shimmering and shining, yet barely visible to earthbound eyes.

Yet to those of us who can finally SEE, my robe is a glowing beacon of remembrance. I am wearing the One and the Many woven together into the fabric of the Greater Reality and it is so blindingly bright in its sweet subtlety that it is all that I can see anymore! All else increasingly fades away as I am led into deeper levels of liquid Light, shifting iridescent glimmers, calling me home.

TEMPLE INVISIBLE #15

Ascending through a sphere of White Light into the capstone of the greatest pyramid on Earth, we realize that the starting point has been reached.

This crystalline capstone emanates a pure, pale Golden Light, irradiating us with its pristine clarity. We have been purified of all Earthly dross and are made ready to continue onwards.

The capstone opens outward like petals of a flower and we rise ever higher. Freedom beckons... Flying with abandon and ease, we proceed upwards, spiralling through the Celestial Heavens. Following the Call that magnetically draws us into yet more distant realms.

Onwards we fly, looking backwards but once to observe the rapidly diminishing pyramid until it disappears into nothingness. We have left the old behind. There is No-Down, No-Return.

Flying further we discover a much larger pyramid ahead. We circle its capstone, but find no urge to enter inside.

Traveling onwards, ever onwards, we pass an array of increasingly bigger pyramids. Circling the capstones and continuing on...

Finally we reach the Eleventh Pyramid. This is the one! As we position ourselves outside of it, we feel a pulling motion. It is as if we were being reeled in. Smaller pyramids move inside the larger ones until they are in perfect alignment. Earthly pyramid in the center; Eleventh Pyramid on the outside. Hovering outside the eleventh capstone, we are finally drawn to enter.

There is no confinement here, for in truth, much of our vast form of Light rises above the capstone, extending all the way into the Beyond the Beyond. We are grounded and anchored far above the ground. Our physical reality is nestled inside in complete positional alignment, yet it no longer defines the parameters of our being.

Suddenly, while remaining anchored in the capstone, the foundation of the Eleventh Pyramid begins to grow beneath us. We can feel ourselves extending downwards, deepwards, into the core of cores. Our heart is aligned with the One Heart. Our eyes look out through the All-Seeing Eye. Our form has become the fully activated Antarion Conversion. All boundaries have been erased.

We have donned the garment of our Starry Overself. The shift in patterning is nearly complete. We stand on the other side of the Doorway. Emanating all-encompassing Love, we beckon our family homeward. . .

TEMPLE INVISIBLE #16

Arriving at the Eleventh Pyramid, all previous boundaries cease to be.

The Doorway has been stretched open. The journey has taken place. The transfer activates, aligning all the pyramids into one congruent whole.

Eleven pyramids incased in One, but there is no confinement, no sense of limitation. Instead limitlessness abounds in No-Time, No-Space. The parameters of duality have dissolved forevermore.

There is no up or down, yet the Eleven Ascending Pyramids have merged with Eleven Descending Pyramids. Capstones overlapping capstones creating the holy sanctum of the One Heart.

In the silent hush of this sacred merger, there is No-Breath, only an enduring instant of No-Time stretched out into the furthest reaches of infinity and beyond. Yes, there is a state of Beyond Infinity to be found by extending the patterning of the Greater Central Sun into a template presently impossible to imagine.

The key is being decoded.

This key could be perceived as a transparent tablet, large enough to fit inside your entire body. There is only one key. It resides within the One. It is accessible to only One. It is not the key to unlock the Door. It is the key to the New Octave, available only when one has passed through the Doorway. It contains the next level of starry initiations through the Eleven Gates. This key emanates from the Greater Central Sun.

It is the key which transfers the 11:11 into the 22.

It is the key which transforms the 22 into the 44.

It marks the end of Time.

It heralds the New Beginning.

TEMPLE INVISIBLE #17

In order to journey into the New Octave, we must move beyond *all* previously established boundaries. This is achieved by a shift in perspective which enables the rigid patterning of duality to be transfigured into a new configuration.

The Antarion Conversion re-forms itself through a process of involution – a journey deep within the Zone of Overlap which then turns itself inside out, forming an entirely new patterning.

The Zone of Overlap becomes the Diamond of the Unseen.

As the Diamond of the Unseen reveals itself, a Shift in Trajectory is experienced.

This Shift in Trajectory extends, transforms and erases the outer parameters of our probable realities. We now discover ourselves to be on a totally new template. We have thus shifted spirals.

TEMPLE INVISIBLE #18

To see the Unseen, we must extend our perceptions into the uncharted realms of the Unknown.

The Invisible cannot be found within the narrow limitations of the template of duality. In the map of the Unknown, nothing will be found within its old positioning.

To see the Unseen, simply look to the area of appropriateness. Here you can surrender your focus, not *trying* to see anything. Now extend the parameters of your consciousness. Look *beyond* where you expect something to be. Look larger! Much larger.

As you merge into and embody your Starry Overself, the Invisible is made visible.

You stand, reborn anew, inside the portals of the Temple Invisible.

A Message To Those Remaining In Duality

Earth is a vast melting pot wherein humanity resides on myriad levels of consciousness within the Template of Duality. Because of this, not all of humanity will choose to move through the Doorway of the 11:11, nor is most of humanity ready for this quantum shift at this time. Yet everyone will surely benefit. Why is this?

**If the spiral turns for one of us,
it turns for all of us.**

How can it be otherwise? All of us are of the One and even if a portion of us *(many or few)* choose to step off the spiral of duality and travel beyond, the effects of this shall be felt by everyone. As some of us graduate and prepare to move onto the spiral of Oneness, we will be passing the old sceptres of leadership and responsibility to those who remain in duality. This shall accelerate their growth process as it did for us when we carried them. As each of us who has chosen to journey through the 11:11 steps off the old spiral, all who chose to remain in duality will be called to step forward into our old positions, thereby causing a massive realignment of the entire Template of Duality.

It is important to remember that in order to open the Doorway we had to achieve a certain level of conscious Oneness while in human embodiment within the parameters of duality. During our process of remembrance we merged with our Angelic Presences and Starry Overselves. This process has had a tremendously powerful and lasting effect upon the energy patterns within the spiral of duality. The calcification of matter has dissolved irrevocably and everything has now been imbedded with starry fragments of our Unified Presence, our great Star of Oneness.

For one brief, shining moment, Angels walked openly upon the Earth, as they did at the beginning. Nothing can ever erase the memory of this achievement. Humanity will never again be allowed to return to the level of forgetfulness that we experienced when we first descended into matter.

A Personal Message For Those Who Choose To Stay:

We are not leaving you behind. How can that be? For we of all people truly know that we are One. And you can never fully separate from part of yourself.

We are choosing to journey beyond duality. We are moving into a Greater Central Sun System. This we must do, for we are Called to go. And as it was at the beginning when we obediently answered the Call for Volunteers upon this planet, now it is our time to travel onwards.

It is important that you understand that we are not abandoning you. Rather, we are clearing the pathway of ascension for all of us, so that at the appropriate time of readiness, the pathway into the Invisible shall be made visible to everyone!

After the passage of what may appear as aeons, a time will come when a new doorway will make itself visible to you. Whether or not this doorway is opened and passed through will depend entirely upon your efforts. It will require your full commitment, your focused intent and your Unified Presence to make it happen. At that time, some of you will have distant memories of when the Doorway of the 11:11 opened and some of your Starry Family ascended into the Greater Reality. This will be your time of greatness, fulfilling your Divine Mission by leading more of humanity homewards.

Once again two wings of Oneness will sweep across your planet signifying that you are ready to ascend. We who have moved beyond, will be ever watching for this sign, encouraging you onwards, rejoicing at your completion, waiting to welcome you into the New Octave...

And speaking from my experience in opening these portals of ascension, there is a warning which must be passed on, though possibly few will hear it and even fewer still will remember when the time is at hand. When you gather together to open your new doorway, watch for a final testing. This will appear when you least expect it. It will come from within your inner circle. A few might move into an unconscious state whereupon they can be used to negate everything that you are doing.

This moment arrives right *after* you think that the task has been achieved, when you are least expecting it. It can be easily circumvented *as long as one or two of you remains aware of the existence of a final testing.* My memories include one of the times when we did not survive our final testing and our entire planet was annihilated just moments before we had opened our doorway. We had gathered together in purity and openness to create our double waves and instead the planet was destroyed. Fortunately, through awareness of the possible energies at play, it did not happen in Egypt at our Master Cylinder. But the potential was there. Remember: becoming free of duality is a major step for all of us, and especially for those who take on the responsibility of leadership.

And for those who still carry within you the fear of the Unknown, perhaps that too, can dissolve away knowing that some of us have already successfully completed the journey. We shall joyously await you on the other side of the Door. While you are completing your evolution through duality, we will ever be with you, enfolding you in the Wings of our Love.

363

In your moments of stillness, call to us and you will feel our Unified Presence, always sending you love, strength, encouragement, tenderness, courage and support. Whenever you need Divine Intervention; simply call out and it shall be given. Our love penetrates everything; it seeps through all veils of illusion and separation. Our Unified Oneness remains as pristine and untouched as it was at the beginning. It is eternal, as are we! Look inside and you will feel us, embedded into the very fibers and cells of your being.

About Star-Borne

Star-Borne is a worldwide umbrella organization dedicated to the awakening and reunification of our Starry Family. We are here to serve in the journey through the Eleven Gates of the Doorway of the 11:11. Our Purpose is to anchor, communicate and uphold *with clarity and purity*, the sanctity of the Beam of enlightened Love which emanates from the Template of Oneness.

Star-Borne's office is presently located in Charlottesville, Virginia, U.S.A. From here we coordinate a broad spectrum of activities including: major planetary activations for the 11:11, Star-Borne Reunions, lectures, workshops, 11:11 Anchor Program, and the networking of information.

Our Star-Borne Reunions are week long gatherings of our Starry Family held twice a year in various locations in the United States. Due to the vast interest worldwide, we are currently planning some Reunions to be held in Australia and Europe. At these Reunions there are many opportunities to make quantum shifts, experience major initiations, release old patterns, and receive practical tools for transformation. Our primary focus is on joyously bringing in the New and aligning into the One Heart.

We also publish and distribute books, audio cassettes, videos, posters and various other products by Solara and other members of our Starry Family. Star-Borne publishes a newsletter called *The Starry Messenger* which serves as the voice of our Starry Family and is sent to many thousands all over the planet. We have a small retail store, *Starbird,* near our office in Charlottesville which features the products of our Starry Family.

Star-Borne Unlimited was founded by Solara in 1987. For many years the office was located in her home and she did all the work of writing, publishing, traveling, organizing workshops, and shipping orders. We have since expanded into a full time staff of ten with beautiful, starry offices. Our few restful moments are spent in the lingering embrace of the New Octave. . .

You may contact us at:

Star-Borne Unlimited
2005 Commonwealth Dr.
Charlottesville, VA, U.S.A. 22901
(804) 293-1111 or fax (804) 977-8433

11:11 Anchors

There are currently thousands of people serving as 11:11 Anchors throughout the planet. The original function of 11:11 Anchors was to prepare those in their area for participation in opening the 11:11. Once that was achieved, the scope of their service has expanded to include the entire twenty year journey into the New Octave.

The 11:11 Anchors serve as Pillars of Light within their community, anchoring and embodying the energies of the New. It is their function to gather together a local group of awakening Star-Borne to support each others growth and transformation, further quickening the movement into the Greater Reality. Each of the 11:11 Anchors serves as a representative of the One.

Due to the vastness of this project and its worldwide focus, it has been impossible for us at Star-Borne to meet with and personally screen and train each 11:11 Anchor. This has led to a diversity of levels of awareness in those serving as 11:11 Anchors. We are now in the process of restructuring our entire 11:11 Anchor Program, asking those who feel a deep alignment of Purpose with the Star-Borne vision to recommit themselves to being Anchors. We are seeking purity of Essence, total commitment to fulfilling your Divine Mission, and quality of being, rather than quantity of numbers in our 11:11 Anchors.

If you feel called upon to serve as an 11:11 Anchor, you may write Star-Borne for an application form. You will be asked to attend either a Star-Borne Workshop, Anchor Training, First Gate Initiation or Reunion in the near future. It will be your task to form a group in your area with regular meetings, facilitating them through new levels of awareness. Most importantly, you are asked to serve as an embodiment of the Highest Truth of your Being, anchoring in your Starry Overself, living your life in No-Time. Remember: The best way we can teach is by being!

This is our life's work, how we can fulfill the Divine Plan on Earth. It is the time which we have all awaited. There is much to do. Our Starry Family stands ready to receive our encouragement, support and guidance on the homeward journey. Until the Doorway of the 11:11 closes at the end of 2011, there is much to achieve. The 11:11 Anchors serve as the pillars of our Unified Presence.

About Solara Antara Amaa - Ra

Once in awhile, someone walks upon this planet, who truly makes a contribution to humanity. Everywhere they pass by, they leave a trail of stars behind them. Such a one is Solara. She serves her Divine Mission with dedication, obedience, total commitment, clarity, courage, tenderness, strength, humor and love.

Traveling widely throughout the planet, she has awakened many of our Starry Family. She has held the purity of the Beam within her heart, anchoring the One into the Many. This great mass awakening and activation of the Star-Borne has been her responsibility. She not only gave birth to the Vision for the Doorway of the 11:11, but served as its center point.

Through her books, tapes, videos, talks, workshops and Presence, Solara is clearing the channel and defining the map into the Greater Reality for all.

For many years Solara carried this sceptre of responsibility by herself. But now sceptres are being passed . . . New sceptres are being raised. Thus, she passes this sceptre on to each of you, that all of us may rise into our empowered Presence, that together our load may be lighter – and united as One, we may complete our glorious homeward journey.

369

Acknowledgements:

Each book that I write is a journey. This grand & glorious adventure into the Unknown is always enhanced by blessed beings whose love, encouragement, humor, and understanding makes my journey easier and my load lighter. I gratefully enfold you in the wings of my love, for without your support it would not have been possible.

Δ Δ Δ

Kumari for traveling with me on the Celestial Barge.

Ah Koo for guiding me through the Eleven Pyramids.

Aqliaqua for true kinship in the One Heart.

Ramariel for embodying True Love.

Grace for her depth of being.

Etherium for his sensitive music and joyful Presence.

Elariul for his indefatigable enthusiasm.

AArela for her drawings and loving strength.

Akiel for his enlightened friendship & inspired editing.

Garjon for his typesetting and super sweetness.

Elestariel for asking so many good questions.

Azuria for serving as my Personal Assistant.

Elona & Zaragusta for their dedication.

Paloma for making the transformations within herself.

Elara Zacandra for her gentle sensitivity.

Δ Δ Δ

Nova for her depth and strength.
Nion for courageously riding the waves.
J.J. Hurtak for *The Keys of Enoch*.
Katrina Raphaell for her always excellent advice.
Aquataine for magnificently upholding the Beam.
Makua & Reta AnRa for wisdom & clarity.
Matisha for singing *The Family of AN*.

To my beloved Starry Travelers:

Alairius, Anders, Antara, Aristia, Aya, Carmen Balhestero, Diamona, Helios Corona, Henry in Sweden, Kala*ai, Lilina & Galadriel, Luna, Mika-Alla, Sha-lin, Solamé, Solani, Solar, Sunyar, Urith Ra-El & Ynaria.

All the Star-Borne Staff for their enduring commitment.

And eternal gratitude to all the shining ones who joined with me at the Master Cylinder in Egypt!

AVAILABLE FROM STAR-BORNE
Books by Solara

11:11 - Inside the Doorway...$15.95
EL*AN*RA:
The Healing of Orion
> A timeless romance set during the intergalactic wars leading to the
> completion of duality...$14.95

The Star-Borne:
A Remembrance for the Awakened Ones
> A vast handbook of remembrance! $14.95

The Legend of Altazar:
A Fragment of the True History of Planet Earth
> A profoundly moving story of Atlantis, Lemuria & Beyond, which triggers
> the core of remembrance...$12.95

Invoking Your Celestial Guardians
> This beloved book transforms lives $6.95

Audio Cassettes by Solara & Etherium

True Love/ One Heart...$10.00
Through the Doorway $10.00
The Lotus of True Love $10.00
Temple Invisible $10.00
Unifying the Polarities $10.00
Archangel Mikael Empowerment............................$10.00
Voyage on the Celestial Barge $10.00
The Angel That You Truly Are $10.00
The Star That We Are $10.00
Remembering Your Story $10.00
Star Alignments $10.00

Video Cassettes by Solara

Solara in Egypt $25.00
11:11 Master Cylinder in Egypt $25.00
Cosmology of the Beyond $25.00
Entering the New Octave $25.00

Other Star-Borne Publications

A Language of Light – Grace
Exquisite poetry written by an Angel $10.00
The Starry Processional – Etherium (cassette)
The beautiful music of the 11:11 Ceremony $10.00
Love All the Way – Matisha (cassette)
Heart filled songs for the homeward journey $10.00
The Eyes of Home – Matisha (cassette)
More songs for our Starry Family $10.00

11:11 Master Cylinder Posters

A. View from above

B. Starry Processional

22" x 28" $15.00 each

Our newsletter, **The Starry Messenger**, is available for yearly subscription for $25.-US, $30.-Canada, $40.-Foreign.

US FUNDS ONLY.
(Please add $3.50 shipping for first item, 50¢ for each addt'l item.)